THE HAWKSHEAD HOSTAGE

Summer has come to the Lake District town of Windermere, where Persimmon 'Simmy' Brown runs her own florist shop. With the shop struggling for money, a contract to provide floral displays for a hotel in Hawkshead couldn't have arrived at a better moment. However, Simmy's association with the hotel soon turns sinister when she finds a body in the lake. Then her friend, Ben Harkness – who alerted her about the body – goes missing and is thought to be kidnapped. While simultaneously trying to cope with her father's encroaching dementia, solving the puzzle seems a gruelling challenge, but Simmy is compelled to uncover the truth...

THE HAWKSHEAD HOSTAGE

THE HAWKSHEAD HOSTAGE

by

Rebecca Tope

Magna Large Print Books
Long Preston, North Yorkshire,
BD23 4ND, England.

British Library Cataloguing in Publication Data.

A catalogue record of this book is
available from the British Library

ISBN   978-0-7505-4463-4

First published in Great Britain by Allison & Busby in 2016

Copyright © 2016 by Rebecca Tope

Cover Photo © garyforsyth/iStock
Cover Design © Christina Griffiths by arrangement with
Allison & Busby Ltd.

Published in Large Print 2017 by arrangement with
Allison & Busby Limited

Magna Large Print is an imprint of Library Magna Books Ltd.

Printed and bound in Great Britain by
T.J. (International) Ltd., Cornwall, PL28 8RW

For Margaret Aitchison, Katherine Knight and Diana Palmer, with thanks for your abiding interest and support

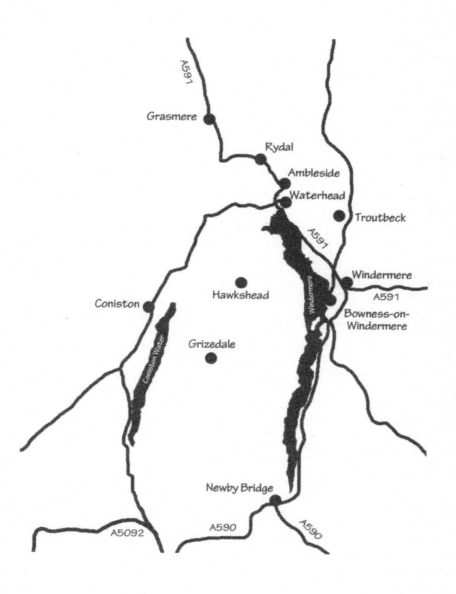

Author's Note

The Hawkshead Hotel does not exist in reality. Ann Tyson's B&B is real, and recommended. Some minor liberties have been taken with the structure of actual buildings in Hawkshead to serve the purposes of the story.

Chapter One

The tourist season had been in full swing for some weeks by mid July, bringing a strong sense of not quite keeping up with all the opportunities that came with it. Persimmon Petals, the Windermere florist shop, was not an obvious destination for any of those who came to the Lake District for their holidays. Where any outlet providing food, sweets, clothes, games or maps was kept fully occupied, the flower shop was doing rather badly. For various reasons, many of the ideas for additional profitable sidelines that had floated up during the spring had not been followed through. Simmy (officially Persimmon) Brown had been distracted by her father's abrupt decline into a worrying loss of capacity, along with her own mild depression induced by the departure of her more than capable assistant for a proper job in a hotel. Melanie Todd now had her foot on the first rung of a real career, often working fifty hours a week and loving every minute of it. Another of Simmy's young friends, Ben Harkness, had been immersed in exams for many weeks, and had then gone off on a fell-walking holiday with his brother and some friends.

Which only left Bonnie Lawson. And Bonnie was a distraction all by herself.

It was a Monday, cloudy and cool, with a threat

of rain. 'Great weather for shops,' said Bonnie. 'All except ours, of course.'

'There are still quite a few weddings and funerals,' Simmy argued. 'Not to mention birthdays.'

'Yeah. Shall I have another go at the window? It needs more red in it.'

'If you like.' Bonnie had created one of her trademark displays in the shop window only two days ago and there was absolutely nothing wrong with it as it was.

Bonnie was missing Ben even more than Simmy was. The two youngsters had established a bond a few months earlier, when Bonnie first arrived at the shop, and were now well known around town as an item. It was either a highly improbable or completely predictable relationship, depending on the level of understanding in the observer. A specialist in couplehood might demur that they were too alike for it to succeed. Casual acquaintances might conclude that they were ludicrously different. The truth was a complicated amalgam of the two.

'How's your dad now?' Bonnie called from the cramped window space. 'Did you see him yesterday?'

'He's not too bad, really. If you stick to conversations about the correct use of English and quirky aspects of local history, he's just the same as always. But underneath, he's still scared. He thinks people are conspiring to attack or rob him. He hates to let my mother out of his sight. She's convinced it's a weird form of Alzheimer's, but can't find anyone who agrees with her.'

16

'Sad. Not much you can do about it, either.'

'I did go there yesterday, even though they were terribly busy. There was a family with three children under five, and a yappy Jack Russell. My mother's thinking she won't let people bring their dogs any more.'

'Does she still let them smoke?'

'In theory, yes. But hardly anybody wants to these days. They automatically go outside, without even being asked.'

Angie Straw, Simmy's mother, ran a B&B that was almost the last of its kind. She kept rules to a minimum, enforced no schedules on her visitors and gave them a generous amount of space both upstairs and down. When it was raining, people might stay all day, playing games, chatting and smoking. Word of mouth ensured a healthy stream of customers who knew what to expect. Those unwary enough to call in on the off chance, with no pre-knowledge of what was on offer, could find themselves shocked by the many deviations from the usual. Angie had at one time compared herself to the famous Baron Hotel in Aleppo, which visitors either loved for its nostalgic lack of luxuries or hated for the same reasons. Now Aleppo lay in ruins and she could hardly bear to think of it.

It was half past ten when the shop door flew open and a whirlwind figure came in.

'Hey, Mel,' said Bonnie, who was idly arranging gerberas according to height. The excitement on the older girl's face elicited little reaction. Bonnie was used to drama.

Melanie threw a grin at her, but headed purposefully for Simmy in the back room of the shop. 'Sim! Quick – I've only got a few minutes. I was going to phone, but came instead. Listen – I've got you a job. Lots of work. A contract for the summer. And I'm not even going to ask for commission.'

Simmy pulled off her rubber gloves and made calming motions. 'Slow down,' she begged.

Melanie took a breath and leant her solid body against the doorpost. 'The hotel wants you to do their flowers, right through to the end of September. They should have thought of it months ago, but they never got around to it. I've been nagging them for weeks. Now they've decided to give it a try. You have to take enough for big displays in all the main rooms – that's three or four, and two more for the upstairs places. Change them twice a week. That's good, isn't it?' She fixed Simmy with her distinctive stare, enhanced by an artificial eye. 'Tell me I did good.'

'That's a lot of flowers. How much are they paying?'

'That's for you to negotiate, not me. I can't do *everything*.' She threw out a hand in a sweep of exaggerated impatience. 'They'll pay the going rate. Business is booming out there. You'd be amazed.'

'Thanks, Mel.' Simmy's smile was slightly forced. 'I don't know what I'd do without you.'

'You *are* doing without me. This is just a little bit of networking. If it works out, I'll get a star for putting you together.'

Simmy tried to see the positives, but mostly failed. Melanie's hotel was in Hawkshead – a tortuous drive from Windermere, unless you took

18

the ferry, and that was still not entirely straight-forward. The new commission would consume almost half a day, twice a week. Bonnie would be left in charge of the shop rather more than Simmy would like. 'When do I start?' she asked.

'Soon as you can. Go and see them today, if you've got time. They've not got much idea what they want, so you can do whatever you like. Tell them it'll have a subliminal effect on the guests and raise their TripAdvisor ranking considerably. They're obsessed with that.'

'Who should I speak to?'

'Dan. He's the under-manager. Next up from me. Sort of. He's mostly okay, anyway, if a bit smarmy sometimes.' She flushed slightly.

'Goes with the job,' said Bonnie, who had listened quietly up to then. 'Bet you're not smarmy, are you, Mel?'

'Can't seem to manage it,' laughed the girl.

It had been of some concern to Simmy that Melanie's outspoken attitude might not fit too well with hotel work. Suffering fools was not her strong point. But she had been astutely accom-modated in the less public aspects of the job, as an administrator. Taking bookings, ordering food, making sure the laundry was done and the carpets kept clean – a multitude of tasks that fell well within her capabilities. 'I don't have to be. Anyway,' she went on, 'I can be perfectly polite when I need to. I was all right here, wasn't I, Sim? Nobody complained.'

'You were great,' Simmy assured her. 'It's good to see you again. I've missed you.'

'But Bonnie's okay, right?'

19

'Bonnie's amazing,' said Simmy with a smile. Bonnie was like a puppy, blooming under approval.

'That's good.' Mel hurried to the street door. 'I have to go. Pop in and see me when you bring the flowers. Take samples – pictures – give them the hard sell. They can afford it.'

'Thank you,' said Simmy. 'Thank you very much. It's brilliant of you to organise it.'

'I know,' said the girl and disappeared.

'Wow. That'll do the finances some good,' said Bonnie, watching the place where Melanie had been. 'She's really something, isn't she?'

Simmy was looking thoughtfully at the same empty space. 'That was so kind of her,' she murmured. She looked at Bonnie, who had been introduced to her by Melanie. 'I owe her a lot.'

'She does it instinctively. She likes to bring people together and sort things out.'

'I'd better follow it up, then.'

'Don't you want to?' Bonnie's small face, surrounded by a halo of fair hair that was almost white, looked up at her, eyes wide.

'I do, of course. It's just such a commitment. It's going to change all our routines and squeeze other things out. What if we get a funeral and a wedding in one week? And three or four anniversaries? It'll be bedlam.'

'I can do loads more than you've been letting me. When Ben comes back, he's going to get Wilf to teach me to drive. That'll make me more useful.'

'Isn't that against the law? Wilf's not old enough to be an instructor. Besides, I wouldn't let you use

20

the van. I only let Melanie do it for a couple of weeks, and then cancelled the insurance again. It costs too much to keep up permanently.'

'Oh. Well, anyway, I can do all sorts of other things. And it's only for a few months. Once the tourists slow down, the hotel won't want you any more.'

'They might. The season never completely stops. And that would be just as difficult, in a way. All that money for three months, and then it just isn't there. It'll cause havoc with the books.'

'Worry about that when it happens,' said Bonnie, with an air of having said this before, a few too many times.

The hotel was on the outskirts of Hawkshead, barely half a mile to the south. It had been a sixteenth-century manor house, on elevated ground above Esthwaite Water, remaining in the same family for centuries. It had grounds that sloped down to the very edge of the gentle little lake. After a period of decline and neglect it had been sold and gradually transformed into a hotel. The story was only sketchily understood by Simmy, gleaned from brief conversations with Melanie since she started working there. The first attempt at providing accommodation had fallen foul of bad plumbing and a curmudgeonly proprietor. The next people cleaned it up but gained a reputation for poor food and high prices. Finally, the third attempt struck lucky, with a flair for characterful furnishings and inventive promotions. Added value was provided in the quieter seasons in the form of ghost walks, local history talks, writing workshops, painting classes and bridge weekends. It accommodated twenty-five guests, thanks to the conversion of stables and barns. The presence of a chef capable of working miracles with locally caught fish ensured a high level of success. Bookings were healthy for the next several months, according to Melanie. And well deserved it was too, thought Simmy, recalling all the efforts that were being made to capitalise on the building and its beautiful surroundings.

As she approached it, Simmy's first impression was of a modest building of considerable age, comfortable in its setting. White-painted, two-storey, with a stone wall marking out the extent of its grounds, the sign announcing The Hawkshead Hotel was of unpretentious lettering and size. No mention of weddings, banquets or conferences. A shrubbery on the left and a car park on the right. On a sunny day, it would look lovely. Even under clouds, it was more than attractive. She might enjoy coming here after all, she decided. The contact was a precious one, with a variety of opportunities leading from it, if she could only be clever enough to exploit them.

Inside, the reception desk was angled across one corner of a good-sized hallway. Already, she could see a place for a floral display, a few feet inside the door. Something subtly scented, in warm colours. She paused, peering round a solid-looking door into a lounge with a bay window, where another arrangement of flowers might be positioned to catch the sunlight, when it came. The window faced south-east, she calculated, with a view of the lake. Any flowers should be muted, to avoid distracting attention from the outside vista, but rather bringing echoes of it into the room.

She should make notes, she realised. Ideas were erupting faster than she could register them. Would Dan, the hotel man, want to provide some input as well, or would it all be left to her?

There was nobody on the desk. It was four o'clock in the afternoon – a time when guests might be expected to start to arrive. But perhaps everyone was already in, or had given later times. Perhaps it wasn't the sort of hotel where a girl sat idly waiting twenty-four hours a day just in case she was needed. There were voices not far away; quite loud voices, Simmy noticed. A woman was audibly shrill, a murmur of men joining in.

Simmy decided to investigate. There was a door beside the desk, leading into a short corridor with toilets on one side. Opposite them a staircase led to the upper floors. At the end were three further doors, left, right and straight ahead. The last was standing open and people were to be seen on a paved area just outside it. There were tubs containing lobelia and pansies and other unimaginative things.

'We have to call the police,' the shrill woman was saying as Simmy approached.

Chapter Two

Her first instinct was to turn and run. No more police involvement for her, not after the miserable events of a few months earlier and the consequences they had had for her father. How was it possible that she had innocently walked into another scene of crime and mayhem? She stood halfway down the corridor, unnoticed and indecisive.

'No need for that,' a man said in a shaky voice. 'She's only been gone a few minutes.'

'But where *is* she?' the woman demanded. 'Where can she have got to?'

'She can't have come to any harm,' the man said. 'There are no ponds, or roads, or... How old did you say she is? Has she done this before?'

'Six. And yes, she does have a tendency to run off,' the woman admitted. 'But this is a strange place. She'll get utterly lost.'

Even Simmy, lingering in the background, heaved a sigh of relief. A child of six was hardly going to stumble into a pond or under a passing car. And besides, neither of those hazards existed. A child of six was inquisitive, drawn to explore hidden corners and make dens under laurel bushes. As if her sigh had been a signal, three people turned towards her at the same moment.

'Who are you?' the woman asked.

'Um ... I came to see Dan about some flowers,'

she said weakly. 'I've obviously chosen a bad time.'

'Did you drive down from Hawkshead?' another man asked. He was young and good-looking and less agitated than any of the others in the group. In addition there were two young women hovering some distance away who Simmy guessed might be Polish or Ukrainian, working as chambermaids. Where was Melanie, she wondered. Melanie would be a welcome addition to this unsettled gathering.

'Yes, I did. Has something happened?'

'My little girl's lost. She was here half an hour ago. I left her on the parterre while I popped up to the room, and when I came back she was gone.' She threw accusing looks liberally around the members of the hotel staff. 'And nobody even noticed her.'

'Well, we should look for her,' said Simmy briskly. 'I expect she's just hiding somewhere – there's obviously plenty of scope for that. What's her name?'

'Gentian.'

Simmy closed her eyes in a moment of fellow feeling for the child. Another botanical name to be endured for a lifetime. Parents could be so cruel, she thought ruefully.

'There are people searching the grounds,' said the older man. 'They're not very extensive. This isn't Storrs, you know.'

Simmy shuddered, eliciting puzzled looks. 'Sorry – you reminded me of something that happened at Storrs last year.'

'A young man was drowned,' he nodded irritably. 'It was stupid of me to mention that place.' He turned to the woman who was casting her gaze all around like a shepherd searching for a lost lamb. 'Mrs Appleyard, please don't worry. Your daughter can't have gone far. If this lady came along the road just now, we can be sure there's no chance that the child went off that way.'

'I would definitely have seen her,' Simmy confirmed. She tried to think. 'What was she playing with – when you left her?'

Expecting the answer to involve some electronic gadget, she was foolishly glad to be told, 'She was making a daisy chain, as it happens. We picked the flowers when we went for a little walk. She'd got the hang of it very nicely.'

'Which one of you is Dan?' asked Simmy, thinking that she should go back to Windermere if her purpose was to be thwarted by a hunt for a lost child.

'None of us. I'm the hotel manager, and this is Jake Bunting, the chef. Dan's gone to have a look around the annexe buildings. Penny – she's the receptionist – went with him.'

'Oh.'

'We're not getting anywhere just *standing* here,' complained Gentian's mother. 'I think we should call the police.'

This is where I came in, thought Simmy. 'I should get out of your way, then,' she said, feeling heartless. 'I don't think there's much I can usefully do. I don't know this place at all.'

The woman reached out and gripped her arm. Her blue eyes stared pleadingly into Simmy's. She was of a similar age, and similar height. Her

26

hair was mid brown, and her clothes barely smart enough for a mid-range English hotel. 'You seem so sensible,' she said. 'Please don't go.'

With an effort, Simmy tolerated the appeal without shaking the woman off. *I've lost a daughter too,* she wanted to say. *Mine was born dead. You've had six years with yours. Think yourself lucky.* 'Let's go in separate directions and call her, then,' she suggested.

As if only waiting for a voice of authority, the group dispersed and seconds later voices of all tones and types were shouting 'Gentian!' across the grass and gravel of the hotel's rear. Simmy saw the manager's face as it dawned on him that other guests would be disturbed in a most undesirable fashion. This, she supposed, was the main reason why so little had been done to instigate a proper search thus far. Hotel managers were likely to be paralysed by any hint of trouble that might reflect badly on their establishment.

His fears were quickly realised. Three more people materialised from the back door, their expressions betraying a readiness to manifest annoyance and complaint at the disruption. There were two men and a woman, the men in their sixties or thereabouts, the woman slightly younger. One of the men was tall, lightly bearded, wearing a yellow straw hat and carrying a newspaper. He showed every sign of having wandered outside in search of fresh Lakeland air, only incidentally finding himself embroiled in a crisis of some sort. The others were clearly a couple, the woman glancing repeatedly at the man with little nervous jerks, as if to check that she retained his approval at every turn. 'Is there something wrong?' asked the husband.

'We're looking for a little girl,' said Simmy. 'She seems to have gone missing.'

Gentian's mother had vanished towards the shrubbery; the chambermaids were also no longer in sight. The manager was standing on a patch of grass, his head stretched upwards as he scanned his domain with an exaggerated alertness.

'She's sure to turn up,' said the tall man confidently. 'Always getting into mischief, children. I had some myself.' He sounded slightly puzzled, as if his own offspring had been mislaid for the past few decades without causing him undue concern.

The child's name continued to resound, the calling slowly moving further off. Then two more people came down the corridor and all was resolved. 'Here she is!' called Simmy, without thinking. How did she know this was the child in question? The answer quickly came to her. Who else would Melanie be holding so firmly by the shoulder, with such a look of triumph? Who else but Melanie, when it came to it, would be the one to find the brat?

Only the manager heard Simmy's cry. He turned and came trotting back, arms outstretched. 'Thank heavens!' he panted. 'Miss Todd – where did you find her?'

'She was under the table in the lounge,' said Melanie, giving the child a little shake. 'Enjoying all the fuss, the little beast.'

Most of the brownie points that Melanie had just earned for herself fell away at this lack of proper disquiet at all the might-have-beens. The child, by definition, was an innocent little angel, potential victim to the evil that lurked behind every wall and hedge. It could not possibly be a little beast.

But it was. Simmy could see this right away. A sly satisfaction sat on the young face. It was a very prepossessing little person, with thick black hair, dark skin and startlingly blue eyes. *Gentian blue,* thought Simmy. 'Your mother's going frantic,' she said crossly.

'I was all right. She always makes such a fuss.' She glared at Melanie in defiance. 'And I don't like it at all.'

'Why? Do you do this often?' asked Melanie.

Gentian shrugged. 'Not really. I just like to be by myself, and she won't let me.'

Word had been passed across the grounds, and now the little girl's mother came scrambling along and grabbed her offspring. She was an awkward person, Simmy observed, wearing high-heeled shoes, at odds with the baggy top and cut-off slacks. Nobody would have ever guessed her to be related to the beautiful child clutched to her breast. Perhaps it had been an adoption, Simmy thought idly.

'I was all right,' Gentian repeated loudly. 'Get off me.'

She was dropped like a kitten turned hostile. 'Oh, darling, don't be beastly.'

'I'm not. It's you. There's nothing to *do* here. Why can't we go on a boat or something? There's just a lot of old people here.' She swept the group with a critical eye. 'Except her. She's all right.'

29

She indicated Simmy.

'I'm not old,' said Melanie.

'You don't count,' said Simmy with a laugh. 'She'll never forgive you for finding her.'

Melanie came from a large family and had no illusions about innocent little angels. She grinned in agreement and changed the subject. 'You came, then,' she said. 'You'd better go and find Dan.'

'He must be the only person I haven't met in the past twenty minutes.' But that wasn't true at all, she corrected herself. There had to be numerous guests as well as some additional staff she hadn't yet encountered. The place was full of people – or would be at the end of the day.

'He said he was going to look for the kid round the stable block, but I think he's having a quick fag somewhere. He's as bad as young Gentian, if you ask me – hiding away so's to get a bit of peace.' She spoke in a whisper, with a glance at the manager. 'He'll get a bollocking from old Bodgett if he's not careful.'

'The receptionist went with him, apparently.'

'What? Penny? Not likely. They loathe each other. She'll have gone for a fag as well – or whatever her thing is. Wait till you see her.'

The kid was being hauled away by an increasingly irate and embarrassed mother. 'I was going to call the *police*,' she said in a loud hiss.

'That's stupid,' argued Gentian. 'I was perfectly all right.'

'Well, if you do it again, I'm going to keep you shut in the room for the rest of the week. Just you see if I don't.'

'He's not really called Bodgett, is he?' asked Simmy.

The manager had gone back inside, leaving Simmy and Melanie alone under the grey skies. A foolish little drama had come to an end with no harm done. The relief was still reverberating somewhere inside Simmy. She had almost forgotten what she had come for.

'Boddington-hyphen-Webster, would you believe? What is it with people and their double barrels these days? They all think they're descended from earls or something.'

'I know.' Simmy recalled a recent rant from young Ben Harkness on the subject. Computers, it seemed, disliked long hyphenated surnames, with ticket bookings and online registrations choking on them. 'It's all very silly.'

'Anyway, come with me and we'll find Dan. He must be around here somewhere. Oh – did you see Jake? He's the only normal person here. Funny, that. Usually the chef is the most bonkers of them all in a place like this. But he's all right, is Jake. Never gets in a tizz. Loves his work.' She sighed.

'Good-looking, as well,' Simmy observed.

'Yeah, and the rest. But he ticks one of the boxes for the stereotype.' She sighed again. 'Seems such a waste, though I know I'm not meant to say that. Don't tell him I said so, but really, it's very unfair.'

'What?' Simmy was still thinking slowly.

'He's gay, of course. Wouldn't you know it? Lives with a chap from Belgium or somewhere, in the village.'

'Oh.'

31

'And here's the last one in the set. Look at her.'

Simmy looked. A very thin woman was coming towards them, wiping her nose with a tissue and feeling the back of her neck with the other hand. She appeared to be around fifty, with careful make-up and smart clothes that looked rather warm for the season. Her hair was a glossy artificial black, which highlighted the pallor of her skin. Her midsection was actually concave, reminding Simmy of the runner Paula Radcliffe, whose body had always caused her great fascination. How did all those organs and countless yards of intestine fit in there, she wondered.

'Hi, Penny,' said Melanie. 'They found the missing kid.'

'Right. Where was she?' The woman's voice was high and forced. Every move she made appeared to take an almost insuperable effort.

'In the lounge. Panic over.'

'Good. Better get back to my post, then.' She laughed, but Simmy could detect no hint of a joke. 'Who's this?' Penny asked, as an afterthought.

'Persimmon Brown, the florist,' Melanie said.

Simmy realised that Melanie was being extremely careful with Penny-the-receptionist. Making no claims for herself, adding no embellishing information, answering questions with the shortest of sentences – all decidedly out of character.

'Right. Fine.' Penny glanced at a small sparkly watch. 'Only another hour to go, thank God.'

They watched her go back into the foyer, and then Melanie led the way along a gravel path towards the annexe, past an arrangement of ornamental trees in large pots on one side, and a row of windows on the other.

'Is she ill?' Simmy asked, thinking about Penny.

'Physically or mentally?' Melanie laughed. 'Actually, I think she might have some sort of health issue. She works short days. Lord knows how she ever got this job. She knocks off at four o'clock, and the manager's wife does evenings and weekends, including Fridays. But I think Penny's tougher than she looks. And she's good with the guests, amazingly. Smiles and simpers at the men, sympathises with the women. She's a great actor. All the staff leave her alone as much as they can.'

'She's scary, then?'

Melanie paused. 'There's just something *about* her. Like a time bomb. You get the feeling if you crossed her, she'd explode all over you. Or else drop down dead in front of you. She goes to the gym a lot. It's obviously killing her.'

Simmy snorted agreement, while thinking there might be rather more to the odd creature she had just met than an addiction to weight training or whatever else people did in a gym.

'That's the dining room in there,' Melanie pointed out, continuing her tour. 'Then there's the kitchen, look. It's all very well organised. Dan lives in. He's got a couple of rooms round the corner. Bodgett's in residence as well, of course. They share the old servants' quarters. He's the butler and Dan's the housekeeper. Funny, eh?'

'It's a whole little world,' said Simmy, thinking there was a sort of magic to hotel life. The core of permanent staff on one hand and the constantly shifting procession of guests on the other. 'I presume there's a gardener and kitchen hands and waiters as well.'

'Pretty much. The dining room staff are mostly foreign, same as the cleaners.'

'And you're always full, right? Twenty-five people to look after, day and night. Very weird, when you think about it.'

'Hospitality,' said Melanie. 'One of the oldest professions.'

Simmy thought again of her father. 'I suppose so. If my dad was here, he'd talk about pilgrimages and ancient customs, or Victorian dosshouses with four to a bed.'

Melanie laughed. 'He would, too. Now come on. I'm meant to be working. Before all this nonsense with the lost kid blew up, I was trying to track down a missing pillowcase. I mean – people steal towels, but you don't often lose a *pillowcase*.'

'Makes a useful extra bag, I suppose.'

'Right,' said Melanie inattentively. 'There's Dan, look. Now, make sure you give me proper credit for putting you in touch with him. I need to keep on his right side.' She indicated a figure still too far off to hear what they were saying.

Simmy gave her a surprised look. 'You sound scared of him, same as you are of Penny.'

'No, I'm not a bit scared of him. But Dan's the real power here. Does just what he likes and nobody dares challenge him. It pays to stay on the right side of him.' Again, she flushed, as she'd done that morning. 'But he's perfectly nice.' It sounded defensive to Simmy.

She watched the man approaching them. He

34

walked with a loose easy gait, unselfconscious and unhurried. Aged about thirty-five, she guessed, with dark colouring. His hair had been cut carefully, to capitalise on its thickness and slight wave. In another age, he might have been mistaken for Clark Gable without the moustache and with an additional three inches of height. 'He should grow a moustache,' she murmured to Melanie. 'Then he'd be perfect.'

Melanie snickered, quickly putting a hand over her mouth. 'Shut up – he'll hear you.'

And that, Simmy suspected, would be a very bad thing.

Chapter Three

Men who worked in hotels ought to be handsome, as a general rule. It endeared them to the guests and made complaints less frequent. Dan fitted the bill in a way, but the veneer of insincerity was almost palpable. 'I'm Persimmon Brown,' she said, holding out her hand. 'I came to talk to you about flowers. I gather Melanie told you about me.'

'Oh, right. Pleased to meet you. Dan Yates.' He smiled at a point some inches from her left ear and added, 'Thank you, Melanie. I think I can take it from here.'

'I'm sure you can,' said the girl, using her uncanny skill at conveying insolence, scepticism or plain disapproval in words that nobody could find objectionable.

'Let's go to my office, then. Follow me.' He set off briskly in the direction of the converted stables, Simmy following like a schoolgirl. Power politics of some kind, she judged. She could easily have walked by his side. She had never worked in an environment where such games were played; all she knew of them came from TV sitcoms and stories told by her former husband. She was aware that there were plenty of people in the outside world who enjoyed throwing their weight around, using tricks like this. And yet Melanie had said he was 'okay', so she should probably give him the benefit of the doubt. Perhaps he was basically insecure or merely amusing himself by toying with her to make life more interesting. Perhaps he had no idea what he was doing and just wanted them to get on as quickly as possible.

'Here we are,' he said. 'They gave me the tack room.' He opened the door into a small boxy addition to the main stable block. An earlier door into the horses' living quarters had apparently been sealed off, and the resulting new wall used for a floor-to-ceiling set of shelves. Simmy looked around, trying to work out the details of the conversion, with a faint idea of describing it all to her father at some point. He took considerable interest in such things.

'Sit down,' Dan Yates invited. 'And tell me what you think of Melanie's ideas.'

'Well ... I'm not sure how much she's discussed with you. We should probably start from scratch, to be sure it's all clear.'

'Quite right. As it happens, the manager and I

had been thinking we needed something decorative, something distinctive, but subtle – to improve the atmosphere. It's all about perception, you see. We want people to remember us as having just that extra hint of luxury. The food is our main appeal at the moment, and the views.'

'Right,' said Simmy. 'I see.'

'Yes, but we need another *dimension*. We're acutely aware of the history here. There have been serious failures in the past. There's a fragility, a vulnerability, to the whole industry these days. We want to consolidate what we have, build on it slowly, without making too many mistakes.'

Simmy nodded. So far, she did at least understand the words he used. He hadn't said 'iterative' or 'quantum' or 'logistics', which was a relief, if only because she might have laughed at the wrong moment if he had.

'So we would like you to supply enough flowers for displays in the main ground-floor rooms and in the solar upstairs. That would be four positions. We'd like scented blooms, nothing too flamboyant. Perhaps you could share any ideas you have at this point?'

'Well ... I did have a few thoughts about your reception area and the lounge. I haven't seen the other places. That big bay window in the lounge – an arrangement just to one side of it, with a lot of greens, would have the effect of bringing the view right into the room. For the reception, I thought lilies and foliage in the blue or mauve spectrum, with some scent, as you say. Nothing that would intimidate or distract, but be welcoming, like coming into someone's house.'

'Perfect,' he approved with a wide smile.

Again, Simmy found herself wishing he had a moustache. His upper lip looked weak and naked without one. She liked facial hair, reminding her as it did of a grandfather who had sported a full beard. She had loved to play with it as a child, and ever after associated beards with warmth and humour and manly strength. Her father had taken to going unshaven at times, but never allowed it to develop as nature ordained.

'Is this just for the summer season?' she asked.

'Initially, perhaps. We'll see how it goes, shall we? We are open all the year round, except for the middle of January. We close for two weeks then and give the whole staff a well-earned holiday. Now, then, we need to discuss money. What do you think?'

She took a breath. Her price lists didn't extend to such a large and regular commission, and every time during the day that she'd tried to work it out, the answer came out different. 'Are you thinking two visits a week? Perhaps Mondays and Fridays? I don't think it could be less than that. Some flowers do fade and droop after three or four days, although there are lots that would last a week if the water was topped up and the temperature wasn't too hot.'

'Twice a week is fine.'

'Well, to cover my travel and time spent here as well as all materials, I would want five hundred pounds a week.' She waited for the explosion at such an outrageous demand. If they paid that, she would find herself able to afford all sorts of things she'd been depriving herself of.

'No problem,' he said, so quickly that she knew she could have gone higher. After all, they charged their guests a hundred and fifty a night. Anyone staying a whole week was already more than paying for the flowers. 'Now, let's give you a guided tour.'

Again, he trotted ahead of her, skirting around the side of the main building and in through the front entrance. They paused on the spot where Simmy had already mentally planned her welcoming exhibit, and then progressed to the lounge where a scattering of guests were on sofas drinking tea. Simmy recognised only one of them – the tall man with the straw hat and a rather appealing beard. 'Afternoon, Mr Ferguson,' Dan addressed him with a smile. 'Had a good day?'

The man nodded coolly and turned a page of his newspaper. Dan showed no sign of offence, but returned to his quiet discussion with Simmy. Again a subtle scent was decided upon, with colours in a very discreet and muted palette. The dining room was inspected, and a position next to the sideboard selected as the best place for flowers. These could be more dramatically cheerful, encouraging diners to take a risk with their fish.

The solar was a fabulous upstairs space, full of light and height. 'Tall spiky things,' said Simmy. 'Fanned out in the shape of a rising sun. Oranges and yellows.' She was transported by the opportunity the job was creating for her. 'Which I'd vary, of course. It would never be the same two weeks running. But still along that sort of line.'

'Excellent,' said Dan Yates. 'That's all good, then. Can you start this week?'

39

'Friday?'

He pouted teasingly. 'Is tomorrow too soon, then?'

'Well, yes, it is, really. I need to order everything, and...' she stopped, fully aware that if she put the order in that evening the flowers would arrive next morning, with nothing to stop her from coming back and arranging them in the middle of the day. Was it not a deplorable laziness that made her pause? 'I suppose it would be possible. Will you supply the pots, or should I?'

'We've got a whole lot in a pantry at the back. I'll show you.'

'Good.'

'The thing is, we've got people coming on Wednesday, who we'd rather like to impress. Americans. A little bird has whispered that they might be rather useful to us, with reviews and all that. Even if you just did the foyer and the solar, that would be a big help. Then come back on Friday for the full monty.'

They were descending the stairs, emerging into the corridor that Simmy had found nearly an hour earlier. Standing there, waiting for the stairs to be clear, was the couple who had reacted badly to the sounds of the hunt for Gentian. It occurred to Simmy that they might occupy a ground-floor room, perhaps accessed through one of the doors at the end of the corridor? She gave herself a mental shake. Too much contact with Ben Harkness, she chided. Always trying to read clues and make deductions, was Ben. She had hoped the habit wasn't catching, but apparently it was. There was no imaginable relevance to the location of

40

guest rooms.

'Hello there,' said Dan heartily. 'Mr and Mrs Lillywhite,' he introduced them to Simmy. 'This lady is going to be supplying us with flowers,' he explained.

The woman smiled tightly, and the man merely inclined his head. 'The lost child is restored then,' he said. 'No more panic.'

'There was never any panic, sir,' said Dan. 'But her mother was understandably alarmed. I'm sorry if you found it disturbing.'

'It was right outside our window,' the man went on, the rumble of discontent hard to ignore.

'My apologies,' repeated Dan. 'I can assure you it won't happen again. As a gesture, permit me to offer you a complimentary aperitif before dinner. I'll give Charles a note now, to be sure it won't be overlooked.'

Simmy thought that Mr Lillywhite might also benefit from a moustache. He could have bristled it and harumphed at being wrong-footed so effortlessly. As it was, his clean, pink face adopted a gracious expression, and he ushered his compliant wife upstairs ahead of him. 'Thank you,' he mumbled. 'Come along, Rosemary.'

Well done! thought Simmy. All her preconceptions about the need for unwavering sycophancy in the world of hotels had been confirmed. This man had to set aside any thought of his own self-respect, for the greater good of satisfied customers. It was done with dignity, and the slenderest hint that he was, after all, in the right of it. The complaining guest would be left at best with mixed emotions. Free drinkies – hooray! But offered so glibly, so willingly – didn't that leave a suspicion that he, the guest, was being humoured like a sulky child? The suggestion that his objections had been foolish, excessive, somehow betraying unfortunate origins, would make him uneasy. Especially as, in this case, something about his wife's chin made the suspicion all the stronger.

Nothing could be further from Simmy's mother's plain-speaking to her B&B guests. If they complained, she cross-questioned them as to precisely what they had expected. She might ask them if such a requirement, whatever it might be, had ever in their experience been met. She might even point out that she did her best in the circumstances, but was only human and had never promised a weekend in paradise. The people almost always apologised for their importunate demands.

Dan took her to a gloomy room that must have been the dairy originally. There were slate slabs for keeping milk, butter and cheese cool, a stone floor and very small windows. On a shelf stood at least a dozen assorted containers, from metal buckets to fancy terracotta plant pots with ornate handles. None seemed quite right for the purpose to Simmy. But there were also three large rose bowls with their own pedestals, tucked against the wall. Made of fine-quality china, it seemed odd to find them discarded so carelessly. 'What are they doing here?' she asked.

'The manager had them taken out of harm's way, a while ago now. He was worried that guests' children might knock them over. Plus he thought they looked wrong with no flowers in them. And until now, we haven't found anyone capable of filling them regularly.' He smiled at her, showing perfect white teeth.

'Can we risk using them, then?'

'If you think they'll do.'

'They'll be fine. But there's only three. What else can we use?' She scanned the room, assessing the options. 'That's interesting.' She went to a large black vase, tall and narrow, with a gold-etched design down the front that looked like Chinese lettering. 'It would be good in the lounge.'

'Isn't it a bit low?'

'We'd have to find something to stand it on. Any little table will do.'

'Okay. Shall we take them in now? Or what?'

She hesitated, wondering how best to organise things. 'If I can take the black one back with me, I can have at least one display ready in advance. The bowls can stay here until tomorrow, and I'll do the arrangements *in situ.*'

'Whatever you say.' She had the impression that he was tiring of the whole subject of flowers, and eager to see her off. He must have things to do, she realised. The end of the afternoon would see people returning from their day out, dinner to be prepared, plans to be made.

'I'll see you tomorrow,' she said. 'Thank you for spending so much time on this. I won't let you down.'

'I'm sure you won't,' he said. 'I have complete faith in you.'

She parted from Dan Yates thinking it would be interesting to get to know him over the summer. Not only him, but also the rest of the staff. And it would be a bonus to see Melanie more often. With a light step, she returned to her car, and navigated the twisting route back to Windermere. Bonnie would have gone home and locked the street door of the shop, but there were all those flowers to be ordered, and some tidying to do. She was busy, she realised. Very busy.

But there might also be time to more thoroughly explore Hawkshead itself. The fact that very few cars were permitted in the centre of the village had deterred her from ever going there other than to deliver flowers from time to time. Now she might find an hour or so to walk there from the hotel, and even have a drink in one of the cafés. Fridays might be organised accordingly. Arrive at the hotel mid afternoon, and award herself a nice summer evening in the fells of Furness, or the edge of Esthwaite. If she had somebody to go with her, it would be all the nicer, of course – but that was unlikely.

It all meant change, anyway, and that was a good thing. Her gratitude towards Melanie burgeoned as she realised just what a big thing the girl had done for her. There was, after all, a florist in Coniston and several in Ambleside, any of which might have got the commission instead of her. She would have to do a good job, if only to justify Mel's recommendation.

Back in the shop she spent twenty minutes ordering a careful selection of flowers, making sketches of the displays she intended to install at the hotel. Ideas thronged her mind, subtle touches that would enhance the impression she hoped to make. The additional work on Friday was even more exciting and she jotted notes for the solar and dining room as well. Only then did she remember that Melanie had said there might be another site upstairs where flowers could be needed. Dan hadn't mentioned it, but it set her to wondering whether there actually was a large meeting room up there. All the winter events offered by the hotel must need something of the sort. She remembered her curiosity about the Lillywhites' reason for going upstairs. Perhaps they'd rented the room for some purpose?

It was sheer greed, she accused herself, wanting to provide yet more flowers. The work would be onerous as it was, and anything more would have to be renegotiated payment-wise. But the more she thought of the lovely old building and all the hidden areas she hadn't seen, the more she wanted to discover. Apart from her own fascination with it, she wanted to be able to describe it to her father and play their favourite game of imagining how things must have been centuries ago.

The original owners were very probably a large Victorian family with servants and regular social events. Dancing in the current dining room; conversing in the lounge; eating in a darker area to the rear, close to the kitchens. There would be eight or nine bedrooms on the upper two storeys, with dressing rooms and large closets now transformed into bathrooms. Alterations would have been considerable, to include en suite bathrooms, for one thing. Walls would have been moved, staircases enlarged or even added. There

45

had to be a lift somewhere. In a combination of preservation and modern vandalism, the building's new incarnation would be unrecognisable to those long-age residents. She looked forward to gradually finding out more, during her regular summer visits.

She had to accept that four large displays was plenty. As she listed her requirements for the wholesaler, she discovered that her five hundred pounds would not yield as big a profit as she'd thought. What a fool, she reproached herself. She should have done detailed costings, instead of plucking a figure out of the air as she had. There would in effect be eight lots of flowers to be specially purchased every week – although some might be carried over from one visit to the next. She would have to be very clever with design and colour, using cheaper blossoms to maximum effect, if she were to benefit as originally hoped.

But it would have unforeseen advantages, too. People would ask who had done the flowers, and make a note of the name. And it would give extra weight to any approaches she might make to other hotels, closer to home. She could send people for a look at the Hawkshead example as proof of her abilities.

And Bonnie would appreciate the additional responsibility. She loved working in the shop, giving up any pretence to other ambitions. 'This is the life,' she often said. 'I've found my vocation. I don't care what Corinne says about getting some proper qualifications.' She was certainly very talented when it came to visual effects. After only a few days in the job, she had transformed the interior of the shop with an almost magical set-up suggesting a kind of highway from street to cash register. She regularly reorganised the front window, too. But she was slow to learn the names of the flowers and the importance of the seasons. She floundered when a customer asked for suggestions and could not do the simplest mental arithmetic.

Her education had been fatally interrupted by anorexia, with exams taken for form's sake and almost certainly comprehensively failed. The results weren't expected for many more weeks, but nobody thought there would be any pleasant surprises. She looked much younger than her seventeen years, a pale little pixie creature who few people could take seriously.

At last Simmy closed down the computer, checked the lights and locks and headed for home. She lived in Troutbeck, at a much higher elevation than the lakeside towns of Windermere and Ambleside. A brisk walk up Wansfell from her cottage would reveal a sweeping view across the lake to the woodlands on its western shore, where Coniston, Hawkshead, the Sawreys and Furness were arrayed between Windermere and Coniston Water. Everywhere in this southern part of the Lake District there were trees and gardens and rich green grass. Only on the high fells did the rocks and heather prevail, assisted by the relentless grazing of sheep.

The names and character of the various settlements were gradually coming into focus for her as she got well into her second year in the area. There was a lot of catching up to do, though, before she could achieve anything like familiarity. New details were constantly coming to her attention – including the existence of the Hawkshead Hotel and the environs of the tiny town from which it took its name.

She fell asleep making mental lists of everything she would have to do next day, and for the rest of the week. It would all fall into place, she was sure. There were plenty of hours in the day, after all. Half-dreaming, she saw before her the faces of Dan Yates and Jake the chef, as well as young Gentian and the harumphing ground-floor guest. They were all admiring a great vase of flowers that she had arranged out on the parterre.

Chapter Four

'How did it go?' Bonnie asked, the moment she stepped into the shop next morning. 'At the hotel, I mean.'

'Really well. Although I have a feeling I didn't ask for enough money. It seemed like a lot until I broke it down, and then it was too late. It's okay, though. I'll just have to be extra clever at what I use.'

'The delivery van's here.' Bonnie cocked her head at a vehicle pulling up outside.

The girl helped the van man to unload, admiring the closely packed blooms as she always did before releasing them from their captivity and giving them a drink. 'Look at this colour!' she cried, holding a pale-mauve primula aloft. 'And what's with all this eucalyptus?'

'That's for the foyer. It's going to be mainly mauves and purples. Eucalyptus is perfect for that.'

'What are the others?'

Simmy produced the black vase. 'This one's going in the lounge, at the end of the week. Today, I'm only doing the reception area and the big space upstairs. It's called a solar, because it gets so much sun.'

'Sounds nice,' said the girl, sounding wistful. 'Wish I could see it.'

'We'll work something out so you can,' Simmy promised, thinking the girl probably hadn't ever seen the inside of an expensive hotel.

By ten o'clock, she had assembled everything she needed and loaded it into her van. She had also checked the computer for new orders and left Bonnie with all the usual instructions for taking charge of the shop. 'I should be back by twelve,' she said. 'Have fun.'

Bonnie's mobile prevented her from responding. 'It's Ben,' she said with an unconscious grin.

For no good reason, Simmy hovered in the doorway while the youngsters conversed. Within half a minute it turned out that she had been right to do so. Bonnie flapped an urgent hand at her, saying, 'Yes, she's here. You only just caught her.' She held out the phone. 'He wants to speak to you.'

'Hi, Ben. How are you?' she greeted him.

'Okay. Listen – are you coming to Hawkshead this morning? Bonnie said you were, when I spoke

49

to her last night.'

'Yes. I'm just leaving. Why?'

'I'm stuck here, that's why. I assumed I'd got a lift sorted, but they've gone without me. Probably my own fault, for boasting about how much I like hiking. Then I went for the bus, but they cancelled the next one. I'm far too knackered to walk to the ferry. It's hot. And Bonnie says you're coming here anyway, so that seems the perfect solution. Don't you think?'

'It's no problem for me. Where will you be?'

'In the car park. The one on the left as you go into the village.'

'You'll have to amuse yourself while I do the flowers in the hotel. Is that okay? I should be finished by twelve at the latest.'

'It'll have to be,' he said ungraciously, before asking, 'but can't I come with you to do the arranging? I could guard the van or something. It's going to be boring otherwise, kicking my heels in Hawkshead.'

It occurred to Simmy that sitting in a van was hardly exciting, but she guessed the boy was in need of a rest. He'd probably fall asleep. 'I suppose so. Stand where I can see you, then, and I'll be there in about twenty-five minutes, I should think.'

'Thanks a bundle, Sim,' he said. 'Can I talk to Bonnie again now?'

Resisting the urge to give Bonnie a repeat set of instructions, Simmy set out. It was a route she was beginning to find familiar, and to savour accordingly. From Windermere to Ambleside the road followed the eastern edge of the lake, often within

50

a few feet of the lapping water. There were huge, high trees along this road, as there were bordering much of the A591, all the way from Ings. They gave the impression that there was a forest just waiting for its chance to become once again the dominant feature it must have been a millennium ago. If people and sheep were sent into an enchanted sleep for a few years, they would awake to dense vegetation on all sides.

Then she was passing the marinas and jetties that formed the southern fringe of Ambleside, curving around the very northern tip of Lake Windermere, and into the twisting little lanes that led to Hawkshead. It was a total of nine miles, and it always took at least twenty minutes. She had to follow behind two cars obviously driven by visitors, so her predicted time of arrival in Hawkshead was exceeded slightly. Ben was standing conspicuously in the entrance to the car park, scanning every vehicle with close attention.

'Had a good holiday?' she asked him, once he was settled, his rucksack at his feet.

'Sort of. Not exactly a *holiday*, though. We walked eighteen miles a day for three days, most of it uphill.'

'How many of you?'

'Five. Me, Wilf, a guy called Tom and two brothers, Mo and Sid. Really they're Mohammed and Sayeed. They're from Sheffield. Wilf met them a while back. Tom's my age. He's here with his family on holiday, but didn't want to spend the whole time with them.'

'Sounds like a good group.'

'They were okay. I chatted a lot to Tom, and he's

quite bright. He's from Derby. I've never been to Derby,' he added thoughtfully.

'How did he get together with you, then – he just walked up to you and asked if you'd take him, or what?'

'More or less. We were in Coniston on the first day, and he got talking to us. We'd got space in one of the tents, so we said okay. No big deal.'

Simmy reflected wistfully on the spontaneous freedom this implied. 'I suppose he had a phone with him, so he could keep his parents posted.'

'Yeah, but he only called once, I think.'

'So you had a good time.'

'Pretty much. Although the food was rubbish. Burnt sausages, most of the time.'

'You poor thing. You do seem to have lost a bit of weight, I must say.' She threw a quick look at his bare legs, which had very little flesh on them. 'Nice and brown, though. I don't remember it being sunny.'

'We had one nice afternoon. Unless it's scorching from the campfires. Or just dirt.' He licked a finger and rubbed it on the skin above his knee. 'It does come off a bit, look.'

She laughed. 'Maybe you should go down to the lake for a wash while I do my flowers. The hotel's grounds go right to the edge.'

'Sounds nice. But I might wander over to Colthouse. I want to see if there's a path through the woods, or if you need to go around the road.'

'Why? What's there? I've never heard of it.'

'Mostly it's a Quaker meeting house and burial ground, but there's an Ann Tyson's House there as well.'

'Sorry, Ben. None of these things mean anything to me. Well, Quakers, a bit...'

'Don't worry about it. It's a thing I've got going with Bonnie. I'll be sure to be back at the van in plenty of time. I know you'll be ages.'

In two more minutes they were at the gateway leading to the hotel. 'Better not park right in the middle of all these Rovers and things,' she said. 'It'll lower the tone.'

'BMW, Audi, Mercedes, Subaru,' he noted. 'Can't see a Rover.'

'Smart, is all I mean. My dad always says you can't get better quality than a Rover.'

'He has no idea,' sighed Ben.

Simmy laughed again. It was good to spend a few minutes with the boy, after not seeing him for over a week. He was always good company – unpredictable, funny and immensely knowledgeable. The fact that she was easily old enough to be his mother seldom presented any difficulty. There had been times when he had felt like the parent and she the child.

'Do you want help with the unloading?' he asked, with a wary glance over his shoulder at the contents of the van.

'No, thanks. I'll have to do it all in the right order. You go and have your walk, if you've really got that much energy. I don't expect anybody would mind if you took the path down to the water. Or you could just stay here and have a little nap.'

'Can't do that. It's no distance to Colthouse from here. Even round the road can't be more

53

than twenty minutes.' He got out of the van and stood admiring the lake, stretching away to the right. 'I quite like Esthwaite,' he said. 'It's so unglamorous compared to most of the others.'

'I'll probably only be about an hour, so don't go far. If I can't find you, I'll come down to the lake and look for you. It's a nice day for a change.'

'It would turn nice, just as I'm going home. It was cold and windy all the time we were in the fells.'

He moved off at a trot, down the moderate slope to the edge of the water. As far as Simmy could see, there were no paths in the direction he'd indicated. Instead there was a fenced-off area of woodland that looked impenetrably dense. The lake lapped almost imperceptibly against the grassy bank. She watched Ben for a moment and then got straight to work.

The next forty minutes were spent in total concentration on the flowers. The black vase had been set aside as destined for the dining room on Friday, so she used two of the rose bowls from the dairy. Somebody – presumably Dan – had brought them into the foyer for her. On closer inspection, she liked them less. They were certainly in keeping with the house – florid Victorian pinks and greens decorated them and their pedestals. One had a long crack in it, and the other looked as if it had been washed in a very hot dishwasher, leading to a patchy fading of the design. They were not a matching pair, and not of the best quality. She would use them for this week, while searching out something better for the future. Her friend Ninian

Tripp could make himself useful in that department, even if he wouldn't have time to fashion something himself. He was a potter, after all, with vases one of his best lines. In time, he could very likely produce a set of perfectly gorgeous items for the hotel.

Thoughts of Ninian always brought their own special set of frustrations. He and Simmy were conducting a sporadic relationship, for which neither of them seemed to feel a great deal of commitment. It was agreeable to spend a night in his isolated little house on Brant Fell with trees all around. It was equally agreeable to have somebody to eat and chat with at the end of a day's work in the shop. But Ninian would never be an object of great passion; nor would he qualify as a father to any baby she might yet manage to produce to compensate somehow for the poor, lost little Edith. As the months rolled by, Simmy increasingly gave up any hope that such a child might ever exist. She was thirty-eight already. Surely her destiny was firmly set now as a flourishing businesswoman with a growing complement of friends in this beautiful part of England that she was still getting to know?

She completed the display for the reception first. Tendrils of scented honeysuckle wove amongst the cool shades of eucalyptus and the bolder allium. The primulas were tricky to position and certain to go limp by Friday. The colours were a risk – not many people would dare combine the orangey shades of honeysuckle with mauve and purple, but – as one of her tutors had often said – in nature almost any combination could be found, so there

55

should be no firm rules when it came to arranging flowers.

Upstairs in the solar, she worked faster, the finished effect clear in her mind's eye. The shape was the thing – a semicircle to represent a rising sun – with the colours falling easily into place. Set against a wall, only one face of the display would show, so she was able to keep it almost two-dimensional. When she stepped back to assess it, she was impressed by her own work. It was undeniably flamboyant, celebrating the light and heat of summer, certain to warm the spirits of anybody who saw it.

She had left her phone, with notebook and wallet, in the van. Carrying her bag of oasis, ribbons, ties and other necessities, she went back to the vehicle. Nobody had spoken to her, and she had not set eyes on Melanie. A few guests had drifted past her in the reception area, but said nothing. A woman she supposed was Mrs Bodgett appeared from a room and fiddled with a few things behind the reception desk, at one point. She looked to be about thirty-five, with enormous false eyelashes and a lot of make-up. She smiled and mumbled something, but it was hardly a conversation.

Out of habit, Simmy switched on the phone, and within a few seconds it gave the little song that told her she had a message. Bonnie, she supposed, with a question about the shop. It was voicemail, not a text, which suggested it might be urgent. With a sigh, Simmy put the phone to her ear, reluctant to discover what mistake the girl might have made without having recourse to advice.

'Simmy!' came a high-pitched voice, full of panic. 'There's a body here. Under the trees, at the very top end of the lake. I don't know what to do. Well, I'll have to call 999. Who knows when you'll get this... Hey!' The phone went silent in her hand, even though she continued to listen for further speech.

It was Ben. The last syllable had been closer to a scream than a shout. For quite a long moment, Simmy merely sat there, inwardly cursing. Because her first reaction was that the boy was having a laugh, playing a joke on her. There had been bodies before, associated with flower deliveries and malign uses thereof. Not until that final word did she understand that this was real, and that the boy was not merely panicked but terrified.

Chapter Five

She ran back into the hotel, intending to find Melanie. But then she realised that help and reassurance were luxuries she could not rely on. Something terrible had happened to Ben, and suddenly it was as if her own most beloved child was in danger. His cry of *Hey!* echoed in her mind, swelling with a host of dreadful implications. He had been alarmed, angry, shocked and scared. It was all in that one little word.

The woman with the exaggerated lashes was standing in the foyer, gazing with modified rapture at Simmy's flowers. Her head was on one side, and a hand extended as if – outrageously – to adjust a bloom. 'Help!' cried Simmy, ignoring pangs of embarrassment at her naked emotion. 'Something awful has happened – is happening – down by the lake. I've had a message. We need to call the police. Quickly.'

The woman fluttered the heavy black fringes over her eyes. They made her look like a caricature of a doll, itself already a caricature of a real child. They made one doubt whether there was a fully formed functioning individual behind them. 'What?' she said.

Penny was behind the reception desk, watching dispassionately and making no move to intervene. Simmy ignored her instinctively. Instead she waved her phone in the painted face before her. 'A dead man!' she shouted. Then she took a breath and understood that it was down to her. She squinted down at the screen and pressed the 9 digit three times. It was not the first time she had done this, but it still felt imbued with horror. Her stomach churned and her legs trembled.

When it came to explaining her problem, she floundered. 'A friend just phoned me to say he's found a dead body, in some woods on the banks of Esthwaite. Then he broke off, as if he was being attacked.' That was what she *should* have said. But it didn't come out like that. 'He's just a boy,' she repeated. 'He said somebody's dead. It's by the lake. I'm at a hotel.' Phrases emerged that made perfect sense to her, but were clearly gibberish to the woman at the end of the line who repeatedly urged Simmy to calm down and to give helpful details such as her actual position. 'Is somebody injured?' she asked. And, 'Can you see what's happening from where you are?'

This seemed to go on for hours, before Mrs Bodgett snatched the phone away from her and tried in turn to provide useful information. Given that she still had little idea as to precisely what Ben had said – or who Ben was anyway – she did not do very much better than Simmy had.

'We should go down there and see for ourselves,' Simmy said, when the emergency person finally agreed to send a police car to investigate. 'Where's Melanie?'

'In the office.' The woman gestured at a door across the hallway, which Simmy had barely noticed. In other hotels she had known, the office had generally been visible by anyone standing at reception through a glass partition or suchlike.

Penny leant forward. 'Who is this Ben person?' she asked in her high voice. 'Not one of our guests?'

'He's a friend of mine. He came with me.'

The gesture of neck and chin clearly said, *Oh well – not a problem for the hotel at all, then.* Simmy felt hot and angry, but said nothing. Panic levels were subsiding, but there was still a great choking cloud of anxiety about Ben's welfare. Melanie would understand, and even assuage to some extent. 'Can you fetch her?' she asked. 'Please.'

Her plea was acted upon by the manager's wife and suddenly there was the big dependable young woman standing right in front of Simmy, calmly prepared to hear whatever might be said. 'Listen,' said Simmy, holding out the phone. 'It's a message from Ben. On the voicemail.'

Melanie competently accessed the recording, a frown deepening on her face. 'Oh dear,' she said. 'That sounds bad.' She blinked in rapid thought. 'What time was this?'

'I don't know. Doesn't it tell you?'

Melanie listened again. 'Eleven thirty-two.' She looked at the clock above the reception desk. 'More than half an hour ago. We'll have to go and see what's happened.' She frowned even more deeply. 'That's plenty of time for him to run back up here, isn't it? Do you know where he went exactly?'

'Something about a place called Colthouse. But he says he's near some woods, doesn't he?'

'There are trees at the top end of the lake. It's all very close. About two minutes' walk from here. Where's Dan?' Melanie addressed the receptionist, wife of the manager, and apparently sole representative of the senior staff. 'Where's your husband? Who's here?'

'You know as well as I do,' said Mrs Boddington-Webster. 'Jeremy went into Hawkshead, and Jake doesn't come in today. The lunches are all done in advance on a Tuesday.'

'What about Dan?'

'Good question.'

'Come *on,*' urged Simmy. 'We have to find Ben. He sounded so ... desperate. Didn't he?' She appealed to Melanie for confirmation.

'He did rather. Not like himself. Something obviously scared him.' The girl's face had been steadily paling since she'd heard Ben's message. 'Why hasn't he come back, or phoned again?'

'I daren't even think,' said Simmy. She began to leave the building by the front door.

'No, not that way. It's much quicker to go out of the back,' said Melanie, already leading the way. The others followed her out, across the gravelled area, past the stables and down a gentle slope to the lake, barely seventy-five yards distant. It was actually part of the hotel's grounds until the final few yards, the water lapping almost imperceptibly at the grassy edge. The ground was unusually flat for the area; no great rising fells or dense woodlands bordered Esthwaite, which dreamt away the days in a glassy calm. As before, there were two or three small rowing boats sitting motionless on the water, with anglers in them.

'Won't those people have seen anything going on?' asked Simmy. 'Should we shout to them?'

'They won't take any notice,' said Melanie. 'They ignore everything happening onshore. I think half of them are asleep most of the time, anyway.'

'Trees. Ben said there was a body under trees at the top end of the lake.' Simmy had been repeating the words to herself as they ran down to the water. 'Must be over there.' She pointed to her left, where a small path wound its way amongst a scattering of rocks towards a patch of woodland. She could see a dead tree and a section of new-looking fencing on either side of it. There was a small field between where they stood and the trees, containing several cows. 'Do you think a cow attacked Ben?' It was a hopeful, almost comical, idea. The 'Hey!' that she had heard might have been addressed to a belligerent animal. 'He might have climbed a tree to escape.'

Melanie made a sound of restrained derision at this. The trees were not large, on the whole, and even if one had proved climbable, they both knew that Ben would not run away from a cow. He would stand his ground and shout at it until it backed off. There were no calves to be seen, and all country people knew that the only cattle to be feared were protective mothers and dairy bulls.

It was the manager's wife who made the first discovery. 'Oh my God,' she said, as she bent down and picked up a black, rectangular plastic object from beside a tuft of long grass. 'Is this your friend's?'

Melanie snatched it and flittered a thumb over the screen. No buttons these days, Simmy noted, with a sense of never having a hope of keeping up. Even in the midst of her horrified suspicions, she could hear her mother commenting on how useless the gadget actually was, however passionately it might be vaunted as indispensable.

'Yes, it's his,' said the girl. 'So he was definitely here.'

'And just as definitely taken away against his will,' flashed Simmy, impatient with Melanie's faint attempt at being positive. 'He'd never go without the phone if he could help it.'

'So where's the body he was talking about?' asked Mrs Bodgett.

They all scanned the ground, moving to the fence and gazing at the dense undergrowth between the trees. 'Nobody could get through there,' said Melanie.

'No,' Simmy agreed. 'How far does the wood go?'

'Not very far,' said the manager's wife. 'There's a tarn through there, called Priest Pot. You can't see it from here – or anywhere, really. It's surrounded by trees and rushes and stuff.'

'Which way is Colthouse?'

The woman pointed. 'Over there. Why?'

'Ben said he might go there.'

'Well, he'd have to go round by the roads. Past the sewage works, up to the recreation field and it's just a little way to the right from there. There's not really any sort of shortcut, that I can think of.'

'How long would that take?'

'Fifteen, twenty minutes.' The woman flapped impatiently. 'There's nothing here. We've called the police for nothing.'

'There's his phone,' said Melanie. 'That proves he was here. We should have a closer look.'

They walked along the fence, the ground muddy in places. They passed the dead tree that Simmy had noticed. For a few feet there was a wooden fence with rails, instead of the barbed wire along the rest of the stretch. 'You could climb over here quite easily,' said Simmy.

'It's been flattened here, look,' said Melanie, pointing at a patch of bent bracken just beyond the barrier. 'Somebody might have been lying there.'

'There's the police,' observed Mrs Manager. She pointed to the road some distance away. A car could be seen turning into the hotel's entrance. 'I saw the markings on the side.'

'We should go and meet them, then,' Simmy

decided. They began to walk towards Esthwaite, following the course of the fence again. 'You know what? I bet Ben saw somebody asleep and thought he was dead. Maybe he was with a girl or something. Or not supposed to be here. So when he woke up and saw Ben on the phone he hit him, or chased him. And Ben dropped his phone trying to get away.'

'Yeah? So where is he now?' demanded Melanie. 'It's way over an hour ago. If he's still running, he'll have reached Ambleside by now.'

The jest went unheeded, because Simmy found herself watching a pair of swans making serene progress across the middle of the lake. They were so far removed from the turbulent worries of human life that she really wanted to join them, for a moment. Not just that, but to *become* one of them. Then she tracked back, her attention caught by a *plop* caused by a fish jumping out of the water. Another creature disporting itself in mindless pleasure, little knowing that a fisherman was out to get it. The lake itself was an oasis of calm, lacking all pretensions, ignored by almost every tourist in the region. The stark disjunction between the tranquil summer day and the extreme concern she felt for Ben was almost enough to justify Melanie's flippancy. It was all mad, after all. Senseless, stupid and insane.

'What's that?' Mrs Boddington-Webster suddenly yelped. 'Look!'

Warily, Simmy followed her pointing finger. Over the fence, where all three of them stood helplessly staring at the water, was a dark lump, almost entirely submerged. 'It can't be,' she said, feeling horribly sick. 'It absolutely can't.'

With no thought for dignity and heedless of her smart work uniform, Melanie scrambled over the wire, her weight making the whole fence sag and buckle. 'Come on!' she yelled, as if the others were half a mile away instead of five feet.

Simmy's long legs helped her negotiate the obstructing fence, but the other woman was a lot shorter and even more smartly clothed than Melanie. She hesitated and then withdrew, her face tight with apprehension. 'I'll go and lead the police down here,' she said. 'There'll be nobody to meet them, otherwise.'

Melanie and Simmy waded into the shallows, the ground soft and squelchy beneath their feet. Simmy wished she'd taken her shoes off. They felt like lead weights as they filled with water. The object they sought was only a yard or so from the edge, the water hardly any depth. They would have seen it sooner if it had not been for the long grass growing below the surface, obscuring nearly everything. Three days of heavy rain the previous week must have caused the lake to expand, washing over ground that was normally dry and grassy.

'It's a body,' choked Melanie. 'A man.'

'Ben? It's not Ben is it?' The idea was as appallingly untenable as that of a nearby nuclear explosion or a huge dragon descending from the sky with outstretched claws. Something that would spell perpetual darkness and oblivion. Something that would render existence less than meaningless. If Ben was dead, there was no more hope for the world. All this went through Simmy's mind even as she spoke the terrible words.

'No,' said Melanie. She was crying. Tears were running down her cheeks. She sat down in the water, holding a horrible sodden head between her knees. 'No, it's not Ben.'

'Who then?' It seemed clear that it was some-one known.

'Dan. It's Dan, from the hotel,' said Melanie.

Chapter Six

'Is he dead?' Simmy asked the question with the merest scrap of hope. The water might be shallow, but the face had been immersed in it, and the whole aspect of the body screamed life-lessness. The uncaring lake and the sky above it had quite given up on him. He was an inert unthreatening mass of meat and nothing more.

Melanie shook her head and said nothing. Then she put two fingers on a place at the side of his head, where the hairline was. Simmy leant down to see, wincing with the horror of it, her throat stinging with bile.

'The bone's broken,' she realised. 'That's ter-rible. That must be what killed him.' She looked steadily at the handsome face and the wet hair. The skin was oddly loose on the bones, the mouth and eyes open. 'Get up, Mel. You don't have to do that any more.'

But Melanie was immobilised. Gradually it dawned on Simmy that there was nothing to be gained from dragging the girl away. Mixed with the horror and grief was a kind of wonder. Mel traced the dead features with gentle fingertips, forcing Simmy to understand how a dead face is no more alarming or repellent than a live one. Why in the world should it be? She had known, for a few minutes, the same truth when her baby had died. But it was a slippery truth, and no two bodies were the same. Shivers of disgust and fear were slicing through her, as she formed part of the unhappy tableau on the edge of the lake.

Again, years seemed to pass. Simmy knew they were breaking rules, that they ought to be doing it all differently, but she felt weak and incompetent. Slowly the gears of her mind began to engage again until her head was almost bursting with questions, memories, implications. Twice before in the past year she had encountered the savage danger of water. A young man at a wedding had been deliberately drowned in Lake Windermere, and she herself had been pitched into water with malicious intent. It would seem that in an area known for its multiplicity of lakes and rivers, those intent on murder saw them as a convenient means of killing.

'What happened, do you think?' she ventured. 'Somebody hit him with a hard object and then threw him into the lake as a way of hiding him? But when would they have done that? Ben saw the body under the trees.' Her heart flinched. 'He must have seen them do it. They must have needed to keep him quiet. He's a witness to the whole thing.' Desperation made her jiggle on the grass, and throw wild looks up towards the hotel from where help should be coming, and yet strangely wasn't.

Melanie merely shook her head. Her tears had slowed, but she continued to sit straight-legged in a few inches of water, Dan's head and shoulders were on top of her at an angle. Simmy began to wonder at the level of emotion shown over the man who had been the girl's superior, and who she had shown very little sign of liking much. Was it no more than a natural human response to the pity of a sudden death, a young man's life cut off so horribly? Her own emotions were stubbornly fixed on Ben and the acute need to find him before a similar fate could befall him.

'Hey, hey,' she soothed. 'You don't have to sit there with him. The police and everybody will be here in a minute. They won't want you getting in their way.'

'I can't move,' whimpered the girl. 'He's so heavy.'

Simmy was not eager to help. They had succeeded in swivelling the body around, so the legs were still in the lake, while the head and shoulders were in Melanie's lap, on a slimy, semi-dry piece of ground. Esthwaite did not have proper banks – at least on its western side. The water merely lapped at the edge of the field, its boundary never the same from one week to the next. Their efforts had created a muddy cloud in the shallows, slippery and sludgy. She looked all around. Why hadn't one of those darned fishermen taken more notice and come to their aid? How could they have missed the fact of something ghastly going on? Perhaps if she shouted to them, they would respond.

But the idea of more people splashing about, asking questions, saying stupid things, was repellent. If the men in the little boats had actually witnessed the slaughter of Dan Yates and the dumping of his body in the lake, then surely they would have flown into action, phoning police and rushing to the shore to do their best to help? As it was, they must have missed the whole thing and thereby rendered themselves useless.

At last – and it was probably well under ten minutes in reality – there was authoritative assistance in the shape of two policemen, the hotel manager and someone wearing a white outfit, who presumably worked in the kitchen. Stupidly, Simmy searched the little group for Ben Harkness, who would always have turned up for the excitement if he possibly could.

The sudden manifestation of a dead body threw everyone into a far more concentrated mode. The policemen had thought they'd been summoned to a smoke-and-mirrors scene, involving nothing more than a dropped mobile phone. Now they had a whole long list of procedures to follow, for which they had not been prepared at all. Their attention was directed for a minute or two to the intervening wire fence, separating them from the tableau in the water. 'We'd better pull it down,' said one.

'Right,' said the other uncertainly. 'Just a bit, right?' Together they pulled up two vertical wooden posts and laid them flat. The fence had been wobbly from the start, and Melanie's assault on it had already accomplished half the job. The wire obligingly lay flat and the policemen walked over it.

'Who is it?' demanded the manager, trying not to look too closely. 'Is it your friend?'

Melanie raised her grubby face to his. 'It's Dan,' she said.

'What?' The manager turned green. 'It can't be. How can it be?'

Nobody spoke. The policemen were both eyeing their glossy black footwear and equally pristine trousers, knowing they would have to get them wet. They also knew that they ought not to disturb the scene of a sudden death. But beyond that, they knew almost nothing. Accident, suicide, heart attack – anything was possible. Distressed colleagues and unidentified women had to be sorted out. One of them put out a hand to Melanie. 'Come on, miss. Let's have you out of there for a start.'

He planted his feet securely and exerted enough force to lever her out of the water. She came slowly, reluctantly, and then stood with bowed shoulders, shivering. The officer looked around the group for something to throw over her, but nothing was identified. 'You need to get indoors and take those wet things off,' he said. But words were not enough to achieve this, and Melanie stayed as she was.

Simmy lost patience, surprising herself as much as anyone. 'There's a boy missing,' she said. 'He's seventeen. He found this body, over an hour ago. He phoned me. Now he's gone. His phone was here, abandoned. We *must* find him before something terrible happens to him.' Her voice rose to a shout. 'We have to look for him.'

To their credit, the officers took her seriously, at least to the extent of looking at her and then looking at each other. 'All right, madam,' said one. 'You're telling us that this young man found the deceased and called you. What happened then?'

'I didn't hear the call. It was on my voicemail. When I found it, I came down here with Melanie and Mrs Bod – I mean the manager's wife.' She ignored Melanie's alarmed gasp at the narrow escape from using the disrespectful nickname, other than to note that the girl was not entirely traumatised if she could worry about such a detail. 'But he said the body was under the trees, not in the lake. The killer must have moved it, and then taken Ben away. Ben's been *kidnapped*.' This time she wasn't shouting, but choking out the word, unable to confront all the implications it carried.

'Killer?' repeated the policeman. His face was paler than before, as if the concept of deliberate murder was far beyond his scope. Perhaps it was, Simmy realised. Perhaps she had more experience of it over the past year than this young constable had. Perhaps, like Melanie, he hadn't yet seen a dead body in all its fresh and gruesome reality.

'And kidnapper,' Simmy insisted.

A connection had apparently been taking place in the mind of the other officer. 'We're not talking about young Ben Harkness, are we?' he said slowly. 'You said the lad's name was Ben.'

'Yes!' Simmy's relief was entirely irrational, but

71

somehow the fact that Ben was already known to this man made a huge difference. 'You'll have to call DI Moxon. He'll understand.'

But she had gone too far. The hotel manager squared his shoulders and laid a hand on a uniformed arm. 'We have a *body* here,' he said thickly. 'My employee is lying here dead. I think that ought to be your primary concern right now.'

'I agree with you, sir. But if there is any suggestion of foul play, we are not permitted to move him. We need a police doctor, a senior officer, photographer...' He was removing a device from his belt and frowningly trying to recall correct procedure. 'Excuse me,' he added, and walked a few steps away from the bewildered group. His colleague, belatedly following protocol, made ushering motions. 'Please move away now,' he said. 'There's nothing more you can do here.' He produced a device of his own. 'If we could just have an identity for the deceased.' He looked from face to face.

'It's Dan Yates,' said the lad from the kitchen, speaking for the first time.

'Actually, his name is *Ai*dan,' said Melanie. 'Dan for short.'

'Do you have details of his next of kin? Is he married?'

The manager took over. 'Divorced. No children. Parents in East Anglia somewhere. I've got it on record in the office.'

Simmy acknowledged to herself that she actually cared quite little for Dan and his horrible fate. She cared about *Ben*, primarily because he had been under her care when he disappeared.

What will his mother say? became her dominant thought, followed rapidly by *and Bonnie!*

She groaned aloud.

Chapter Seven

In the hotel foyer, Simmy noticed her newly arranged flowers with surprise. Such a lot had happened since she'd done them that she felt they ought to be looking wilted by this time. Instead they were fresh and undeniably beautiful. The sinuous shape created by the eucalyptus and honeysuckle suggested, with the very faintest of hints, an air of sensuality and luxury, heightened by the scent. She waited for everyone else to reach the same conclusion – but they all seemed far too distracted. As she ought to have been herself, of course. But then she remembered poor Dan Yates, and how pleased he would have been to find how capably she had met his requirements. Along with that thought came, an alarming one: would the hotel management still want her to provide flowers twice a week, now their under-manager was dead? Would they close down out of respect – or what?

Such selfishness, she reproached herself, was a disgrace. The world of flowers and holidays and harmless fell-top walks had been shaken by violence and confusion. It was of no help at all to remember that she had encountered not just murder but kidnap in the recent past. To have it happen again was so appalling, she just wanted to dig herself a hole and hide away in it. A filament of guilt was gaining ground inside her, too. Not only for her selfishness, but for her failure to hear Ben's frantic message on her phone when he first called her. How could she have been so stupid as to leave it in the van? She couldn't have saved Dan, but she might well have been in time to interrupt Ben's captors, and save him from abduction.

People were swirling about, asking questions and making demands. Not a single hotel guest was amongst them, for which Mr and Mrs Boddington-Webster must surely be thankful. There was more than enough confusion already with the staff all clamouring for information. Melanie seemed to form a still centre, silently distressed, her soaking clothes marking her out as especially significant. Simmy herself was wet, but nowhere near as much as Melanie. And because nobody knew her, or understood her part in the story, she had been shifted to the outer edge.

Finally, reinforcements arrived in the shape of DI Moxon, already well known to Simmy and Melanie. With a singularly unprofessional smile, he went first to Simmy, both hands extended. 'What happened?' he asked.

She waved at the manager and his staff. 'Their colleague's dead, down in the lake. And Ben's missing.' She choked on the last word. 'He's been abducted. There's no other explanation.'

'Okay. Leave it to us,' he said, in a tone that did little to inspire confidence. 'Don't go away, though. I gather you're a crucial witness.'

'What time is it?' Only then did she remember other commitments and obligations.

'Um... Twenty to three.'

'It's not, is it? What will Bonnie think? Why hasn't she called me?' Then she remembered. 'Your men have got my phone. There's a message from Ben on it. She must be going crazy, wondering where I am.'

'Call her on the hotel's phone, then.'

'Right.' At first glance there was no phone available on the reception desk. 'Where is it?'

He made a small gesture of impatience. 'Ask someone.' His gaze fell on Melanie. 'Miss Todd's here as well?'

'She works here. She knew Dan. I think, actually, she must have had *feelings* for him. She's very upset.'

'So I see.' He sighed. 'Well, let's get some sort of order established. One thing at a time. Don't go away,' he said again.

Simmy went around the same circuit of panic, paralysis, mistrust and misery as before. She could see that Moxon had an uphill struggle ahead of him, when it came to achieving order. Melanie, still wet and shocked, was leaning against the reception desk. The skeletal Penny was standing back, eyes wide, making small shooing motions with her hands. The manager and his wife were whispering together, apparently arguing over the best place to put the police personnel. It was a miracle, Simmy thought foolishly, that nobody had knocked her flowers over.

She went to her former assistant. 'Have you got your phone?' she asked. 'Bonnie will be going mad, wondering where I am.'

Melanie took a breath and gave the question

some thought. 'I think she might have called. Somebody did.' From a mysterious pocket in her cotton jacket, she extracted a phone. 'I didn't think I should answer it.' She looked at Moxon with a mixture of respect and impatience.

'It still works, then? It didn't get wet?'

'Seems okay.' Melanie's voice was flat. She was shivering and plainly shocked.

Simmy felt guilty at her lack of concern for the girl. She took the phone, but made no attempt to use it. Other things must come first. 'You need to go and change your clothes. Somebody ought to have made you some sweet tea by now. It's so *disorganised*,' Simmy complained. 'It's *hours* since Ben disappeared and nothing at all's been done to find him.'

'That's because Dan's not here. They're all incompetent except him.' Melanie spoke loudly, obviously not caring who heard her.

'Come with me, then.' Simmy felt suddenly adult and capable. She led the way through the door she had noticed earlier, into a large office. There were computers, a telephone, filing cabinets, and a long row of keys with big plastic tags hanging from hooks. She pushed Melanie onto a padded, upright chair and looked round for a coffee machine. There was no such thing. Nor were there any spare clothes. 'This isn't much use,' she grumbled.

'What did you expect?'

'I don't know, really. Where do you keep your normal clothes, for a start?'

The girl hesitated and her cheeks went pink. 'At home. I haven't got anything here.' She sounded defensive. Simmy remembered that Melanie's original plan had been to acquire a job that provided accommodation, to enable her to escape from her crowded and noisy family home, but the Hawkshead Hotel had failed her in that respect. She mostly used the ferry across Windermere, and then caught a rare bus to Hawkshead, which saved some time and meant she didn't need to use a car. Simmy was ignorant of the details, since the girl had ceased to work for her. But in any case *home* now seemed impossibly inaccessible.

'They want me to stick around for a bit, but I suppose I could pop into Hawkshead and try to buy you something. You can't go all afternoon like that. Look at you!'

Melanie's legs were not just wet but muddy, her shoes ruined. 'I'm going to leave awful marks on this chair,' she said. 'Not that I care.' She plucked at herself. 'There'll be some spare clothes somewhere around,' she said vaguely. 'Something I can borrow.'

'Who from? Mrs Bodgett's miles smaller than you. Those girls, whoever they are, are little, as well. Not to mention Penny,' she added with a giggle.

'There's another one. Camilla, she's called. She's my sort of size. But she probably won't have anything. And she might not be in today.' Melanie tailed off, her teeth chattering. 'I am a bit cold,' she admitted.

'And in shock.' Suddenly, Melanie's needs dropped down Simmy's list of priorities. At least she was here and alive. 'Mel – I have to do something about Ben. His parents ought to know

77

what's happened. And *Bonnie*.' She kept forgetting Bonnie, who had been so cruelly abandoned without explanation, making all sorts of a mess running the shop, no doubt.

'Yes,' Melanie agreed. 'I'll go to the kitchen and make myself some tea or something. They've got a little room where they change. I can borrow an apron.' A flicker of a smile crossed her face. 'A big white apron to wrap round me.'

Simmy let her go, and simply sat there for ten minutes, listening to voices and car engines coming from beyond the room. She was shocked herself, with squelching shoes and a fair degree of dampness around the lower legs. Everybody else had allotted tasks, the staff no doubt despatched in all directions to assemble all their colleagues and ready themselves for questioning. The only window looked over the parking area, revealing a steady increase in vehicles containing officials.

Finally she gave herself a shake and lifted up one of the phones on the office desk. She keyed the number for her shop, her heart pounding as she rehearsed what she would say. It was not answered very promptly. 'Bonnie? Are you all right?' she began.

'Sort of. Where *are* you? Something's happened, hasn't it?'

For a wild moment, Simmy wondered whether Ben had miraculously shown up at the shop, telling the story of his adventures to his girlfriend. How else would she know there was something going on? 'How do you know?' she asked.

'It's obvious. Your phone's off. Melanie isn't

answering hers. And Corinne came in a bit ago and said there was weird stuff on the police radio.'

Corinne acted as a kind of foster mother to Bonnie. Her social circle included a number of people Simmy regarded as somewhat disreputable. Like Melanie, she knew everybody in Windermere and Bowness, having lived there all her life. Listening to the police radio had become a habit some years ago, according to Bonnie. 'She's always expecting to hear something about people she knows,' Bonnie had laughed. Sometimes she did.

'Yes, well...' Simmy said. 'I'm sorry to leave you on your own for all this time. Have you had any trouble?'

'Not really. Nobody much has been in. Tell me what's going on. Why do you sound so peculiar?'

'The police are here. There's been a death. I've got to answer some questions.'

'Wow! And Ben? I bet he's having a right old time, then. He loves anything like that.'

'Actually... We've lost him.' It sounded ridiculous, as if he was a dog or a carelessly mislaid toy.

Bonnie gave no hint of concern. 'He'll be doing his own investigating,' she chuckled. 'Who died?'

'Dan Yates. The under-manager. Melanie's very upset. She's in shock. We found him, you see. In the lake.'

'What lake? I thought you were at Hawkshead somewhere.'

'Esthwaite.'

'Oh, right. I always forget about that one. It's not much of a lake, is it? Did he drown himself in it?'

79

'Not exactly. Look, Bonnie – it's all rather complicated. I have no idea when I'll be back. You can close up, if you like, and go home. And if Ben calls you, please let me know right away. And the police.'

'Why do they want him?'

'He's *missing*. He probably saw the people who–' she stopped herself just in time. 'He might be a witness to a crime.'

There was a small silence. 'Missing? Lost? What do you mean? How *can* he be? Wasn't he with you?'

'He went for a walk – down to the lake and to a place called Colthouse. He phoned me about seeing Dan's body. I missed the call. It was on my voicemail. After that he just – disappeared. We found his phone.'

'Oh. And you're scared something awful's happened to him. No, no. That wouldn't be it. He's too clever to let it. He'll be fine. He's just tracking them or something. You know what he's like.'

'Yeah. You're probably right. So – if he does phone...?'

'I'll tell you. Is your mobile on again now?'

'Oh, no. The police have got it. Well, you'd better call the police, okay? I don't matter.'

'I will shut the shop, then,' said Bonnie decisively. 'And I'll go and talk to Ben's mum, if she's home. She can drive us up to Hawkshead to look for him.'

She made it sound so blissfully simple. 'I'm not sure...' Simmy began. 'Shouldn't she be told by the police first?' At some point, she had given the Harkness address to one of the policemen. Helm

Road was in Bowness, ten or fifteen minutes' walk from the centre of Windermere. If Bonnie was determined to go there, nothing Simmy said could stop her. Ben's mother mostly worked from home, in a very well-appointed office at the top of the house.

'It's okay, Simmy,' said the girl. 'It's going to be okay.'

It was tempting to believe her. 'Oh, well,' she said feebly. 'I'm going to be here for ages yet. I'll try to catch up with you this evening.'

She was interrupted by the door to the office opening and DI Moxon coming in. His face was a mixture of briskness and solicitude. Their relationship – such as it was – went back ten months or so and she had gradually learnt more about him since then. She had shared her own painful past with him, administered urgent first aid to him, and eventually met a wife she had never suspected existed. She was still not entirely sure that she liked him. He had a strong aura of the police, with the odd lack of human understanding that seemed to go with the job. Much of what she said to him apparently came as a big surprise, although he seldom manifested disapproval or criticism. He seemed to find her instructive, she often felt, with her instinctive feeling for people's emotional states.

He was even more baffled and amazed by Ben Harkness. Only Melanie gave him any comfort, with her comprehensive knowledge of local networks and connection to elements with which the police were habitually familiar.

The detective was holding a clipboard in one

hand, like a charity fundraiser or somebody doing a street survey. It struck Simmy as incongruous, for some reason. 'Hello,' she said.

He nodded and said, 'I've just been speaking to Miss Todd,' he told her. 'She's been extremely helpful. I think I've got it straight now.' He tapped the clipboard. 'Names of all the staff, who was on the premises this morning. List of guests. G5.'

She frowned at him. She'd heard of a G5, but could not remember what it signified. And why was he reporting to her as if she was his superintendent? 'G5?'

'The form that has to be completed whenever an unexpected death occurs. Last seen by... Next of kin... Name of his GP. That sort of thing. I always like the G5,' he finished wistfully. 'It was a very clever invention.'

'You can't have got all that from Melanie,' she objected. 'She was in here only a minute ago.'

'Fifteen minutes at least,' he corrected her. 'She's all fixed up with dry clothes, and wanting to go home. Somebody will take her in a little while. And you're right, of course. We've been talking to several others as well.'

Simmy blinked at the strange rush of time that this implied, but forced herself to stick with the most important details. 'So who was he last seen by? Dan, I mean.'

'That's not certain. Probably Miss Todd, but possibly Mrs Boddington-Webster. He works complicated hours.'

'He lives on the premises, so I suppose that's not too much of a problem.'

'Yes, we've looked around his room.' He

cleared his throat. 'Did you know that Miss Todd has been spending some nights here with him?'

'What?'

'I don't expect I should be telling you, but there's no way we can stop it coming out. I imagine most of the staff are aware of it, anyway. But she told me that you didn't know. She seems embarrassed about that. She poured it all out the moment I had her on her own.' He preened slightly at having elicited such intimate information from a girl he knew had never entirely trusted him. The Todd family had an uneasy relationship with the police, despite Melanie's dalliance with a constable named Joe.

Simmy hesitated, feeling surprisingly hurt and offended. Why should Melanie tell her who she was sleeping with, anyway? However close their friendship might have been over the winter, it had effectively ended when Melanie moved on with her career. And Simmy was, as she reminded herself regularly, old enough to be Mel's mother. She reproached herself for her excessive reaction, and fought to stifle the unworthy feelings. 'Well, that explains why she cried over him,' she said faintly.

'How well did *you* know him?'

'Not at all. I only met him once, yesterday. He seemed very competent. Professional.' Melanie had used the word *okay* about him, she remembered. Typical British understatement, apparently. 'Have you told Ben's parents he's been abducted?' she burst out. 'That's what matters now. I mean – if you find him, you'll probably find the person who killed Dan as well. Won't you?'

He raised two steadying hands. 'That's rather a

leap,' he said. 'But yes, one of our people went down to Helm Road an hour or so ago.' He looked at his watch. 'Maybe a bit less than that,' he amended.

'They'll be frantic.'

He tilted his head. 'I'm not so sure. They'll be used to the boy going off on his own adventures by now. And we certainly won't be using the word *abducted* to describe what's happened.'

'What else would you call it?'

'Simply that nobody seems sure of his where-abouts. That we'd like to speak to him about an incident near Hawkshead.'

Simmy sighed. 'Well Bonnie won't swallow that, for one. Remember Bonnie Lawson? She and Ben are going out together, or whatever they call it these days. She *loves* him. She's going to be searching for him.'

'So you've told her?' He gave her a heavy look, like a reproachful schoolmaster.

'I have.'

'Oh, well.'

'She's just as likely to find him as any of us,' Simmy said. 'They've got a very special bond.'

'We'll take all the help we can get,' he said, with a hint of a smile.

She had to force herself to ask the next question. 'How exactly was he killed? Dan, I mean. Was it that place on his head?'

He understood only too well how resistant she was to this kind of detail. Detective Inspector Nolan Moxon had a habit of reading Persimmon Brown better than she would have liked him to. Where others might puzzle him, she often appeared to be clear as a diamond. It made them both uncomfortably vulnerable and exposed. She had believed initially that he was simply in love with her, while she found his physical presence faintly repellent. Now she had met his wife and seen that he had a solid marriage despite a recent spell of trouble, it was all more complicated. She liked him better now and felt less sorry for him. He had improved his appearance recently, too. Over the winter he had often seemed a trifle unwashed, his hair greasy and his clothes unchanged. There had been subsequent hints of depression and marital distance to explain all that. Furthermore, there had been an intimacy between them that went beyond the ordinary. They had witnessed each other's extremes and the resulting relationship could not be denied.

'We can't say for certain,' he said carefully. 'The police doctor is always very cautious about that until there's been a proper examination. There is, as you say, evidence of a blow to the head. And he was moved from the attack site to the water. We found the spot where the assault took place.'

'The place where we found Ben's phone,' she said. 'I suppose we shouldn't really have touched it.'

He smiled. 'Anybody would have done the same.'

'Why would they move him, though?' She heard the word *they* echoing. 'Do you think there could have been more than one of them?'

He nodded. 'One person couldn't do it alone.'

Simmy had not even begun to consider this idea. Instantly, it made sense. 'Of course,' she nodded. 'A group, perhaps? Some sort of gang? So some of them killed Dan and dumped him in the lake, while others took Ben away.' She visualised a bunch of hooded youths, up to something dreadful in the woods when Dan came across them. Perhaps they hadn't meant to kill him. She almost smiled. It would surely be easy for the police to catch up with a whole gang, and make them relinquish the captive Ben. But then she thought again. 'But *are* there gangs around here? In Hawkshead?'

'Not that we know of. But they come from the cities on motorbikes. Glasgow, even, sometimes.'

'On their summer holidays?' She had an image of a battered charabanc full of Glaswegian yobs, waving bottles of beer and looking for trouble. 'I'm not sure–'

'No,' he interrupted. 'Neither am I. But we've got to start somewhere.'

Outside the office there were raised voices. Simmy realised that she and Moxon were probably monopolising the vital heart of the hotel's operation, even though the phone hadn't rung and nobody seemed anxious to come in. There would be guests returning from their days out on the fells before long, and the manager was unlikely to want them to walk into the maelstrom of a police investigation. If the short-lived hunt for a small girl had raised complaints, how much more objectionable would a murder investigation be!

'You won't need to question all the guests, will you?' she asked.

'We'll want to know where they all were this

morning. Routine enquiries, as they say.'

'The management will hate it.'

'Too bad. A murder enquiry trumps just about everything. Nobody gets a choice in the matter.'

She shivered. 'It sounds so horrible. My mother would say—'

'Yes, I know what your mother would say,' he interrupted. 'Now, I'd better go and see what's happening out there.'

She thought of her flowers, now so irrelevant and trivial. She had been so proud of them, only a couple of hours ago. It didn't seem fair. All she wanted was to carry on her business, bringing colour and scent and beauty into people's lives. Instead, there was fear and pain and mystery. She got up from the chair and followed the detective into the foyer, where the first person she saw was a woman she had only met fleetingly before. But she knew immediately who it was and the recognition was mutual.

'Where is he?' the woman cried. 'What have you got my boy into now?'

Wordlessly, Simmy just stared at Mrs Helen Harkness, mother of the missing Ben.

Chapter Eight

The injustice of it struck deep. She had been doing the boy a favour, giving him a lift. By rights, it was a job for his mother or father – but they were too busy, otherwise engaged. Moxon came to her rescue. 'I don't think Mrs Brown can be held responsible,' he objected.

'No, no. I'm sorry.' Helen's eyes were wide, her movements jerky. 'I don't know what I'm saying. Although...' She looked back at Simmy. 'It's not the first time, is it?'

Simmy couldn't argue with that. Her very first encounter with Ben had been at the scene of a fatal shooting. Since then there had been other complicated police investigations in which they had been embroiled. Almost from the start, Ben had been passionately interested, deciding that his vocation was as a forensic scientist. Brilliantly clever, his way appeared smooth for the coming years of further education, his eventual career beyond question. He had attracted favourable attention from an American university, with a promise of a postgraduate place some years hence. Meanwhile he was stacking up A-levels, with one more year at school still to go.

'I don't know how worried I should be,' the woman said. 'As a rule I'd trust him to know what he was doing. But I've never had the police come to the door before. He's never gone *missing* before.'

Helen Harkness was in her early fifties, mother of five children and a very successful architect. Ben was the second child, his great intelligence something the family had long ago accepted as a mixed blessing. Impatient with his siblings, awkward in social situations, he had gone his own way almost from the start. Both his parents erred on the side of neglect, by modern standards. But thus far, they had never found reason to regret their parenting style.

'He's a resourceful lad,' said Moxon clumsily. 'But given that he's still under age, we're very much taking this seriously. Nobody will be more relieved than me when he's found,' he concluded, perhaps rashly. Surely, thought Simmy, his mother and father would be more relieved than even the most dedicated police officer.

'So where are you looking?' demanded Mrs Harkness.

Moxon grimaced, showing his teeth and sucking in a long breath. Simmy glanced around at the other people still gathered in the reception area, noting as she did so that her floral display was still quietly trying to enhance the general atmosphere, and failing quite badly. There was no sign of Melanie or Mrs Boddington-Webster. Penny had evidently abandoned her post on the reception desk and was nowhere to be seen, either. The two chambermaids were sitting together on a small, padded bench, looking even more bewildered than before. A woman in a suit and high heels stood beside the reception desk, clicking fingernails on its surface in a parody of typing or piano playing. Simmy had not seen her before. Nobody was giving her any attention. A uniformed policeman guarded the door into the corridor that Simmy had used on her first visit.

'Can I go?' Simmy asked Moxon. 'You know where to find me.'

'Er ... not just yet. No. Hang on, if you don't mind.' He spoke without looking at her, still apparently groping for a response to Ben's mother's question.

'Well, I'll be in the garden,' she said. 'It's too crowded in here.'

He let her go without protest. She walked across the gravel to the lawn at the side of the main building, where there were seats scattered about. It had a view over Esthwaite.

Frustration over Ben was making her jittery, so that sitting still was almost impossible. She understood for the first time the full meaning of the word 'wired'. It was as if electrical filaments were firing in all her limbs, as well as inside her head. There had to be a solution to the crisis, an explanation for what had happened. The abductors must have left clues – they must *want* something. Either they would kill their captive or make some sort of demand using him as leverage. Except that none of this fitted the scanty facts. Much more likely that they had panicked when they realised he had seen Dan's body, and his killers, and been bundled into some sort of vehicle simply to prevent him from calling for help. Which he had been doing, Simmy remembered miserably, and she had stupidly failed to heed his call. So then, they would drive him away to a remote spot – in which the whole region abounded, after all – and then what? Leave him tied and bound, to starve to death? Arrange for him to escape after a period of time in which they could get far away? Drug him with some mind-altering substance that would dislocate his memory and perhaps leave him permanently damaged? Her imaginings grew darker and more terrifying, her anguished concern for her young friend less and less bearable.

She paced around, sometimes managing to sit

90

down for a few minutes before jumping up again. The afternoon was sunny and much warmer than in recent days. She once again lost track of time, but became increasingly aware of thirst and hunger. She had consumed nothing since breakfast, and it now must be over halfway through the afternoon. Where could she get a drink? she wondered. When would Moxon finally get around to properly interviewing her?

There was no very obvious police activity, except for the usual tape marking off the area where Dan's body had been found, but the doctor, photographer, and the body itself had all gone, blessedly quickly. Simmy had learnt for herself that sometimes a murder victim could lie where it fell for the best part of a day while authorities circled around it. Moxon and a few others were conducting interviews somewhere inside the hotel. Down on the little lake there were people in rowing boats, just enjoying the water, not even pretending to be catching fish. The mismatch between her thoughts and the world before her eyes made everything worse. And then, as if to reinforce the same feeling, a child's cheerful chirruping broke into the gloom.

'Race you, Mummy!' it yodelled. 'Right round the hotel and in through the back.'

'Oh, no, Genny. I'm exhausted already.'

Genny – short for Gentian, of course. Why not have opted for Jennifer in the first place and have done with it, Simmy wondered sourly. The child itself now came hurtling around the corner, elbows pumping with the effort, despite her mother's refusal to participate. 'Oh! Hello,' she said,

91

spotting Simmy. 'What are you doing?'

'Nothing much.' She had been unconsciously pacing up and down the grass, sometimes watching the boats on the lake and then turning away to gaze up at the road into Hawkshead. 'Have you had a good day?'

'It was okay. We went to Bowness and had ice cream.'

'Gentian, you ungrateful child. We did *far* more interesting things than that.' Her mother had come within earshot, evidently relieved that the race had been aborted. She gave Simmy a look of appeal. 'She's never satisfied,' she complained.

Simmy just smiled wanly. It wouldn't be long before the woman realised that things were not as they ought to be at the hotel, but Simmy was not going to be the one to explain. There were sure to be details the police wouldn't want spread around. And Gentian showed ominous signs of being unhealthily thrilled by any hint of murder and mystery. Another little Ben Harkness in the making, in all probability.

The front entrance to the hotel was not visible from where they were standing, so they were not prepared for the sudden appearance of the woman in the smart clothes and unsuitable shoes. She was scowling down at a mobile phone, barely looking where she was going.

'She looks cross,' said Gentian cheerfully and loudly.

The woman inevitably heard her and redirected her gaze accordingly. 'I bloody well am,' she said. 'What sort of a hotel is this, where they can't even handle a simple enquiry? And why are there police all over the place?'

Simmy gave her a cool appraisal. To anybody with half a brain, it must be obvious that something bad had happened. 'Do you work here?' the woman asked her.

'No, I don't. I think the hotel staff are in the middle of a crisis, don't you? They might be a bit too busy to deal with casual questions. Why don't you just phone them tomorrow?'

'Highly unprofessional,' the woman sneered. 'They'll never prosper if that's their attitude.'

'What crisis?' demanded Gentian's mother. Simmy had quite forgotten her name, if indeed she had ever heard it. It struck her that these two women had much in common. Both expected instant attention and servility. Something had given them each a powerful sense of entitlement. Neither could permit a little matter like a murder or abduction, divert them from their own wishes – unless the victim happened to be connected to them, of course. Then all hell would break loose.

'I'm sorry. It's not up to me to explain it. I'm sure neither of you is the least bit involved. I suggest you just get on with ... whatever, and wait for things to get back to normal.' Which they never would, of course, she realised. Not with Dan Yates dead and gone for ever. Not with the taint of murder hanging over the place for years to come.

'You were here before,' Gentian's mother accused. 'Who *are* you?'

'Nobody important.' She found she was rather enjoying the withholding of information. It went against so many social expectations, where gossip ruled supreme and nobody could let a question go unanswered. It made her feel special and rather powerful. She resolved to do it more often in the future.

The effect was also gratifying. The woman's mouth fell open and her cheeks darkened. 'Sorry,' Simmy added, 'but that's all there is to it.'

'Well, I just hope we can get tea in the lounge, as usual,' the woman huffed. 'That's all I can say.'

The one in the suit had clearly had enough. 'I'm leaving,' she said, as if this would cause acute consternation in her listeners. Simmy wondered why she'd walked around the side of the hotel in the first place, instead of going directly to her car. Then she reproached herself for her own paranoid suspicion. Anybody might feel drawn to give the place a good look, besides wanting to catch a view of the lake.

Gentian did a little skip, merely to remind everybody that she existed. 'I want lemonade,' she said. 'They do *amazing* lemonade.'

This reference only served to make Simmy feel more desperately thirsty than before. Perhaps she could join the guests in their quest for tea. It sounded as if it must already be that sort of time. As if in confirmation, two more cars came along the drive, crunching over the gravel. In a collective move, the three women and small girl all shifted position so as to see who emerged from the vehicles. They drifted across the lawn in a smooth arc until they were level with the corner of the hotel. The first car to arrive disgorged two people. Simmy recognised the middle-aged couple she had seen on Monday. The woman, who Simmy remembered was called Rosemary, was carrying a bulky carrier bag, while the man remained fussily locking and then checking the car doors. They looked as if they'd spent a strenuous morning shopping – which seemed unlikely, given the location, despite the galleries and china shops in Hawkshead. The smart woman, to Simmy's surprise, went over and spoke to the Lillywhites. Spreading the poison about the hotel, Simmy supposed, or trying to elicit another lot of complaints to use as ammunition. She couldn't hear what was said, but it looked amicable enough. To judge from the body language, the couple were not displeased by the approach, showing no hint of indignation or concern.

The second car contained two men in their twenties. Only when they had climbed out and were standing shoulder to shoulder staring at the hotel did Simmy guess they might be police detectives. How many more people would be shipped in before the day was done, she wondered. Then one of them turned and bent over the back seat of the car. When he straightened again, he was holding a large camera with a long lens.

'Surely they can't be reporters,' she muttered.

But it would seem that they were just that. They observed the various cars scattered around and apparently recognised one or two of them. The one without the camera spotted Simmy and headed for her. 'Sounds as if there's been some trouble up here,' he said.

'Oh?' Again she enjoyed the sensation of deliberately withholding information.

'Do you work here?'

'No.'

'Who are you, then?'

'I might ask you the same question.'

'We can see DI Moxon's car, as well as another police vehicle. We've heard the call for a body to be taken to the mortuary. And there's also something about a missing person. A boy, by the sound of it. So stop messing about and tell us what's going on.'

'Why on earth should I? You still haven't introduced yourself.'

'We're from the *Gazette*. We thought there might be a statement by now. The police actually find us pretty useful, you know,' he finished defensively.

'Surely the statement would be made to all the media people together? Surely it's very intrusive of you to come here hoping for special treatment? If somebody has died, then don't you risk upsetting the friends and relatives?'

'Oh, you're no use at all,' he snapped and turned away from her. His eye fell on the Lillywhites, who had still not made it into the hotel, and he headed for them. Simmy relaxed, knowing the couple could have nothing interesting to impart. Her main feeling was concern that careless words spread by the media would jeopardise the search for Ben. At the very least, it would make his captors more careful. As she watched the frustrated journalist ask his probing questions, she was rescued by the detective inspector hurrying out from the main entrance.

'Jamie Murray – get away from these people,' he said, sounding more irritated than angry. 'You should know better.'

'Mr Moxon, sir. Can you give us at least the basics?'

'Not until we make our official statement. 6 p.m., in Hawkshead. The main car park, most likely. Until then, you are officially requested to say nothing. This is all extremely sensitive. Your editor will already have been contacted, most likely. Now go away and leave these good people in peace.' He addressed the Lillywhites. 'I'm afraid there's been some trouble here today. Could you come with me, please, and I'll go over it with you. I'm Detective Inspector Moxon,' he added. Then he noticed Simmy. 'Mrs Brown. Oh lord, I'm sorry.'

'You forgot about me,' she said.

'I did. Listen – I don't think we'll need you for now. Thanks for waiting. You must have things to do.'

'When do I get my phone back?'

'Oh – that's a good question.' He tapped a front tooth for a moment, and then said, 'I can't see that we need it now. Go and ask for it. Say I told them to give it to you. Once it's gone back to the station, there's a stack of paperwork to fill in before it's returned.'

'Thanks,' she said, aware that he was making a special exception for her. Then she waited until the reporter and his friend had driven away before speaking again. 'The only thing I want to do is find Ben. And I imagine you know better than I do how best that should be done.' She could have added that she urgently needed a drink, but that would have felt unworthy and selfish. She had no wish to

97

go back into the hotel, a prey to staff and guests and all the things they might want to ask her.

'Who's Ben?' asked Mr Lillywhite. 'I must say, this is all very disconcerting. Police everywhere and somebody lost. It's not another disobedient child, is it?'

His wife gave a little chuckle at this, which made Simmy look at her. She had not seemed to be the chuckling sort, the last time they'd met. Perhaps her submissive demeanour was no more than ingrained habit, concealing a more robust personality. Or perhaps the laughter was merely a nervous tic. There wasn't anything funny, after all, in people going missing.

'It will all become clear to you after we've had a little talk,' said Moxon ponderously. 'The guests will all be returning soon, I imagine, and we'll be speaking to you all over the coming hour or two.'

'But why?' asked Mrs Lillywhite. 'Can't you tell us what this is all about?'

Simmy left Moxon to it, found the man with her phone, and finally escaped to her van. Only as she started the engine did she wonder where she ought to go. Ben's rucksack was still on the floor where he'd dumped it, looking forlorn and abandoned. It made her think of Dan Yates's possessions in his room, never to be handled again by their owner. Fear for Ben gripped her, along with a terrible sadness. Her place was rightfully beside poor, shocked Melanie and the bewildered Helen Harkness. They and Bonnie all loved Ben in their various ways. They would all have theories and suggestions about what must have befallen him.

On the driveway she had to squeeze past a silver-coloured Audi driven by the tall man who was the other person she had met on Monday. And then, turning in from the road as she was turning out, a big four-wheel drive thing containing several people promised to add to the throng. It had darkened glass in the rear windows, so she couldn't see everyone, but the driver was a man with sharp features and curly hair. Beside him sat another man, almost bald except for two white strips running above his ears. Two more men were in the back, but she barely registered their appearance. Only then did Simmy recall what Dan had said about expecting some important American guests in the near future. Could these be them, she wondered. And if so, what would they make of the chaos they were about to walk into?

Chapter Nine

A minute's drive took her to the turn into Hawkshead village with its numerous souvenir shops, tea rooms and pubs. Her throat felt terrible – she was in desperate need of a cup of tea. It was approaching five o'clock, though, and that was closing time by the ancient schedules that operated up here. In many ways Hawkshead was fixed around the 1950s – a fact much relished by Simmy's father. 'Even in the height of summer, they close by five,' he said. 'Although you can generally find a pub open, I suppose.'

She did not want a pub. She wanted a little

99

table on the pavement and a pot of well-brewed tea all to herself. Hurriedly parking and pouring money into the machine, she then headed towards the village centre. Almost instantly she set eyes on a café that matched her requirements. The door stood open and she trotted in, holding her purse in readiness.

No problem, according to the woman at the counter. She could have all the tea she liked for two pounds. The first swallow was ambrosial. The world settled down again, for the few minutes it took to drain three teacups. She ignored the insistent pangs of hunger that now materialised once her need for fluid had been satisfied. But she could not ignore the temptation to justify the parking fee by making a little circuit of Hawkshead while she was there. It would be the first time she'd had a chance for a proper look, apart from a few flower deliveries made to properties close by. There were people in quantity, sitting at outdoor tables, strolling down the streets, walking their dogs. Very few vehicles impeded them, so they filled the middle of the road as well as the pavements, such as they were. The late afternoon light had a, clarity that drew her attention to the stonework of the church, set on a hillock above the little streets, with a graveyard on yet higher ground behind it. Its clock told her the time was ten minutes to five. Ben had been gone for several hours – more than long enough for truly dreadful things to have happened to him.

Everything in Hawkshead was packed in close together and higgledy-piggledy. The buildings had obviously come in a haphazard fashion, narrow streets winding around and between them, as well as crooked little alleyways. There were square gaps clearly designed for a horse and carriage to go through, and sudden spaces between the buildings that pedestrians could use. Standing at any point, it was possible to view almost the entire settlement. She stared about her as she strolled along, noticing a large shop offering superb quality gifts, including Wedgwood and Moorcroft china. There was a chemist shop, too, and a National Trust outlet selling expensive tea towels and jigsaws. All the buildings looked historic and a few of the streets were cobbled. She could see three pubs, at least – as well as the same number of tea rooms. She spotted a gallery full of fine paintings, and then a surprisingly utilitarian Co-op, which stayed open until 10 p.m. Dominating the whole village was an empty shop that had once sold books. Its abandonment added a dimension of dereliction and financial difficulty to what had at first seemed to be quite a thriving little place. The sounds were all of human voices, with music wafting from some unidentified point. A dog barked and a baby cried. The absence of traffic made a huge difference, she realised. When a delivery van or misdirected car did appear, it was at a crawl, seeming embarrassed to be there. Her father was right, she decided. Hawkshead was stuck in a bygone time.

But she couldn't linger any longer. Just a quick visit to the Co-op for something to eat, perhaps, and then back to Windermere, where she had things to do and places to go.

Going back to her car, she noticed again the four-wheel drive vehicle with the four men in. It had just parked close to her, and the men were getting out. She heard one say, in an American accent, 'Did the right thing there, pal. No way we'd want to stay out there tonight. We can try again in the morning. Thank the Lord for Mattie, hey?'

Another man said, 'Can't see the problem with the hotel, anyhow. They'd have been happy to have us an extra night.'

The first man turned round, looking annoyed. 'Listen – we booked for Wednesday, we show up Tuesday. That looks bad. They've got plenty of problems already. We'd just get their backs up.'

'Don't let's quarrel over it. It's done now.'

Simmy tried to make sense of this exchange, with difficulty. The men seemed respectable enough, giving no grounds for suspicion. Whatever reason Dan might have had to impress them, it would have to wait for the following day. Like everything else, she decided wearily.

She went first to her shop, to check that Bonnie had left it secure. Where was Bonnie now, anyway? If Ben's mother was up at Hawkshead, who would the girl find to share her anxiety? Corinne, presumably, or Ben's brother Wilf. In any case, Simmy found herself feeling superfluous. There was one new order on the computer, and a mildly chaotic list of takings in the till. Not a busy day by any standards, when it came to the business of selling flowers.

Almost without thinking, she walked down Lake Road to the large house where her parents lived. Beck View had five bedrooms, four of them let out to Bed and Breakfast guests. In July, the constant stream of customers kept Angie and Russell wholly occupied. Since Russell had begun to cause concern, Angie had looked increasingly tired and unhappy. It was a situation that Simmy feared would require drastic decisions before another year was out. As she got closer, she resolved to be of practical help to her mother, and possibly even refrain from telling the story of the day's events. No good could come of it, and in her father's more fragile condition, he might find it damagingly upsetting. It would be enough to spend some time with them, while more capable people than she conducted the search for Ben Harkness.

She had to go around the back since her father had started to insist that the front door be kept constantly locked and bolted, day and night. It was only by a strenuous exertion of will that Angie had managed to convince him that no harm could come from leaving the back unlocked while they were at home. 'One of us is always in the kitchen, anyway,' she said. But such assurances meant little to a man suffering from such paranoia as Russell was. He easily argued that it was not true. In the end Angie simply said, 'Well, you'll have to live with it, then. I'm not going to be made a prisoner in my own home by your demented imaginings.'

It was exactly the sort of thing you were not supposed to say, but somehow she got away with it. Russell's wretched little Lakeland Terrier was given the role of guardian of the back door whenever his people were somewhere else in the house, and that enabled an uneasy compromise to be made.

And through it all Simmy knew that her mother was experiencing a persistent sense of herself as the victim of a certain betrayal. She knew because she felt it herself. It was as if Russell's accord with his wife's attitude to life had always been a pretence, which he could no longer sustain. He had merely gone along with her cavalier approach to warnings of danger and patchy adherence to rules because it had seemed the easy way. Now, something had shifted and the real Russell Straw had emerged, timidly seeing robbers and murderers behind every tree. It infuriated and alienated Angie, who made no secret of the fact that she now liked him a lot less than she once did.

For Simmy the feelings were even more complicated, because they included a large dose of guilt. It was because of the succession of alarming and dangerous situations she had fallen into since moving up to the Lake District that Russell had lost his nerve. Or perhaps it had begun even earlier than that, when her perfect baby daughter had died unborn, thereby demonstrating that the universe was unstable and hostile and in no way to be taken for granted.

She deliberately rattled the door and stamped her feet as she entered, to give due warning of her presence. Guests would most likely be arriving at just this time, with all the explaining and settling that went with it. A Tuesday was not usually a popular day for B&B guests to start their holiday, but by July there were always individualists who constructed their own itineraries, regardless of usual patterns. Angie would be weary from changing sheets and duvet covers, as well as probably getting in fresh supplies for the immense breakfasts she continued to offer.

As luck would have it both her parents – and the dog – were in the kitchen. Coming through the small storeroom between the back door and the main room, she had a moment to observe them, slumped in chairs on either side of the Aga like two aged characters from a Victorian novel. The Aga was emitting its usual wasteful heat, even on a warm day in July, making the kitchen uncomfortably hot. 'No wonder you're both half-asleep,' she said cheerily. 'It's stifling in here.'

'It's the Aga,' said Russell.

'I know it is.' His statement of the obvious caused her a pang of distress. Her father had always prided himself on imparting new information and anecdotes, very often surprising in their detail. He had explored almost every inch of the southern Lakes, as far as Grasmere to the north and Kendal to the east. He read forgotten little histories and produced nuggets from them, often for the entertainment of his guests at breakfast time. Simmy hoped that this still happened.

'Where have you been? I hear the shop's been closed all afternoon.' Angie spoke incuriously, most likely assuming there had been a distant flower delivery to make.

'I went to Hawkshead, actually.'

'Ah!' said Russell. 'The town that time forgot. I spent a night there some years ago and it was the quietest night of my life. No traffic, birds, radios. It was uncanny.'

'I'd never walked through it before. It's a funny mixture of old and new. Galleries and upmarket

105

souvenir shops, as well as little tea rooms and cobbled streets. I guess it's all focused on tourism now. None of it's really authentic. The bookshop's closed down.'

'Ann Tyson's House hasn't changed much. You can imagine how it was three hundred years ago. That was where I stayed, before we came to live here.'

'Did you? And Esthwaite's nice.' She winced at the realisation that the calm little lake would never feel 'nice' to her again, with its grim associations.

'Taken over by fishing folk. Not much use to anybody else. Been the same for over a century now.'

'Maybe that's why it's so unspoilt.'

He looked at her with a little smile. 'Maybe it is, old girl. You could be right about that.'

'Why Hawkshead, though?' asked Angie with a faint frown.

'Oh, I didn't tell you, did I? I've got a big flower job at a hotel there. It goes on all summer, and maybe longer. Although—' she realised too late that when the news finally emerged about Dan and Ben, her mother would make an instant connection. Miserably, she concluded that she would have to tell them at least something of the story.

'What?'

'There was some trouble this afternoon. It involves Ben Harkness. He's missing.'

'That boy!' scoffed Russell. 'Always into something. He'll turn up.' He spoke as if Ben were twelve, rather than seventeen. 'He must be somewhere.'

'Obviously,' snapped Angie. 'What happened

then, P'simmon?' Only her mother called her that, and only her mother could say it exactly right. It was always a funny little pleasure to hear it on her lips.

'Well...' she glanced at her father, wondering whether there was any way to get him to leave the room. 'Haven't you got things I can help you with? I know you're busy this week.'

'Only one lot have arrived so far. There's another couple and a family with a small child. They'll be here at any moment. They're late, actually.' Angie consulted the large clock over the door. 'I hope they're not standing outside – the doorbell doesn't always work.' She threw a wrathful look at her husband, which he failed to observe. 'Russell – can you go and have a look? Make sure there's room for them to drive in and unload. And can you *please* leave the door unlocked, just for a bit?' The final part was uttered in a supplicatory tone that carried with it the knowledge that it was almost certainly spoken in vain.

'I can watch out for them if you like,' he offered.

'Yes, do that.'

As soon as he had gone, she turned to Simmy. 'Is that what you wanted? To get him out of the way?'

'I suppose so. The thing is, there's been a murder at the Hawkshead Hotel. Melanie and I found the under-manager dead in the lake. And Ben's disappeared. We think the killer – or killers, more likely – took him because he'd seen them. Something like that, anyway.'

'Mere. Esthwaite's a mere, not a lake.'

'Shut up. You sound just like Dad. What does it matter? Didn't you hear me?'

Angie sighed. 'I heard you. I'm just too tired to adequately respond, I suppose. Is it the hotel where Melanie works now?'

'That's right. And apparently she's been seeing the man who was killed. She's very upset.'

'It all sounds *highly* upsetting. What about Ben's mother? She must be distraught.'

'I saw her briefly. She seemed very calm, actually.'

'Shock,' Angie diagnosed. 'Disbelief.'

Simmy nodded, saying nothing.

'So why aren't you out looking for him?' Angie went on. 'Were you the last person to see him?'

'Probably. He went for a walk by the lake – *mere* – and found Dan's body. He called me, but I didn't hear the phone. It was in the van. So he left a message. It was cut off. He made a sort of shout and it went dead. We found it down where he'd been walking. There was no sign of him. He just disappeared.'

'But the body was there?'

'Sort of. I mean, yes it was, but it wasn't under the trees like Ben said, but in the water. Melanie and I fished him out. Poor Mel,' she finished miserably.

'He wasn't drowned, then?'

Simmy stared at her mother's face, without actually seeing it, her inner eye filled again with the image of the dead face. 'No. He'd been hit on the head. Moxon says there must have been more than one person. They lifted him over a fence and dumped him in the water. A horrible thing to do.

Melanie sat there with him on her lap. All dead and soaking wet and heavy.'

'Poor Melanie,' Angie murmured. 'What a dreadful thing.'

'The really terrible thing is Ben, and what must have happened to him, because he saw them, so they kidnapped him to stop him talking.' She was gabbling, trying to explain the theory of what had happened.

Angie sighed and gave a sceptical look at her daughter. 'You can't be sure that's how it was. That boy's got plenty of native wit. He'll turn up any moment, you see.'

'No, Mum. I'm sure he's in trouble. Nothing else would make any sense.' Her voice rose. 'And if that was it, then they won't ever be able to let him go, will they?' The idea of Ben being permanently silenced returned to her with renewed force. It paralysed her with fear and horror. 'I would be looking for him if I thought it would do any good. But where would I start? There isn't a single clue.'

Angie glanced nervously towards the front of the house, clearly hoping her husband couldn't hear them. She spoke in a low voice. 'Calm down, for heaven's sake. There must be *something*. If the same person or people killed the hotel chap and then abducted Ben, there'll be footprints and – I don't know. All that forensic stuff.'

'I don't know, Mum. There might not be anything useful. I can't believe they could find much in that marshy ground, and there aren't any CCTV cameras down there, either. I don't think the hotel has anything like that.'

'They must have taken him off in a car.

Somebody will have noticed it. Where will it have been parked?'

Simmy finally got herself in check and regarded her mother with surprise. 'You're really thinking about it, aren't you?'

'Well, you've got me worried now. I like that boy. He's an original. We can't let him come to any harm.'

'A bit late for that.'

'And what about Bonnie? What does she say about it?'

Simmy moaned. 'I don't know, Mum. I suppose she's as helpless as the rest of us. I left her all alone in the shop, so she closed up early. I have no idea what she did after that.'

'She'll want you, won't she? You're getting to be like another mother to her.'

'No, I'm not. She's got more than enough mother figures already. *Everybody* mothers her, because she looks so small and fragile. She's seventeen and a lot more streetwise than I'll ever be.'

'Hmm. And Melanie? She's only young, as well, and it sounds pretty traumatic, what she had to go through.'

Simmy felt crushed by the needs of so many distraught females and her mother's apparent assumption that she, Simmy, could somehow be of help to them. She also felt a pang of guilt at having allowed Melanie to slip from her thoughts. 'She was very horrified. Moxon says she was sleeping with him. She cried when we found him. I thought it was just the shock, but now I suppose it was more than that.'

'This murderer has obviously done an awful lot

110

of damage,' said Angie coolly.

The understatement was too much for Simmy. It brought home to her – as understatement so often did, of course – just how immense the damage actually was. Whatever happened next, a man was dead. The hotel would be thrown into disorder. The police investigation would disrupt its daily doings, and probably drive some guests away. It could spell disaster for the business, just as it seemed to have found its feet. And that was at the trivial end of the spectrum. The other end scarcely bore consideration.

'I don't know what I should do,' she wailed. 'I can't see anything I *can* do. I've told the police everything I can think of. I don't even know if I'm supposed to go back on Friday with more flowers.' She knew it was unworthy, but she did wonder about the promised five hundred pounds a week for the rest of the summer. To lose it before she even had it felt cruel. Yet more damage inflicted by the cursed killer. No punishment would be vile enough for this person or persons who had done such a terrible thing.

'We must keep all this from your father,' urged Angie. 'He won't take any more, the way he is now. I've got him signed up for a course of CBT, and that won't work if he has proof that his fears are all quite justified.'

'CBT?'

'You know. Cognitive behavioural therapy. They make you focus on the positive and examine your fears in the light of logic and reason. For most people, that makes them see that there's nothing to worry about.' She pulled a face. 'Not exactly so

111

in our case. He's terrified for you, you know. If he gets the slightest hint that you've brushed up against another murder, I daren't even think what that'd do to him.'

'I know.' More damage, Simmy realised. Ripples spreading forever outwards, from a moment of violence.

'So we've got to be normal. Can you do that?'

'I don't know,' Simmy admitted.

'You do see, don't you?' Angie was uncharacteristically intense. 'It really matters. I can't go on with him as he is. If we can't get him right, well...'

'God, Mum – you're not saying you'd leave him? What happened to "in sickness and in health"?'

'Don't give me that.' Angie's eyes flashed in anger. 'Don't you *dare*.'

Simmy was both contrite and intimidated. 'Sorry,' she said thickly. 'Look, let me do something useful for a bit, and then I'll go. I'll chat to Dad first, shall I?'

'He knows Ben's missing.' Angie sighed. 'I hope he's not going to dwell on that.'

'Sorry,' said Simmy again. 'What needs doing?'

'You can lay the tables for breakfast and check the cereal. Sugar bowls. The dishwasher's full. I still haven't emptied it from this morning. Most of the tablecloths are okay, but one had jam on it. It'll have to be changed.' She frowned. 'I hadn't realised how much your father did that he's not doing now. He just sits about. It's infuriating.'

'Leave it to me,' said Simmy, with a sense of relief. She could lose herself in the details of providing an old-fashioned breakfast for about eight people next morning. Angie used sugar bowls, butter dishes, milk jugs, where almost all other B&Bs had gone over to tiny paper sachets and fiddly plastic pots. It cost her more in wastage and washing-up, but she was determined to maintain her standards, regardless of the rest of the world.

Half an hour later, she was no calmer and no less guilty. Her thoughts had flittered from Melanie to Bonnie; then her father and Helen Harkness took centre stage. There were unpleasant patterns forming, all involving people suffering from profound distress, caused almost entirely by deliberate malice. Much of her guilt feelings arose from her constant wish to remain detached from unpleasantness. The rest came from the knowledge that she had taken Ben to the hotel and let him get himself abducted as a direct result.

It was past seven o'clock and she was hungry again despite the snack she'd had in the car, thanks to her visit to the Hawkshead Co-op. The guests had noisily arrived, with far too much luggage and no idea of where they might spend the evening. Simmy had remained in the dining room, invisible, but well able to hear what was happening. Evenings in a B&B were seldom easy. It was one more reason to wonder why people chose them in favour of a hotel. Angie did at least provide a room with a television and lots of games, but she preferred that people didn't eat in there. They were supposed to go out and patronise one of the many restaurants in the area. The people with small children regarded this as an inconvenience, despite clear advance information that nothing was to be had at Beck View itself.

But finally all was quiet and she emerged from the room now spread with immaculate table-cloths and everything else in perfect order.

'Can I make a sandwich or something?' she asked her mother, who was in the kitchen again. 'Then I should go.'

'Help yourself,' said Angie. She was once again slumped in one of the old chairs that stood either side of the Aga. These, as well as the dog, were incongruous elements in a place that was now and then inspected by hygiene officials. The Beck View kitchen was closer to that of a farmhouse than a modern guesthouse, despite the large gas cooker and two big refrigerators. It also had a scrubbed pine table and a walk-in pantry. None of the inspectors found the courage to complain.

Russell looked up from the other chair. 'I've hardly seen you. Did you say something about the boy, Ben, being lost?'

'I expect they've found him by now. It wasn't much to worry about,' lied Simmy, her face growing hot. 'Now, then – I think I'll have cheese and tomato before I go.' She bustled about, making a production of her sandwich. 'Lovely!' she said, after the first bite.

She finished it quickly and gathered up her bag. 'I'll drop in again, in a day or so. Give me a call if you want anything. Shopping. Sheets changing. I can always come for an hour after work.' She made herself sound blithe and useful, a sort of parody of a home help. The idea that her own parents, still so young, might need such a thing, made her wince.

'Thanks, love,' said Angie. 'See you soon, then.'

114

She drove home, up the hill to Troutbeck, more miserable than she could remember feeling since she came to the Lake District.

Chapter Ten

Wednesday dawned deceptively quietly. Simmy woke early and lay in her tangled bed contemplating the coming day with apprehension. She reviewed her own place in the picture, forcing herself to acknowledge that she had learnt quite a lot about murder in the past nine or ten months. She had seen for herself how people who seemed quite pleasant and normal could take a knife or a bludgeon to another person. And then they could behave with sufficient ordinariness to conceal what they had done. They walked amongst society with nothing to disclose their true nature. Simmy had spoken to some of them, all unsuspecting. Had she, then, also spoken to the killer of Dan Yates? Was it Mr Boddington-Webster, or his wife or the handsome gay chef? The bony Penny or the mother of young Gentian? Perhaps one of the other hotel guests she had mingled with on Monday? What about the smart woman who had seemed so impatient? What a good act that would have been, if so. The list was uncomfortably long and did not include a number of others she had not even met. Better not to even try to second-guess who might want Dan dead. Besides, hadn't Moxon implied that there were a number of people involved? Her initial assumptions of a feral gang of disaffected youths rampaging the serene Cumbrian countryside had receded overnight. Such an explanation was both too easy and too unlikely for serious consideration.

At least there was no suspicion resting on Melanie, given what Moxon knew about her from earlier incidents. To some detectives, she might stand out as a person of special interest. Romantically attached to the victim, and therefore prone to jealousy, insecurity, rage, frustration. Technically, for such theoretical investigators, she might come at the very top of the list. But Melanie would never have abducted Ben, causing his mother such distress. And Moxon seemed certain that the crime had not been achieved by a single person. Who in the world could Melanie employ as a sidekick?

Would Bonnie come to work, she wondered. Would Moxon seek her – Simmy – out at the shop, or ask her to come for an interview at the police station? She ought to get up and find her phone and see whether anyone had left her a message. Unlike many people, she did not take the mobile to bed with her. She left it downstairs, turned off and ignored. Since the loss of her baby she had decided that nothing could be of sufficient importance or urgency to justify a midnight call on a mobile phone. The landline would awake her, pealing up the stairs to her room. So would a loud knock on the door. Only her parents mattered enough for such an arousal, and even they would probably wait until morning for any imaginable communication.

Heavily she rolled out and blundered to the bathroom. It was fully light, the days still very much longer than the nights. The birds no longer belted out their dawn chorus, but they were out there teaching their young ones the ways of the world, with agitated flutterings in the branches outside her window. July was a time for consolidation, the summer firmly established, the rigours of winter far ahead. Summer flowers were abundant, lush and colourful. Scarlets and vibrant oranges; velvety purples and deep, dense crimsons were all clamouring for admiration in her own garden. She had an especially exuberant clematis romping along her back fence, thick with pinky-purple flowers and deliciously scented. While her garden was far from the perfect creation she had in mind when she moved there, it was certainly a credit to her, after little over a year in the making.

All of which brought feelings of resentment against the person or persons who had killed Dan. She wanted to immerse herself in her flowers instead of dwelling on the horrors that had been unleashed. The resentment mutated quickly into a determination to find Ben. If he had not turned up, of course. Perhaps all the panic was already over, and nobody had thought to tell her.

Because there was not a single message on her phone. Nobody had told her anything, or asked her a question, or suggested a course of action.

There was no other course of action than to go down to Windermere and open the shop as normal. The weather was even warmer than the day before, bringing people out in shorts and singlets, relishing their good fortune. Even less likely to be buying flowers than ever, Simmy thought sourly. They would be taking small boats out onto the water, or packing picnics and heading for Kirkstone and beyond. Detective Inspector Moxon would be sweating in his interview room, or driving around in search of clues to the identities of the killer-kidnappers. Would he go back to Hawkshead, or leave all that to his SOCO people? One thing Simmy had learnt was that a killing committed out of doors was troublesome when it came to finding evidence. Where they might normally erect a tent over the designated spot, in this case that wouldn't work at all. Even if they discovered flattened grass and footprints under the trees, it would all have been so contaminated and muddled by Simmy and Melanie and Mrs Bodgett – not to mention the trampling down of the fence by the policemen – that little useful information could hope to remain. Poor old Moxon, and whoever his superior might be. They'd be struggling hard to implement any of the usual procedures listed in their books of How to Solve a Murder.

Which meant, presumably, they would focus mainly on the staff and guests at the hotel. The people who knew Dan and might have some idea as to why he had died in such a terrible way.

The thing that most hurt her head and scrambled her thoughts was the dual nature of the crime. Murder *and* abduction. The urgency had to be to find Ben, because that would solve both crimes at the same time. So endless interviews and forensic nit-picking felt like the wrong sort of effort to be making. By the time she was at her shop, she felt like screaming with frustration. It was all a fog, with nothing substantial to go on at all. Even knowing Ben as well as she did was no help. He was not in control. Somebody was hiding him – keeping him from revealing who they were and what they'd done. But they couldn't hide him for ever. So they would have to kill him. And that made her head hurt a lot more, as well as her heart and lungs and most of the rest of her. The sheer brutality of the thought was enough to make everything inside her go tight and sore.

Everything in the shop was as she'd left it. Except that there was a hand-delivered letter from DI Moxon's wife, asking if it would be possible to create and deliver a birthday bouquet for her mother in Newby Bridge, the following morning. At any other time, this would have been a welcome commission. Simmy liked Sue and would have enjoyed making up something special for her. Now it seemed a great effort to even think about it. Limply she turned on the computer, and put in an order for a special delivery of lilies, gerberas and gladioli. Then she phoned the number in the note and confirmed that she would do as requested. It was all she could manage not to leave a message for the detective inspector – knowing he would be sure to keep her informed of any important developments. His wife could not ethically be brought into the matter, anyway, as they both well knew. 'Thanks a lot,' she said. 'I know you've got other things to worry about at the moment.' It was a subtle attempt at sympathy, and Simmy appreciated it.

'We've got to make an effort for a person's eightieth,' she said staunchly. 'I hope she'll have a lovely day. I'll take the flowers around ten, then.'

Then she set herself to freshening the displays, putting pots and buckets full of blooms out on the pavement. Bonnie's perfect window called in vain to unheeding passers-by. What was the point, Simmy asked herself gloomily. If Ben was gone, a bright light would be permanently extinguished, and the world would never be a place to enjoy again. She had thought the same when her baby died, and it had turned out to be very nearly true. But there had been sweet times since then – many of them provided by young Ben Harkness.

She was aware of a growing need for company. It seemed very unlikely that Bonnie would turn up. Certainly there would be no Melanie. That left her friend Julie, perhaps. Julie was a local hairdresser, who had taken Simmy under her wing and shown her around Windermere in the early months. They ate and drank together at regular intervals, but the friendship never progressed beyond that point. They liked each other, but there was too little common ground for a genuine bond. Simmy was not especially good at female friends, anyway. An only child, she was never sure of the boundaries or the obligations.

And then there was Ninian Tripp. Ninian had been fading out of her life for a few weeks now, leaving little trace of himself. A self-employed potter, his aversion to commitment was wholesale. Simmy had pretty well given up on any idea of establishing a sensible relationship with him. He clearly didn't see things as she did, with no thought of 'settling down', as one's mother might say.

At nine-thirty, however, her solitude was broken by a woman coming into the shop. Simmy looked up and met the tear-blurred eyes of Helen Harkness. Her first reaction was one of resistance. This was going to hurt and she flinched. Then she pushed back her shoulders and took a deep breath. 'Any news?' she asked.

Helen shook her head. 'I've been up all night. I mean – you can't go to sleep at a time like this, can you?'

There was little to say to this, so Simmy just shook her head. Here was a very much reduced version of the woman she had seen the day before. Tall, confident, in her late fifties, Mrs Harkness had sailed through life thus far with every expectation of success. Five children and a dependable husband, a thriving professional career – nothing could have prepared her for the events of the past twenty hours or so.

'I mean – Ben's always been a bit wild. Kept us on our toes with his antics. But we never imagined him as a *victim*. It's all wrong.'

Simmy gave this some consideration. 'And yet there's something rather vulnerable about him, I suppose,' she said. 'He's very young. And not exactly *physical*.'

'I know.' Again the eyes met Simmy's. 'Thank you.'

'What for?'

'Speaking plainly. Not trying to pacify me with

platitudes and reassurances.'

'Well, you're Ben's mother, aren't you? He must have got his outspokenness from somewhere. How are the others coping?'

'The girls think it's all rather exciting, although they try not to show it. I made them go to school as usual, with strict instructions not to talk about it. Apparently the police are keeping an embargo on any mention of Ben from the news people. It's too risky, for some reason. I don't really know what I think about it – sometimes I think the police don't believe Ben's been abducted at all. Wilf's gone terribly quiet. Their father's up in Hawkshead tramping round just looking for him. It's a natural instinct, of course, but how do you search the whole Lake District? He could be *anywhere*.'

'Have you seen Bonnie?'

'Not since yesterday. She came to the house while the police were still there. I suppose we should be worrying about her. She didn't come to work, then?'

Simmy shook her head. 'She'll be looking for him as well, I expect. Although I don't know how she'd get to Hawkshead.'

'There's a bus. Or her foster mother might take her. I forget her name.' Helen frowned in alarm at her own memory lapse. 'Gosh, my mind's going,' she cried.

Simmy laughed. 'Corinne. She might, I suppose.' The image of all Ben's friends and relations scouring the fells for the lost boy was a depressing one. Like a lot of tiny ants trying to cover an entire field. A hopeless quest, as Ben himself might say.

'The trouble is, I can't see any reason why they would let him go. It's been going round and round in my head all night. If he saw them killing that hotel man, they'll never be able to risk him going free, will they?'

Fresh images of Ben with his tongue cut out, or his brain destroyed in some way, gave Simmy's insides another twist. 'We might have got it all wrong,' she said, hoping that didn't sound like an empty reassurance. 'We have been jumping to conclusions with hardly any evidence, after all.'

'I think they must be right, though. What other explanation can there possibly be?'

'I don't know.'

'You must be wondering why I came here. I hardly know myself, to be honest. I just thought you'd probably understand. And you were the last person to see him, according to the police.' There was no hint of the previous day's reproach, and yet Simmy's guilt levels rose significantly at these words.

'I should have kept my phone with me. Then I'd have got his call and none of this would have happened. I keep thinking about how he must have felt when I didn't answer.'

'You can't be sure of that. Would you have just dashed down there right away? And even then, would you have been in time to stop them taking him?'

'I think I would. It's no distance, after all.' She remembered how she had delayed for what felt like ages before going down to the lakeside, after hearing Ben's message. 'But you might be right. I might have persuaded myself it wasn't anything very important.'

Helen sighed. 'I can't blame you. I'd have been the same, thinking he was just playing one of his usual games. Although–'

'I know. It didn't sound like a game.' She relived the whole episode again, trying to envisage what must have happened. 'I wonder what they did with him. There must have been a van or something near that farmhouse at the end of the track. Or by the sewage works. There's space to park there. That's quite a long way from the lake, though. You can't get a vehicle across the field. Do you know where I mean?'

'Not exactly. I saw it yesterday, but didn't take it all in.'

'Well, you go down a track, like a little road, which leads to the hotel and the farm past the water treatment place – whatever it is they do there. The track doesn't go anywhere else. There must be a small gate or stile or something into the field, if you park there and want to walk by the lake. You'd go past the trees – there's quite a lot of very dense woodland – and then it's just more fields and water, with the hotel slightly above you. There's no road down to the lake that I can think of, for the whole length of it, on that side.' She remembered something else. 'What about Colthouse? I still can't work out where that is. Ben said he and Bonnie are interested in something there and he was going to walk over for a look. Did he do that, I wonder?'

Helen shook her head helplessly. 'How would we know, unless somebody saw him? We can mention it to the police, I suppose.'

'It might just confuse them. He was definitely beside Esthwaite when it all happened, because that's where we found his phone.'

'The police will have worked it all out. They might have found some footprints.'

'Ben will have tried to leave clues. He'll have dragged his feet, or dropped a tissue or something.'

Helen smiled wanly. 'You're right. But how will they ever find it, if he did? I saw cows down there, for a start. They'll have trampled everything.'

'Yeah.' She was still forcing her thoughts to stay with Ben and how he might have reacted. 'It's possible, I guess, that they didn't drive from there. They might have somehow got to the other side of the lake. What if they had a boat? What if they walked through the trees and up a track or something well away from the hotel, coming out in Hawkshead?'

'It's hopeless,' moaned Helen. 'We'll go mad if we keep on like this. Will the police ask everybody in Hawkshead if they saw anything?'

'They'll ask a lot, I assume. I don't know *what* they'll do, to be honest.'

They sagged helplessly, having no way of answering their own questions. 'We'll have to go and find out,' said Simmy. 'We can't just hang about here sending ourselves insane.'

'There's a family liaison woman at the house. But she hasn't got anybody to liaise with because we're all out. I feel bad about leaving her on her own. Isn't that stupid.' Helen gave a short laugh. 'Imagine what our grandmothers would say to such mollycoddling. All terribly well intentioned,

125

of course, and hopelessly irritating in practice.'

'Scary, too,' said Simmy. 'I mean – doesn't that imply that they think something awful has happened to him?'

'Precisely. She's there to mop me up when the bad news comes.'

'My mother would send her packing. Or else behave so fantastically inappropriately that she'd be appalled.'

'Ben's very impressed by your mother,' said Helen absently. 'And you too, of course. He talks about you a lot.'

'Don't,' said Simmy, suddenly on the brink of tears.

'You're right. We can't stand here getting mawkish. That's not doing anybody any good at all. So why don't we get in my car – which is right outside on double yellow lines – and go and find that boy of mine?'

Simmy waved Helen towards the door, still fighting back her emotion. Sure enough, the big Freelander was right outside the shop. Quickly locking the shop door, Simmy climbed into the passenger seat. She felt instantly superior to the other motorists passing by. The fact that such a vehicle would be awkward in some of the narrow country lanes on the way to Hawkshead was beside the point. It conferred an additional status on her and Helen, both of them already high on the list of importance in the police hunt for Ben. They could do anything they liked, she realised, including parking illegally and abandoning the well-intentioned FLO.

'But where will we start?' she asked, half-speaking to herself. 'We already decided it was hopeless.'

'We're going to the camping site. I've got a feeling. An intuition, even. There are caravans coming and going all the time, nobody asking questions. What a great way of keeping somebody out of sight.'

'He'd break a window or shout for help or kick a hole in the side. Caravans are quite flimsy.'

'Not if he was tied up. And gagged.'

Distressing as such images were, they were at least based on the assumption that Ben was alive and essentially unhurt. Helen started the engine before Simmy had fastened her seatbelt, and went charging much too quickly through Windermere's upper reaches towards Ambleside. She had lived in the area all her life, Simmy remembered, and must know what she was doing. Lake Windermere lay firmly in their way, necessitating a nine-mile drive up to its northern tip and then down the other side to Hawkshead, which was barely four miles away as the crow flew. Nothing could be managed quickly.

'There isn't actually a huge hurry, is there?' she asked. 'I mean, not enough to risk killing us both, or getting stopped by traffic cops.'

'I should have done this last night. I feel as if I've only now come to my senses. Why did I let that detective bloke talk me into going home? I was only at the hotel for an hour, and then they took me back. What a stupid thing.'

'I don't know. He could be right.' Their expedition was already seeming rather foolish to Simmy. 'But I can see it feels better to be doing something. And nothing's happening down in Windermere or

Bowness, is it?'

'Right.'

Around the southern edge of Ambleside and into the tiny twisting lanes they sped. As a passenger, Simmy noticed details she had not observed before. Stone walls that they missed by millimetres when passing oncoming traffic; great moss-covered trees that seemed to belong to an earlier age. Even on a sunny summer's day, it was gloomy. She found herself looking out for places in which a hostage might be hidden. Hillocks and ancient ditches, tangles of undergrowth and even one or two stone-built huts all offered potential prisons. Who knew what caves and holes had been tunnelled under the hillocks? Anything was possible. 'It's absolutely hopeless,' she muttered aloud.

'Stop it. Sometimes you just have to go with your gut. He's my *son*, flesh of my flesh. If I have to tear up every tree in Cumbria with my bare hands to find him, that might well be what I'll do.'

Hawkshead felt almost familiar to Simmy this time. Sure enough there were tents and caravans scattered around a field on their left, with Esthwaite invisibly to the south of them. Helen pulled onto the side of the road and looked all around. 'Can't see any footpaths,' she observed.

'Have you got a map?'

'Not with me. There's a tarn over there, I remember. It's called Priest Pot and was once part of the actual lake. We took the kids there for a picnic, years ago. We had to trespass across a field and climb over a wall to get there. We went into

128

the Quaker burial ground, as well. My kids always did like graves.'

Simmy waited patiently for a point to all this. When none came, she said, 'So Ben knows the area?'

'If he remembers us coming here. He must have been about ten.'

'He's been hiking all round here for the past three days. He'll have worked out the tracks and things.'

'That was Furness and Satterthwaite, I think. It's all much too tame down here by the water. But he's no fool when it comes to finding his way around. He loves all that sort of thing.'

'I keep thinking he's clever enough to outwit the average criminal. And then I remember his talents are mostly theoretical. I mean – he's only seventeen.'

'He did go to tae kwon do for a while when he was about fourteen. He might remember some of that.' Helen sounded very dubious. 'The fact is, I have no idea what the average criminal might be capable of. And who's to say this one's average, anyway?'

They had begun walking down the side of the camping ground, eyeing the apparently deserted tents and caravans. 'We can't just bang on all the doors,' said Simmy.

'We could, actually. There are only a dozen or so. I still have my hunch that this'd be a good place to keep him.'

'Mrs Brown?' came a man's voice from behind them. 'And Mrs Harkness? What on earth–?'

Both women turned to face DI Moxon, who

129

was flanked by two uniformed officers.

'Oh, hello,' said Simmy.

His expression was a complicated mixture of compassion, reproach and irritation. 'You decided to join the search, I suppose.'

'That's right. We thought the caravan park–'

'We're ahead of you. Every single one was searched before eight this morning. If you'd gone any further down here, you'd have seen ten of Cumbria's constabulary working their way right across the fields and woods between here and the lake. A diver has gone into Priest Pot, for good measure.'

'Oh, God!' said Helen. 'You don't think...?'

'We have no reason at all to think anything. We're simply looking for evidence.'

'A murder weapon?' said Simmy, feeling herself channelling Ben Harkness. That was exactly the question he would ask. 'You must know for sure how Dan was killed by now.'

'Blunt instrument to the side of the head,' came the reply, delivered with a surprising readiness. 'Likely to be a hammer – or something with a handle.'

'And it killed him there and then?'

'So it seems.'

'Have you found the exact place where Ben saw the body? Melanie found some flattened bracken, by that dead tree. I suppose it's all churned up now by cows and everything.'

He gave a boyish grin of pride, which Simmy found endearing. This man had in some ways never quite grown up. His responsibilities and areas of social uncertainty both made him quite earnest. He could also be a lot more forthcoming than she imagined he was supposed to be, at times. This was evidently one of them. 'Actually, we have found it. It's all gratifyingly clear, given the circumstances. And it was on the woodland side of the fence, where the cows can't reach. We even found some fibres on the fence.'

Simmy felt a burst of hope. 'From the killer's clothes?'

'Afraid not. Only Mr Yates's. We're thinking there definitely had to be at least two people involved. It seems they carried him along the inside of the fence to the water, then retraced their steps to the dead tree and climbed back over.'

'But how does Ben fit in?'

Moxon grimaced. 'That's the bit we can't explain. If there were more than two attackers, one of them might have held him while the others moved the body. Or he might have stayed of his own accord, trying to stop them. Or...' he glanced unhappily at Helen.

'Or they knocked him out, to keep him quiet,' the woman supplied calmly. 'But if they'd killed him, they would have just left his body there with the first one. They'd have no reason to take one without the other, would they?'

'That's right,' said Simmy admiringly.

'Or he might have run away from them,' Helen went on. 'And still be hiding in those woods. It could take days to search them properly.'

'Not so,' said Moxon. 'We've searched them thoroughly, and can say with certainty that nobody at all is hiding in them.'

'You've done a lot, haven't you?' said Simmy.

131

'In the time, I mean.'

'Thank you, ma'am,' he said, with not a hint of a twinkle. 'We're all extremely anxious to locate young Mr Harkness as soon as humanly possible.'

'And the best way to do that is to track down the people who killed Dan and abducted Ben,' Simmy summarised.

He nodded and then looked at Helen. 'We would really prefer you to be at home, you know,' he said gently. 'There's a chance that your son will somehow make his way there, and to find an empty house ... well, we wouldn't want that, would we?'

'A small chance,' said Helen. 'Let's face it. In fact, it's so small as to be unworthy of consideration.'

'I wouldn't say that.'

'He'd go to the police station before he went home,' said Simmy with certainty. 'If he did somehow escape, he would want you to know all about it. He'd want to make sure you caught these people. He'd want you to praise him for being so resourceful and brave.'

Helen smiled. 'That's all true. Thank you, Simmy.'

'What for?' Hadn't they already been through this bit?

'For reminding me just who Ben is. For helping me to believe that he's very likely enjoying himself, wherever he is, and certainly not worrying about me.'

Detective Inspector Moxon blew out his cheeks in amazed admiration. 'You women!' he said. 'I don't think you've read the book that says you should be helpless with anxiety, or hysterical. That sort of thing, anyway.'

'I was awake all night, and I spent at least half of it in tears, if that makes you feel better,' said Helen.

'I'm ashamed to say I slept quite well,' Simmy admitted. 'There's only so much worry a person can handle, and I've got Bonnie, Melanie and my father on my mind as well as Ben. I think I must have used sleep as an escape from it all.'

'Why are you out here wandering about, instead of ... doing whatever it is you usually do?' asked Simmy of Moxon. 'Interviews, background searches – all that stuff.'

He gave her a stern look. 'I know what I'm doing. I need to be within reach of the hotel for most of today. That's where we've set up the incident room. It has to be close to the scene of the crime, you see.'

'Oh, yes. I suppose that makes sense.'

His sternness deepened and he made a sound of protest.

'Sorry. That sounded awful. So, you want us to go away, right?'

'You must be losing business,' he said, with unaccustomed obliqueness. 'I know for a fact you'll be getting at least one order today.'

She waited, with a little smile. 'Oh yes?'

'My wife's mother will be eighty tomorrow. Sue wants to send a spectacular bouquet as a surprise.'

'All done and dusted already,' she told him. 'I spoke to her this morning. The flowers are coming later today.'

'I'm impressed.'

'Well ... thanks. I appreciate your custom.'

'You're the best in town.' They savoured the little moment. 'So, you'll be needing to get back, then. Can't neglect the business, you know. And there really isn't anything you can do here.'

The moment was spoilt. What concern was it of his if she chose to abandon her duties for a morning? 'How do you know Bonnie isn't manning the shop?'

He cast his eyes upwards. 'Because little Miss Lawson has been bothering us here since before nine o'clock. Apparently she's another one who decided the caravan park was worthy of investigation.'

'So where is she now?'

'Back at home, I hope. I popped her into one of our cars that was going back to the station.'

'And where's Melanie? Just so I have the complete set.'

'She's not at the hotel. I'm assuming she's at home, getting over her experiences of yesterday. She was very shocked.'

'Yes, I know. It was her first sight of a dead body.'

'So she's not helping with enquiries?' asked Helen Harkness.

They both stared at her, reading a host of sinister and outrageous implications into her words. 'Not at all,' snapped Moxon. 'Why do you say that?'

'Oh, no – I didn't mean... Just that she knew the man who died, and is so fond of Ben. I didn't mean...' She stumbled to a halt.

134

'No, I'm sorry I snapped. You struck a nerve, that's all. Not everybody gets Miss Todd, after all.'

Simmy thought she could see what he meant. 'Some people think she *should* be helping you with enquiries? Is that it?'

'Some people being my superintendent, for a start,' he agreed ruefully. 'Now then, we can't stand here all day, can we? I suggest you go and find a coffee in the village, and then get back to Windermere. I should be in at least five places at once.'

'Come on, then,' said Simmy to Helen. 'We're not doing any good here.'

Unresistingly, Helen followed her back to the car. 'Maybe we should leave it here, rather than pay for parking.'

'Up to you. I don't imagine anyone's going to object, once they know who you are.'

'Hawkshead hates cars, you know. They've been very brave about it, considering.'

It took them about four minutes to reach the heart of the little old village, where they opted for a café set below the church. They could see the high-class souvenir shop and the chemist and a lot of other buildings.

'I can still *feel* him here somewhere,' said Helen. 'It sounds mad, but I really can.'

Chapter Eleven

Bonnie Lawson sat quietly in the back of the police car, as she was taken home to Windermere. She had hitched a ride to Hawkshead at seven that morning with a man in a white van who was very vaguely known to her by sight. He had overtaken her just before she reached the bus stop, and made her a better offer than public transport could supply. She had no fear that there would be any misbehaviour on his part. Men had never been much of a bother to her, despite most people's assumptions. Suffering from anorexia in her early teens, the counsellors and therapists and teachers had all started from the premise that one of her mother's boyfriends must have abused her in some way. She had almost come to believe it herself, but the truth was much more complicated and bizarre. One of the many things she adored about Ben Harkness was his easy acceptance and extraordinary understanding when she told him the story.

They *had* to find Ben. She was consumed with a passionate urgency that made her heart race and her fists clench. It was completely beyond acceptability that he should be gone for ever. If that happened, then she would starve herself to death in a month. There would be no sense or purpose in the universe, and she did not want to be part of it. Her need for him frightened her so much that she found herself turning it around, into his need for her. She was going to be the person who found him. The moment these dozy policemen dropped her at home, she'd be off again, back to the search. She'd hang about until they'd gone, hoping Corinne was still in bed, and then get right back to Hawkshead.

But the police turned out to be less dozy than she'd thought. 'We need to speak to your mother,' one said.

'She's not my mother. Even if she was, I'm *seventeen*. You're treating me like I was ten.'

'You're behaving like someone who's ten. You're still a minor, and you're putting yourself in harm's way.'

'Oh, shut up,' she muttered. The words were irritatingly familiar. People had been trying to show her what was in her best interests, and what she was doing to harm herself, for years now. Since getting to know Ben, she was even more certain than before that she knew better than any of them.

'I didn't hear that,' said the man. He was about thirty, plain-looking and trying hard to follow the rules. But he was also human and sympathetic. Like most people in Windermere and Bowness, he was faintly familiar to her. Bonnie had known countless foster brothers and sisters, had been in and out of school, accompanied Corinne to all kinds of meetings and clubs, mostly associated with folk music or dogs. Once you removed all the faceless tourists, the core population was close-knit. They mostly knew each other.

'Is this the house?' asked the other man, who

was driving. He peered through the windscreen at the upper windows. 'The curtains are still closed.'

'She sleeps late. I've got a key.'

'We have to speak to her.'

'Good luck with that.'

But they were determined, and Corinne finally came down, bleary-eyed and ratty-tempered. 'Bon? Aren't you at the shop today?'

'I went to look for Ben. The cops brought me back. They found me walking down to the hotel where he went missing. I hitched.'

'I told you not to do that.' Corinne sighed. 'They haven't found him, then?'

Bonnie considered a burst of tears as a useful strategy, but decided against it, not least because she was worried that once she started, she might not easily stop again.

'She shouldn't be out there on her own,' said the conscientious policeman. 'There's been a murder, don't forget.'

Corinne sighed again. 'They'll be long gone, won't they? And nobody's going to kill Bonnie. Why would they?'

Good question, thought Bonnie. So why would they kidnap Ben? The explanation that everyone seemed to have accepted without question was still niggling at her, not ringing true at all.

'All the same–'

'Right, right. I won't let her out, then. How long do you want me to keep her tied up? She does have a job, you know.'

'Just use your common sense,' said the policeman impatiently. 'It's for her own good.'

He left then, scratching his head at the vagaries of women who didn't know what was good for them.

'I *know* he's still around Hawkshead somewhere,' Bonnie insisted. 'Will you take me back there, Con?'

'What about Simmy and the shop?'

'She won't be expecting me. She won't even have opened up, I bet you. She loves Ben, same as I do. And there's Melanie as well. She's going to want us with her. What do they expect us to do – just carry on as if things are normal?'

'My exhaust is falling off. Those roads'd finish the job. I was going to take it in today. What time is it?'

'Not even ten yet. I was out early.'

'The cops'll just bring you back again, and give me a bollocking for letting you go.'

'I'll be more careful. Oh, go on, Con. The exhaust's been rattling for weeks. Another day won't hurt it.'

Corinne's career as a foster mother was scheduled to end with Bonnie. Over the last decade and a half more than fifty children had passed through her hands, most of them under three years old. She could have carried on, except for the growing demands of her new interest in travelling the country at weekends to festivals, and a less easily defined weariness with it all. The Social Services had never fully got to grips with her ways, and constantly nagged her to tone down the excessive number of dogs around the place and – which was their final straw – her smoking. 'You'd never have been accepted in the first place if we hadn't been so desperate,' they said.

But her methods had worked. The children gained confidence in the world under her rather sloppy care. They were fed, cuddled, sung to and laughed with. In most cases they came to believe that life might be okay after all. She kept in touch with them when they left and often passed unofficial reports back to the authorities if she thought they were being harmed. She had saved one little boy from serious abuse, by the straightforward technique of collaring the abuser in the main street and shouting at him in the plainest possible language. At least twenty people passing by got the message, and gave him to understand that he was expected to reform or suffer the consequences. As it turned out, the consequences happened anyway and his life was effectively ruined. The Social Services cringed away from the whole incident, appalled by the direct action. One social worker called Corinne a vigilante, which she cheerfully agreed was accurate.

Bonnie had been a special case from the start. Older than the others, in and out of hospital, hopelessly behind with schoolwork, she had forced Corinne to focus. By this time they were much more like friends than mother and daughter. While family therapists might regard this as far from ideal, they were both thoroughly satisfied with the arrangement.

'Oh, all right, then. But we're never going to avoid attention with the noise the damn thing makes.'

'You can drop me outside the town. Colthouse or somewhere. Actually, I might start there. Ben talked about it once.'

'I've never heard of it.' Corinne, like Melanie Todd, had a strong preference for buildings and streets over the wild empty spaces of the fells. Never a walker, sailor or swimmer, she also liked to have a lot of people around her.

'Quakers,' said Bonnie vaguely. 'He was on about the Quakers. There's an old Quaker place there.'

Corinne gave up with a deep sigh. 'Let me get my shoes on, then,' was all she said.

Bonnie was reluctant to admit that she did not exactly know how to find Colthouse either. 'Use the satnav,' she urged.

'You do it, then.'

Bonnie commanded the gadget to take them to Colthouse, and for seven miles they did as it ordered. Then, Bonnie found fault with it. 'It's trying to take us through Hawkshead. We don't want that.' She peered at the diagrammatic map on the little screen. 'Take the next fork left,' she said. 'I think there's a sort of loop on a smaller road.'

'My God. Do they come smaller than this one?'

'Just do it.'

They followed a tortuous route through Low Wray and High Wray, with the satnav doing its best to persuade them they were in error. They could see Lake Windermere not far off on their left. After High Wray they turned westwards, curling around a hill with a stone construction just visible on the top, and then a few degrees more southwards towards Esthwaite. Bonnie was concentrating as hard as she could on the layout,

141

noting the position of the sun and the many place names that were signed along the way. 'This must be it!' she cried, after another half-mile. 'Whoopee!'

'Congratulations,' said Corinne drily. 'I can't just leave you here, can I? You'd never be found again. It's the middle of nowhere.'

'It's practically on the edge of Hawkshead. I'll be fine.'

'No, Bonnie. If anything happened to you, they'd put me in jail. Plus, it would be a waste of all my good work.'

'There are walkers all over the place. I've got my phone and a bottle of water. It's a lovely, dry, warm day. I'll be fine,' she repeated.

'But why this place? It's got nothing to suggest Ben was here. It's crazy to even think it.'

'Yeah, probably. But it's only half a mile from where he went missing. There's houses and a road, and the caravan park's only five minutes away. It's a *feeling*, okay? It makes more sense than you think. I just want to have a look. He'll have tried to leave clues, and I'm more likely to recognise them than anybody else.'

A car hooted behind them. Corinne drove into the entrance to a farmyard and let the other vehicle pass. Bonnie jumped out, and then leant back through the passenger window to say, 'Wait for me in Hawkshead, then. Give me half an hour, right?'

'I thought we wanted to avoid Hawkshead.'

'Tell you what – isn't there a garage there somewhere? Where Percy used to work? They might fix your exhaust while you wait.' Connie merely shrugged, and Bonnie went on, 'I'll call you, I promise. Look – it's twenty to eleven now. I'll phone at eleven, exactly. Nothing's going to happen in that time.'

'Famous last words,' said Corinne, but she drove away as instructed, the exhaust making a noise like a souped-up motorbike.

Bonnie waited until the car was out of sight and earshot, and then gave her surroundings a long careful examination. There was a sign beside her indicating the old Quaker Meeting House that was accessed through the farmyard. This much she already knew from Ben. It had a quirkiness that appealed to him. She walked through the quietness, barns on both sides, passing a stone trough with an iron pump above it. The Meeting House was behind a stone wall, gazing serenely at the trees before it and giving no hint that Ben was ever there. Turning back, Bonnie went down the slope to where the small road met a slightly larger one. On the corner was the burial ground that she and Ben had discussed more than once.

She had withheld a lot of her thinking from Corinne, as well as from the police and Ben's mother. It would sound childish and silly to all of them. It very likely *was* childish and silly, a game she and Ben had been playing on and off for weeks. Using Google, along with scraps of history from local websites, and a few old books, they had been constructing a computer-based game based on the year 1780. It was a vast, sprawling virtual tour of all the people and places that were significant in that year, in the county then known as Cumberland. The central thread

143

was a quest for objects connected to William Wordsworth, who at the time was a schoolboy in Hawkshead, along with his brother Richard.

Bonnie suspected that a lot of the purpose behind this project was to educate her in a range of disciplines, from history to computer programming, and including geography and logic. She was given small areas to work on and encouraged to come up with ideas of her own. Within days it had become the greatest possible fun. To her amazement she found Wordsworth's *Prelude* a brilliant read, and accounts of his childhood in hefty biographies downloaded onto her Kindle only enriched her grasp of his life and times. It thrilled her to find so much of her home area described by such a famous poet. Ben had watched with an almost paternal delight as his protégée blossomed under his tutelage.

Wordsworth had lodged with an elderly couple who had been shopkeepers before they retired. Bonnie and Ben became increasingly interested in the Tysons, Hugh and Ann, devoting much of their game to the young poet's time in their care. They built up a fully furnished version – teaching themselves some crude graphic skills in the process – of the Hawkshead house, with candles and rush matting and pictures on the walls. Then Bonnie had discovered that they'd all moved to Colthouse, most likely in 1784 and requested Ben's permission to include that in the game.

'Not our year,' he ordained. 'You can't muddle things up like that.'

'It's not certain,' she persisted, showing him the results of her researches. 'And there's more scope if we have him walking into town from there every day. Plus we can include his other two brothers, who came to join them around then. It's all here in the poem, Ben. Look.'

And she had won him over, at least on that small point. In the process she had stumbled across some wider history, discovering that 1780 was a dramatic year in all sorts of ways. Most of it involved war with America, but there were also some fairly major riots in London, which she found very diverting.

'We can bear it in mind,' said Ben doubtfully. 'What were they rioting about?'

'Anti-papists,' she read. 'Gordon Riots.'

'Hmm,' was all he said. 'Isn't that all in *Barnaby Rudge*? Charles Dickens,' he added.

Bonnie had let it go for the moment. History was turning out to be a terribly large subject, woven in with literature and science and all sorts of other things. But she established that much of Colthouse had remained unchanged since 1780, including the Quaker element.

All that had been on the Friday just gone, the day before Ben and his friends had set off to go hiking near Hawkshead. Neither of them could properly visualise Colthouse, although Ben had an idea his family had gone there for a picnic at one time. 'I'll get a look at it while I'm up there, and take some photos,' he said.

Which was why she wanted to go and check for herself now whether she could find any sign that he had done as he intended. Listening closely to Simmy's account of the boy's movements, she concluded that he could have had time to walk

145

over to Colthouse and back before running into trouble and dropping his phone. She also wanted to discover whether there were any pictures on the phone, which would not be easy. The police would presumably have the sense to look – but she could hardly expect them to tell *her* what they found.

When she had talked to him about the Meeting House, Ben had directed her to the burial ground instead. Now she went into it and paused. There were rows of plain stone grave markers, on sloping ground above the road. There were wooden seats, long grass, brambles and patches of fern. She closed her eyes and called Ben to mind. *Where are you?* she called silently. What had become of the bond between them, that they couldn't send telepathic messages? Did it mean he was dead or unconscious? The idea was literally stunning. It prevented any coherent thought, like a thick, damp blanket being wrapped around her head. But she threw it off, telling herself that she was by far the most likely person to come to Ben's rescue. Nobody knew him better than she did.

One aspect of their game – which would remain at the notes stage for probably at least another year, and then somebody far more skilled at computer techniques than Ben would have to take it on – was secret messages. 'The best ones are the most obvious,' said Ben, and he had demonstrated a few while they sat on a patch of rough grass on the edge of Rayrigg Wood. First he plaited three tough grass stalks together to make a short green rope. Then he pulled together the stems of eight or ten tall fronds of bracken, being careful not to break any of them, and bound them with his cord. The result was a fan of bracken which was highly visible to anybody alert enough to spot it, while at the same time just an innocent overgrown patch of vegetation to almost any casual passer-by. 'It works with anything with a fairly long stalk,' he said. 'Nettles are good, or docks.'

He encouraged her to experiment with her own variations, which she did with enthusiasm, weaving together stalks of timothy grass that she had cut down. She bent them over, leaving their distinctive seed heads as a fringe at the bottom. She then hung the finished product on a low elder branch. 'Would people think it was something sinister?' she wondered.

'They wouldn't think anything,' he assured her. 'But you really ought to leave them growing, not cut them down. They dry out and die too quickly your way.'

She remembered the wondrous model that Ben and Simmy had made the previous year and used for a window display at the shop. That had been created from sticks and dried seed heads and leaves. 'This is a thing with you, isn't it?' she had said. 'I bet you could build a whole house from dead branches if you had to.'

'I bet I could, too,' he agreed.

So when she saw a clump of ferns, their feathered stems held together with a twisted length of rushes, she knew for certain that Ben had been there. What she did not know was what the message conveyed. If her theory about the timing was correct, then it probably conveyed nothing at all, but was merely an example created for the game and photographed, while Ben killed time. Simmy had told him to get lost for an hour or so, and this was a typical example of how he might amuse himself. The unfortunate fact was that it must have been created before he went back to the lake and got himself abducted.

It told her nothing directly about where he was and what was happening to him. But it greatly boosted her confidence that he was all right. Ben was simply too clever to allow himself to be wiped out by a gang of criminals. She and Helen Harkness had agreed on that the previous day, although Helen had repeatedly dissolved into tears of despair as well. Bonnie had left her as soon as she decently could, afraid that the negative stuff would wash off on her if she wasn't careful.

Which meant that she had to get herself to the hotel, doing her best to work out Ben's route and then trying to understand what had happened next.

She left the burial ground and looked around. The way lay over a stone wall, across a field and then into a very inhospitable-looking wood. It would be a slow and difficult walk, pushing through prickly vegetation, probably marshy underfoot, with fences on all sides. Somewhere in the middle of it all was the invisible Priest Pot. Ben wouldn't have done it readily. Instead he'd have gone around by the road, so Bonnie opted to do the same.

Hawkshead was only five minutes away, by road. Then she worked out, after a brief moment of confusion, that she had to turn left at the junction and carry on down the road that led towards

Satterthwaite, on the western side of Esthwaite. The hotel was off to the left, with a helpful sign to show the way.

She walked briskly, knowing she was due to phone Corinne in another minute or two. She paused beside a bend in the driveway, from which she could look down to the place that had seen such dramatic activity the day before.

'I'm fine,' she reported, when Corinne replied. 'Give me another hour, and then I'll walk back up to the road and find you. I want to pop into the hotel and see if Melanie's there. Did you find the garage? I passed it just now and didn't see you.'

'What road do you mean?' came the irritable reply. 'This place is a nightmare. There are roads and tracks everywhere. I still haven't found the garage. Tell me exactly how to get there.'

'It's a bit late now. They looked rather busy. I'll need you to drive me back. Tell you what – go to the car park and I'll find you there. You'll have to pay.'

'Bloody hell, Bon. What am I meant to do for all that time?'

'Go and have coffee. Then go back and wait for me in the car park, right?'

'This is crazy, you know. A total waste of time.'

'Yeah. You could be right.'

But Bonnie knew she had to keep looking. What she'd seen in Colthouse confirmed her hunch that Ben had been there.

Chapter Twelve

She toyed with the idea of reporting her find to the police. There were good arguments both ways – they would gain a better idea of Ben's abilities and be more alert to clues. But they would also get most of it wrong. They wouldn't listen properly and even if they did, they'd say – rightly, in a way – it wasn't relevant. Even though she felt a growing need to confide in *somebody*, she didn't think the cops, even the familiar DI Moxon, would meet her requirements.

Which left Melanie. The hotel was just ahead of her up a gentle slope, its big windows looking out on the serene little lake. She could see a group of police people along the banks of the mere and some incongruous blue tape zigzagging amongst the trees.

The police people were irritating. She couldn't see much prospect of their finding anything to show where Ben was now. There was a gaping hole in the story between his phone call to Simmy and the discovery of the dead man from the hotel. When Simmy had told her about it, she had fixed all the details in her head and used them obsessively ever since in an effort to understand what had happened. But there must be a lot more that Simmy hadn't told her.

She had never been to the Hawkshead Hotel, never even known it existed until Melanie started working there. Some girls might be intimidated by it, but not her, she thought proudly. Nothing intimidated Bonnie Lawson, other than the small matter of an abiding phobia, and even that was under control now, she assured herself. Since meeting Ben Harkness this was much closer to being true. But she loitered on the path, her eyes fixed on the building that offered bedrooms at more than a hundred pounds a night. It was a world she did not understand.

A figure caught her eye, on the upper floor, coming out onto a balcony that ran along half the length of the main building. She could see nothing more than a silhouette, the person apparently wary of being noticed. She couldn't be sure, but it looked like somebody young, probably male, but not certainly. Most likely a junior member of staff skiving off for a quick smoke, or just a bit of sunshine, she decided. She'd have to ask Melanie what the rooms with balconies were like and who was staying in them.

The moment she saw the hotel car park, she wasn't sure she dared go any further. It was full of police cars, vans, and a gaggle of people with big cameras and other equipment. Bedlam, in other words.

So instead she extracted her phone from her backpack and called Melanie. 'Hi, it's Bonnie. Where are you?' she said as soon as it was answered.

'At home. Where are you?'

'At the Hawkshead Hotel. I thought you'd be here.'

'They told me to take a day off. I wasn't fit to

151

work.' The girl sounded stuffed-up and incredibly stressed.

'Why – because of the bloke who was killed?'

'Mostly, yeah. And Ben. If he's dead as well...' Her voice choked.

'He's not dead, you idiot. You should be here trying to find him, instead of going to bits.'

'How?'

'Well, by working it out. He'll have left clues. You *know* him, Mel, nearly as well as I do. You know what he's like. Nobody's going to kill him.'

'What clues?'

'I don't know yet. But you were right *there*. You and Simmy found his phone. You saw how it all was, before the police got there. You might have seen a clue without realising.'

'I saw Dan's dead body. I dragged it out of the water. I keep seeing it, every time I shut my eyes. I got soaking wet and nobody gave me anything dry for ages. I hate everybody at that bloody hotel. I hate the police as well.'

Bonnie tried to imagine how it was to be Melanie at this moment, with not much success. Not a lot made sense to her. 'Did you catch a chill or something, then?'

'No, of course I didn't. They just *ignored* me. Even Simmy forgot all about me. All anybody cares about is Ben Harkness and what's happening to him.'

'Don't *you* care?'

'Yeah, I s'pose I do, but if you say he's alive and unhurt, then that's all right, isn't it? Not like Dan – who's *dead*.'

Something finally clicked. 'You were in love

152

with him? Is that it?' She frowned. 'But you never said. You told Simmy he was smarmy. When did all this happen?'

'He was smarmy to the guests, but really he was a great guy. Really sweet. Kind. Special.' Her voice clogged up again.

'You never said anything. Simmy didn't know.'

'So?'

Bonnie could recognise a dead end when she heard it. 'Can I talk about Ben's phone now? Did you look at it before the police got it? Did you check it for photos?'

'Why would I do that?'

'So what *did* you do?'

'Looked at a couple of the calls, to check it was his. I just had to see your number to know it was.'

'So it wasn't locked?'

'No. It just came on when I tapped it. It's the latest smartphone. That family's got so much money.' Resentment came through loud and clear.

'I need to see the pictures.'

'The cops are sure to look at them. What's in them?'

'I dunno, but there might be clues. What if he got a shot at the people who kidnapped him?'

'The police'll find it. End of story. And that hasn't happened, has it, because then they'd have named the people they want and sent descriptions out and all that. Listen, Bonnie – why don't you just *ask* them? If they think you've got a useful lead, they'll be glad to listen to you.' Melanie sounded exhausted, the words painfully limping out of her.

'Yeah.' Bonnie was reminded that Melanie,

153

against all habit and expectation of her family, had until very recently been going out with a police constable. She had no fear and not a lot of respect in her attitude towards them. 'Except I'm not meant to be here. They've taken me home once today already.'

'Huh?'

'I came over early, and they caught me wandering around, and took me back to the house. But I got Corinne to drive me back up here again. I couldn't just sit and wait for something to happen, could I? It's *Ben*.'

'Oh, I don't know, do I? There's nothing *I* can do.'

'No. Right. Sorry.' She finished the call thinking Melanie was as bad as the police when it came to getting her drift. Why wasn't she here, doing all she could to catch the people who killed her precious under-manager or whatever he was?

She noticed people on the lawn at the side of the hotel, some of them holding glasses. Gin and tonic, she supposed. Two women, four men and a small girl. What would they think if she strolled up and started talking to them, she wondered. She looked down at herself, assessing her own appearance. All her clothes were of good quality – not that anybody cared about that. Her shoes were fairly new trainers and her shorts a dark-blue denim. As for her hair, it always made a good impression, being so fair and frizzy. It haloed her face, making her look like a young angel. She could pass for fourteen easily and twelve with an effort. But people would wonder where she'd come from. They would know she wasn't a guest at the hotel. Her mind raced with possible cover stories, until she fastened on one that seemed workable.

She walked up to the group, focusing on the child, as if too shy to address adults directly. 'Um ... hello? I think my mum is here. She called my dad and told him to drop me off, because something's happened and all the shifts have changed.' She frowned. 'Sorry,' she added, scraping the grass with one toe.

'Why aren't you at school?' asked one of the women.

'Um...'

'Why didn't your father bring you right up to the door? Nobody would drop their kid at the bottom of the drive and leave her to walk,' said a man sceptically. 'How old are you?'

'I'm nearly fifteen. I don't need him to come with me. But I've never been here before. My mum works as a cleaner, making the beds and all that. It's nearly the end of term, and we've got work experience on Wednesdays. They said I could do the same as her, for a week or two.'

It sounded hopelessly garbled to her own ears. Was fifteen old enough for work experience? She doubted it. But these people were mostly pretty old, and weren't likely to know much about it.

One or two of the people exchanged glances, but most of them seemed indifferent to her and her story. The small girl eyed her curiously, though. 'What's your name?' she asked.

'Charlotte,' came the answer in a flash. 'What's yours?'

'Gentian.'

155

'That's nice.' As of a week ago, she actually knew what a gentian looked like, with its deep, unique blue. Simmy had some in pots in the shop, and Bonnie had used them in her window display.

She glanced at the adults, trying to work out how they connected to each other. There was a long-boned, elderly man with thick white hair, beard and baggy trousers who seemed to have a lot on his mind. He held a long glass with a slice of lemon floating in the drink. A straw hat lay on his lap. Another man, quite a bit younger, but still nowhere near young, was leaning against a white-painted metal chair, on which sat a woman with a big red handbag on her lap. Husband and wife, thought Bonnie. The other woman had to be Gentian's mother, and the remaining two men were hard to examine because they had their backs to everybody. One was mostly bald, with just a ring of silver hair.

'So, what's going on, then?' Bonnie asked. 'Why is the car park full of police cars?'

Gentian eagerly supplied an answer. 'A man was murdered, down there, his body was in the lake and he was all wet and *dead.*'

'Oh my God!' squealed Bonnie. 'Is that *true?*'

'It's a terrible tragedy,' said the man with the wife. 'Turned the whole place upside down. We're thinking of leaving early. These two gentlemen have only arrived today and they can't believe what they've walked into.'

The two gentlemen ignored his reference to them, other than to walk a few steps further away from the group. They were not holding drinks. Bonnie could only see that they were nicely dressed and seemed vaguely foreign.

'When did it happen?' she asked.

'Yesterday. I would think your mother would have told you about it by now,' said the seated woman. 'If she's a chambermaid here, she'll have been interviewed by the police.'

'She didn't. I was with my dad. They're not together, you see.' She could hear herself floundering, inventing as she went on.

The woman eyed her sharply. 'I'm not sure I believe your story.'

Time to go, Bonnie realised. 'Oh! Well, never mind. Don't worry about it. I'll go and find her. Thanks, Gentian. See you around.'

Gentian gave her a wistful smile and Bonnie realised how glad the child had been to meet someone closer to her own age. There was something bleak and unnatural about a solitary child amongst a lot of adults. The mother looked rather a sourpuss and none of the others showed any interest.

With thumping heart, Bonnie went through the front entrance of the hotel. What could the police do to her anyway, she asked herself. It was a free country and she could go where she liked. *Free country?* She heard Ben's ghostly laugh. *Where did you get that idea? Haven't you noticed that people have stopped saying that lately?*

Ben wasn't free. There didn't seem to be much doubt about that. But neither was he dead. There was no choice but to believe that he was very much alive and straining every brain cell to devise a way to escape. And Bonnie absolutely had to help him.

157

In the hotel foyer there was a surprising silence. No people, no voices. The first thing she saw was Simmy's lovely display. The eucalyptus trailed exactly as planned, with the many small blooms cleverly nestled in the heart of the tendrils, the whole thing a magical blend of colours. It said *elegance, luxury, competence*. It clashed almost ludicrously with the scene out on the lawn, where people were inclined to blame the hotel management for the untidy fact of a murder in their grounds. You couldn't blame them, Bonnie supposed. They'd expected peace and quiet and Lakeland beauty, not police interviews and all kinds of worry about what might happen next.

She was at a loss as to what to do. She couldn't remember what she thought she *might* do. Originally her plan had been to find Melanie and ask her for more details about what had happened the day before. Then she'd shifted her attention to Ben's photos. And now she was just wasting time and making herself vulnerable to being rounded up yet again by the police.

But she was lucky in that respect, although it took a while to realise it. Two uniformed officers, a man and a woman, came out of a room on the left, and gave her identical careless glances. They thought she was a guest at the hotel, she supposed – although surely they knew them all by this time? Perhaps they'd only just got there – something fresh and crisp about their clothes suggested this might be so. Certainly they hadn't been on duty all night, or sent to crawl around under trees looking for footprints. She gave them a hesitant little smile, which they barely acknowledged.

158

The hotel itself had a peculiar atmosphere. Where was everybody? Were the people on the lawn the only remaining guests? Wouldn't it be more fitting to close the place down, and stop people from coming or going? Or were those still here all under suspicion, kept close and watched for incriminating behaviour? She ran through them again in her head. A tall elderly man; a middle-aged couple; a woman and her daughter (where was the father?); and two foreign-looking men. Was that all, she wondered. What about the staff? Wasn't it likely that one of them had killed the Yates chap out of some work-related grievance? There must be somebody in the kitchen as well as the manager and at least one cleaner. That presented quite a list of suspects – and what if one of them had Ben hidden away, tied up and gagged and left to starve?

She checked her phone for the time. Eleven forty-five. She'd have to go and meet Corinne in the main car park in another few minutes. The last hour had been a complete waste, which felt like a disaster from Ben's point of view. She was just messing about playing games instead of employing observation and logic as the boy had taught her. Everything is connected, he had said. And – if you work out what a person wants, you can understand why they do things. None of that felt helpful now. She wasn't sure it was true, anyway. How could all these people be connected except through the accident of all being together in the same hotel on the same day? Or was that what Ben meant? For the moment, they *were* connected.

All she could do was leave and walk back into

Hawkshead. She'd probably be late, but it wouldn't matter. She felt heavy and useless, and then smiled to herself at the thought of what Ben would say about 'heavy'. She weighed about half of the average seventeen-year-old, and he could lift her with one hand.

Oh, Ben, she sighed.

On the steps of the hotel, she collided with a man who was trotting up to the front door.

'Why am I not surprised to see you again?' he asked, with a surprisingly warm smile.

'Oh, hello. Sorry,' she mumbled.

'You're like a rubber ball,' he told her, with an odd expression. 'That's an old song, even before my time,' he explained. 'Bouncing back to me.'

'I was hoping I wouldn't see you, actually. Why are you so cheerful? Have you found him?' The possibility filled her with light and air. She rose on tiptoe with it.

'No, no. Don't get your hopes up.'

'Oh.' She sank back and scowled. 'Well...'

'Why are you here? Precisely, I mean. You can't be thinking he's hidden in the hotel somewhere.'

She blinked. The idea hadn't occurred to her, but now it seemed to offer a smidgeon of optimism, as actually imaginable. 'There must be all kinds of sheds and cupboards and things,' she said. 'Have you searched them all?'

'Exhaustively.'

'Right. Why are all the people still here?'

'We can't very well banish them. Well – we could, I suppose. But we don't need to. We've got an incident room set up, which is causing them plenty of inconvenience. And we've asked them to turn away anyone booked from today on. They're not happy about that, either.'

'So that's seven guests still here, then?'

Moxon's gaze was on one of the white vans, where two men sat in the front seats, the door open for air. 'They're behaving extraordinarily well,' he murmured. 'Must be because there's a lad missing. Makes them more sensitive. Of course, they're only local. The national ones are terrible.'

'Who?'

'Oh, they're reporters. Asserting their rights to park where they like, so long as it's a public space. The hotel could tell them to go, but they don't see any reason to. They're probably hoping for a favourable write-up if they don't upset them.'

'Guests?' she prompted.

'I make it five, actually. The Lillywhites, young Gentian and her mum, and Mr Ferguson. That's all.'

'So who are the two men over there?'

They were still standing on the steps, the lawn perfectly visible, twenty yards away. The group had barely altered since Bonnie had left them.

'Good question.' He examined them carefully. 'They must be the Americans the manager was so worried about. They were due to arrive today, and he couldn't get hold of them to stop them coming. I wonder if he's spoken to them. I thought they said there'd be four of them.' He sighed. 'I suppose I'll have to speak to them.'

'They look more Mexican than American.'

He laughed. 'So they do. I'll tell them they can stay, anyway. They can't do much harm.'

161

'They look as if that's already been settled. Who says they have to get your permission?'

'Careful,' he warned her.

'Sorry,' she said, with no hint of repentance. 'I've got to go,' she remembered. 'Except...'

'Yes?'

'The photos on Ben's phone. Can I see them? I think they might be helpful in finding him.' She tried to speak as one adult to another, forcing him to take her seriously.

'I expect you can,' he said easily. 'Why not?'

'Now?'

'It's not here. The boffins have got it in Kendal.'

'Oh.' The frustration was intense. 'Can we go and get it?'

'Not at the moment, no. Now, look – I'm going to drive you up to Hawkshead and hand you over to your ... whatever she is. Responsible adult, I suppose is the phrase.'

'But...'

He gave her a look that suggested he knew he'd been wrong to dismiss her so easily. 'You knew him better than anyone, I'm guessing. How long had you been going out together?'

'Seven weeks,' she said promptly.

'Why do you want to see the photos?'

'It's complicated.'

'Get in the car and tell me while we drive. Don't catch the eye of those reporters. They'll be noticing you anyway and trying to guess who you are.'

Bonnie cared nothing for reporters. 'It'll take longer than that. You won't understand if I don't explain everything.'

'We can make a start.'

So she tried to make him understand the game, and how clever Ben was, and how she'd found the message at Colthouse. She was nowhere near finished by the time they got to the Hawkshead car park. They sat in the stationary car, still talking. At first glance, Bonnie couldn't see Corinne's motor.

He was obviously interested. He asked sensible questions and kept checking that he'd got it right at every point. 'So you know for certain that Ben went to Colthouse yesterday?'

'More or less. It's just possible it was earlier than yesterday, but I don't think so. The rushes hadn't gone dry at all, which they would have done. There'll be a picture of it on the phone, with the time and date. He'll have wanted it for the game, you see. To be included as one of the ways people can signal to each other.'

'This is one of those adventure games that people play on their computer, right? Doesn't it take thousands of pounds and months of work to create one of those? Or am I out of date?'

'They're not all like that. But we'd need technical help to get it up and running, yes. We're still just collecting images and ideas for the narrative, at this stage. The latest idea was to have a young Fletcher Christian in the cast. You know who he was?'

'The mutiny on the *Bounty*. How does he connect, then?'

'He went to school with Wordsworth, and lived around here somewhere. Simmy knows about him.'

'Ah – Mrs Brown. Did she open the shop late this morning? Or is she out searching for Ben as well?'

'I don't know. I haven't given her a thought all day.'

'And where's Corinne?'

'Good question. She said she'd be here.'

'Okay, then. Phone her, and tell her you're going to Kendal with me.'

'Can I say I'm helping you with your enquiries? I've always wanted to say that.'

'Say what you like,' he told her.

Chapter Thirteen

Simmy and Helen Harkness sat with their coffee at a table set on the pavement. They were within sight of most of the centre of Hawkshead, watching people come and go, a majority of them wearing hefty backpacks and carrying sticks. 'I never saw much point in walking for its own sake,' Simmy remarked.

'It's addictive. I did it obsessively in my twenties, all the Wainwright stuff. It was exhilarating. I learnt my way around, at the same time. I could go on Mastermind specialising in Cumbrian villages.'

'And have you passed it all on to your kids?'

'You mean Ben? A lot of it, yes. I took them up all the fells when they were little. The girls never liked it much, and Wilf got sick of their complaining. Ben was the keenest by miles. He and I did an epic hike from Bassenthwaite to Ulverston when he was fifteen. He must have told you about it.'

'Not that I can recall. How far is it?'

'About sixty miles, I think. We took it slowly over four days, and spent the nights in a tent. It was amazing. I'll never forget it.' Simmy watched as the present reality returned to Ben's mother's awareness and tears filled her eyes. 'He's my special one. I don't suppose I need to tell you that.'

'He is very special,' said Simmy, with a sniff. 'We've absolutely got to find him.'

'We won't do it sitting here, will we?' Helen had her mobile on the table beside her. She fingered it thoughtfully. 'There must be somebody we can call,' she said. 'Isn't there always somebody these days?'

'Like who?' Simmy stared at her uncomprehendingly. 'What do you mean?'

'Bonnie. Melanie. Even the Moxon man. Just to find out the latest news. I feel as if we're in a void, knowing nothing.'

'You could try Bonnie, if you've got her number. I have a feeling Melanie won't be much use.'

'Why not?'

'The man who was killed – she was going out with him. Or at least, staying overnight in his room. I think she was getting very fond of him.' Simmy thought again of Melanie's tears at the sight of Dan's body. It now seemed to be a matter of urgency to check how she was today. 'I feel bad about it, taking her down there where we found him.'

165

'You couldn't have known. You were looking for Ben, if I've got it right.'

'Yes, but Ben's message said there was a body. I should have thought before letting her go with me. Melanie's very young, and actually quite naïve in some ways.'

'You're joking. That girl's the most streetwise I ever met.'

'Maybe she is by Windermere standards, but that's not saying much, is it? Through all the things that have happened since last autumn, she's been at a distance. This is the first time she's been faced with anything really horrible. But of course we had no idea it was Dan who was dead – and I never dreamt she loved him, either.'

Helen shook her head impatiently. 'It's too late to worry about him. And Melanie will get over it.'

Simmy had initially felt glad to have the company of an older woman, as a change from the youngsters she habitually mixed with. Now she was less sure she liked it. Bonnie and Ben and Melanie were so clear-sighted and definite about everything. Their freshness and zeal were invigorating. Helen Harkness was none of these things, and although Simmy knew it was very unfair to judge her in this time of wild anxiety, she was finding the morning increasingly depressing. Everything she said seemed to be dismissed or belittled.

'What do we do now, then?' she asked with a sense of defeat.

'Well, look who it isn't!' came a voice from the pavement. 'Fancy meeting you here.'

They both turned to see Corinne standing there,

166

hands on her hips, hair all over the place. Here was another older woman, Simmy thought glumly. Corinne had to be in her mid forties at least, despite the multiple piercings and long skirt. Corinne ignored any suggestions of respectability or obligation to conform, not entirely unlike Simmy's own mother. Her girlishness was alternately appealing and irritating. Her opening remark was firmly in the latter category.

'I expect we're here for the same reason that you are,' said Simmy rather sharply.

'Yeah. Hi, Helen. This is all a real bugger, isn't it? Bonnie made me drive her up here, so she can get on with searching for your boy.'

Simmy looked down the little street. 'So where is she?'

'First Colthouse, then the hotel, so she says. Got some idea in her head. Those two – they were like twins, with their own secret language. I had a pair once, for a few months. Jabbered away in gibberish, obviously understanding each other perfectly. Made me feel a bit weird, to tell you the truth.'

'At the hotel?' Simmy stared. 'On her own?'

'She'll be fine,' Corinne said, taking a chair from another table and sitting down. 'Bonnie's always fine.'

'That's what we thought about Ben,' said Helen. 'But there's some dreadful people out there, capable of killing. I don't know how you can say Bonnie's fine, or how you can let her just go off on her own.'

'Don't give me that,' Corinne flashed angrily. 'Besides, who are you to talk?'

167

Simmy watched them both as they realised how foolish and damaging such an exchange was. They both grimaced and then slumped in their chairs. 'Sorry,' said Corinne. 'That was way out of order.'

'She's got her phone, obviously,' said Simmy.

'And she's already called me once. I'm to meet her in the car park in a bit. Where are you parked?'

'I left it out by the campsite,' said Helen. 'We walked in from there. This place is lovely, isn't it? You think it's a warren, at first, and you'll never find anywhere – then you look again, and it's absolutely tiny. The whole village is right here before your very eyes.'

'Shame about that bookshop,' said Corinne, eyeing the large, empty building. 'Right in the middle of town like that. Makes it look depressing.'

'Too big for most businesses,' said Simmy, with an air of knowing all about shops and premises. 'You'd need good turnover to cover the rent.'

'It's been like that for two years or more,' said Helen. 'Somebody must be losing money on it.' Her architect's eye roamed over the big, square edifice, clearly speculating on how it might be brought back to life. 'You could make a flat on the top floor, for a start.'

'Don't!' moaned Simmy. 'That's what Bonnie keeps saying about the upper floor of my shop. I've started keeping things up there, to show her I need it for storage... Do you want coffee?' she asked Corinne. 'Because we were just thinking of leaving. Although we don't know what to do next.'

Corinne gave a self-deprecating grin. 'Well, as it

168

happens, I haven't had a thing today. My mouth's disgusting. Would it be a real pain if I had a quick cup?'

'Not really. I could phone Melanie and see how she is.'

'And I ought to check in with that liaison woman,' said Helen. 'I've been gone for hours. Something might have happened.'

'They'd call you if it did,' said Corinne. 'Do they come to you, or have I got to go in to order a coffee?'

'Quicker to go in,' Helen advised.

Simmy called Melanie first. The phone rang for several seconds. 'Hello,' came the eventual response. 'Simmy? Has something happened?'

'No. I just wondered how you were. Are you at work?'

'No, I'm not. I've just had Bonnie asking me the same thing.'

'Really? So how are you?'

'Don't ask. I'm a mess. It's nice of you to think of me, though.'

'Are you on your own?'

The hollow laugh sounded more like the old Melanie. 'What – in this house? Did I tell you my mum got another dog? A mad puppy that does nothing but torment the other one all day. And shits everywhere, obviously. It's not safe to walk across a room. And the old man's off, for some reason. Says he's cricked his neck, lazy bugger.'

'You might be better off at the hotel,' said Simmy, without thinking. It was axiomatic that Melanie spent as little time as possible in her family home. One major motive in opting for a career in hospitality was that most places provided accommodation. The Hawkshead Hotel had been a disappointment in that respect.

'Why?'

'Well … sorry. That was a daft thing to say. But you need to be out of the house. You'll just stew about everything if you stay there.'

'What do you suggest?'

Simmy couldn't think. She was at Helen Harkness's mercy, unless she got a ride in Corinne's ramshackle vehicle. They were not one inch closer to finding Ben and the morning was virtually gone. 'It's all rather a muddle at the moment,' she admitted. 'I'll phone you again in an hour or two, and we'll work something out.'

'I haven't forgotten about Ben, you know,' said Melanie, suddenly sharp. 'I get that everybody's much more worried about him than Dan.'

'It's not a matter of either one or the other, is it? It's all the same thing.'

'Not quite. Ben's most likely still alive, and Dan isn't. That's different, actually. About as different as you can get, the way I see it.'

The *most likely* sent a blade across Simmy's chest; she could feel it as a genuine pain. 'You need to come here and help us find him,' she panted. 'His mother's here, and Corinne. Bonnie's at the hotel, apparently. Come and help us. We should all be together.'

'I might come and find you later,' Melanie conceded. 'Bye, Simmy.'

Finally, Simmy thought, she'd reached the crucial point. The people who loved Ben *should* all be together. Not just for each other, but for him.

They would create a force field against whoever was holding him and by sheer willpower come to his rescue. At that moment, it seemed possible.

Corinne's coffee arrived and she drank it in a single draught. 'That's better,' she said. 'Now, come along ladies, we've got to get ourselves organised. The morning's been a complete waste, so far. Unless Bonnie's come up with something. That wouldn't surprise me.' She looked at Helen's phone. 'What time is it?'

'Five to twelve.'

'Blimey! Come on, then. Back to the car park.'

They walked in the road for most of the way, as did everyone else in Hawkshead, thanks to the absence of traffic. The occasional exception had to crawl through the pedestrians enduring dark looks along the way.

Corinne's car was under a tree in a corner, its scratches and dents concealed by the shadows. 'Will she find it?' worried Simmy. 'It's not very visible.'

'She knows I always tuck it away if I can. Don't worry about it.'

Helen was slightly behind them, walking with a limp that Simmy hadn't noticed before. 'Have you hurt yourself?' she asked, wondering how that could be possible.

'No, no. It's arthritis. I'm scheduled for a new hip at the end of this month. I've been putting it off, thinking I was far too young, but they've persuaded me. It's my own fault for spending most of my life at the drawing board. I'm convinced that's made it worse.'

'But what about all that fell walking?'

'Good question. I probably didn't mention that I've hardly been anywhere for a couple of years now.' She winced. 'It gets worse as the day goes by. Mornings aren't too bad, as a rule. And of course I didn't think about it at all today.'

'You poor thing,' Simmy sympathised. 'I had no idea. What about that sixty-mile hike you did with Ben?'

'I was doped up with painkillers a lot of the time. It was my final flourish. I enjoyed it all the more for knowing that.'

'But you'll be okay again once you've got the new hip.'

'*Two* new hips, eventually. Let's hope so. Things can go wrong, you know.'

Simmy could see fear in the woman's eyes. 'Not to be undertaken lightly,' she said. 'I'd be pretty scared at the prospect. But I'm sure it'll be fine. Anything must be better than constant pain.'

'I try not to make a fuss,' said Helen with a hint of self-mockery.

'Hey! Look!' Corinne had reached her car and was removing a sheet of paper from under the windscreen wiper. 'Someone's left me a note.'

She held it out so the others could see it and read it aloud. 'Hope this is the right car. A boy asked me to say he's okay. It was early today. Sorry I can't stop. It's probably all a joke, anyway. He was with a woman and said his name's Ben. Sorry, I don't want to get involved in anything.'

They all stood rigid with shock. Then Simmy took it and read it again. 'But *where* was he? If he could tell this person which car is yours, why couldn't he tell them what's happened?'

'Who's the woman he was with?' said Helen.

'The kidnapper. It must be,' said Corinne.

'We've got to think this through,' said Simmy, wishing Melanie were there. Or DI Moxon. Or – best of all – Bonnie. 'It says "early today", so that must be before we got here. So did this person hang around all morning looking out for your car? Then when it turned up, put this note on the windscreen? That's very public-spirited for someone who doesn't want to get involved.'

Corinne rubbed her face vigorously. 'I've never known anything so weird.'

'You would if you'd known Ben all his life,' said Helen. 'He likes to make things complicated.'

'Not this time,' said Simmy with certainty. 'If he could have said more, he would have. He knows this isn't a joke. He'll have been sure that Bonnie would come looking for him, and assumed she'd have to get Corinne to drive him. Look at the registration.' She pointed at the front of the car. 'W456 OBY. That's fairly memorable. If someone was controlling him, stopping him from talking to anyone, he'd have to keep it very short. I bet this note was written by an old woman, who lives around here somewhere. I can just imagine him pretending to bump into her or something like that, and asking her to leave this note.'

'No, no,' said Helen. 'Far more likely to have been a kid. An adult wouldn't take any notice of him.'

'You could be right. Look at the paper,' said Simmy. 'It's been torn out of an exercise book. Probably a schoolbook, don't you think?'

'Written with a felt tip, not a biro,' said Helen.

'As if that meant anything.'

'It means he's okay,' said Simmy, feeling a rush of emotion. 'That's the main thing.'

Helen was still examining the note. 'All the spelling's right. A young kid wouldn't write like this. It's quite nice writing, as well. Looks more like a girl than a boy, if my lot are anything to go by.'

'It's not anybody we know, obviously,' said Corinne. 'I hope this is the right car. If they knew us, there wouldn't be any doubt about it, would there?'

'Obviously,' Simmy repeated. '"He said his name's Ben". So how could it have happened?' She closed her eyes to think. Then, 'So he's in a shop or somewhere with the kidnapper, who's a woman. A person, who might be a teenager, maybe let out of school now the exams are finished, the same as Ben, is close to him. Ben whispers, "I need you to help me. Can you watch out for a blue Citroën, number plate W456 OBY, and put a note on it, or talk to the people in it, and say Ben says he's okay?" That's all it need have been. He might have repeated the number. Then the person spends the morning watching for the car, but didn't want to approach directly, because it all feels pretty dodgy. Ben might just have said – "tell them I'm okay." That would only take a few seconds.'

'Isn't it a huge risk for the kidnapper to take him into a public place? He'd be sure to try to fool her and escape.' Helen looked extremely confused and unsure. 'Although ... well, some of it does sound like him, I must admit.'

'It does,' said Corinne. 'Clever little beggar.'

174

'Except – what does it really mean, that he says he's okay?' asked Simmy. 'He's really not, is he? He's *alive*, which is probably what he meant.'

They were standing at the front of the car, still passing the note back and forth, staring at it in turn as if to force a secret code to materialise if they only knew how.

'Hiya!' came a girlish voice from the rear of the car. 'What're you all doing?'

'Bonnie.' Simmy's first, rather odd instinct was to hide the note from the girl. But as Helen was holding it, she had no way of doing so.

'And me,' said a man, coming up behind Bonnie. 'I found her at the hotel – again. She's obstructing police investigations. We were just going to call you and then drive off to Kendal, but Bonnie had to go to the Ladies first. She was a long time.' He said it with a quiet smile, entirely removing any criticism from the words. Then he paused. 'Has something happened?'

'Um...' said Simmy.

'Hi, Nolan,' said Corinne with exaggerated matiness.

Simmy's eyes widened. How come she was on first-name terms with him? Something to do with foster children, she supposed, although she'd been under the impression that her charges were all much too young to fall foul of the police.

He rolled his eyes, and sighed. 'Watch it,' he said. This time there was no smile.

'What's that?' Bonnie had seen the paper in Helen's hand.

'A note,' said Helen, proffering it not to Bonnie, but to the police inspector. 'From Ben. Sort of.'

Moxon took it as if it might explode in his hand. He glanced at all the ungloved fingers, which he rightly assumed had touched it, and sighed.

'Let *me* see,' said Bonnie, threatening to snatch it. Moxon held it high, out of her reach.

'Please,' she begged.

'Wait.' He read it slowly, his brow creased in bewilderment. 'Well...' he said at last and handed the paper to Bonnie. 'Hold it at the very edge,' he warned her.

She read it in a single glance and then turned it over. Nobody, not even Moxon, had thought to do that. It had a grey smudge on it from the wiper blade, but nothing else. Bonnie sighed.

'What were you looking for?' asked Simmy.

'A sign,' she said. 'So Ben never touched this. He told someone else to do it.'

'Have you any idea who?'

'Someone who believed him and who had enough brain to remember the car number or description. Or who knows me and Corinne. "Early today". That's the important bit. Pity they don't say an exact time. Then we could check the movements of all the women on the list.'

'List?' queried Moxon.

'Of suspects. Hotel staff and guests, basically.'

And Melanie, came the thought unbidden to Simmy's mind. She kicked it away in horror. What was the matter with her? How could she be so idiotic, so treacherous, so *peculiar* as to think such a thing? Just that Mel was one of the hotel staff, of course. That's all it was. Obviously.

'We could have fingerprinted it,' said Moxon. 'Still can, of course, but we'll have to eliminate

176

you three ladies. And I don't suppose it'll be of any help.'

'The person would have to be on your database,' nodded Bonnie. 'And I don't think that's very likely.'

Simmy watched as he pursed his lips, in a silent reproach to the liberals who had ensured that no comprehensive database containing the prints of every individual in the land existed. Except, that was going to be DNA, wasn't it, Simmy asked herself.

'We worked out what might have happened,' said Helen, and repeated Simmy's theory almost verbatim. 'We thought a kid – a *big* kid like Ben – was the most credible. But one that doesn't know Ben. Of course, they go to a different school from here. It's the John Ruskin. Ben goes to the Lakes.'

'Yes, but there's no sixth form at the JR,' said Bonnie.

'So?' asked Moxon, a trifle impatiently.

'So it's more complicated than you think. If a person is over sixteen, they could go to a school somewhere further from where they live.'

'This isn't helping,' said the detective. 'As I see it, there are two very significant facts here. First, the boy is alive and well. Second, he's with a woman.'

Bonnie danced in frustration. 'There's no *clue*,' she wailed. 'Why didn't he leave a proper clue?'

'Maybe he did,' said Helen. 'You know what he's like.'

'You don't think this whole business is one big game to him, do you?' Simmy felt a sudden gust of rage at the very idea.

'Do they know...?' Moxon asked Bonnie. 'All that stuff you just told me?'

'Um ... probably not.'

'What?' said Corinne, Simmy and Helen in unison.

'It's just this game we're putting together. It's nowhere near finished. Just odd bits and pieces, really. But it's what we've been doing for a month now. At least. It's educational,' she added defensively. 'History and plants and all sorts. It'll make a fortune when it's finished.'

'It just might at that,' Moxon confirmed. 'But first–'

'First we have to *find* him,' said Helen loudly. 'Instead of just standing here.'

Simmy gave voice to her main difficulty. 'I still don't get why his kidnapper would go out into the streets with him, for anyone to see. How did she know he wouldn't be recognised? Or make a run for it?'

'She could have threatened him,' said Corinne. 'After all, he knows she's killed one person already. She could have said his sisters, or Bonnie, would be gone after if he didn't do what he was told. He might well believe it.'

Simmy recalled a highly unpleasant and frightening threat made to her parents not so long ago, and nodded. 'Makes sense,' she said.

'Look – I have to get back to the hotel,' said Moxon. 'My superiors are not going to believe that any of this is helping with the murder investigation. The manager wants us to pack up and go by this time tomorrow, and until we've got every last detail out of all those people, that isn't going to happen.'

'It *is* helping, though,' said Simmy. 'Now you know the killer – or one of them – is a woman. You just have to work out where they all were early this morning, and see who was missing.'

'Just,' he repeated with a touch of scorn. 'They're all coming and going the whole time. The guests, especially, can't be kept from doing what they want. That child, Gentian, drives her mother mad if she isn't kept amused.'

'I saw her,' said Bonnie. 'I saw most of them, actually. So did you.' She looked at Simmy. 'There were two swarthy foreigners as well. They look like drug dealers.'

'Stop it,' ordered Moxon.

'What about that woman in a suit?' Simmy asked suddenly. 'Was she there as well?'

Moxon and Bonnie exchanged a look. 'Suit? What sort of suit?'

'Dark-blue, short skirt. High heels. She was in the foyer yesterday, getting impatient. Then she went outside for a bit. Then she drove away. You must have seen her, when she was talking to the Lillywhites. You were right there beside her.'

'Was I? I don't remember.'

Simmy looked under her eyebrows at him. She was at least as tall as him, and this look was one she had developed since meeting Ben Harkness. It conveyed, *Have you really thought about what you just said?* and *I think you might want to try that again.* It worked very effectively.

'Do you know her name?' he asked.

'Of course not. I got the impression she was trying to book into the hotel, and nobody was

179

paying her any attention. She was fairly miffed about it. Then I wondered whether she might have some connection to the Americans that Dan was so worried about. That seemed to make sense. They wanted to impress these people, because they could bring in extra business. That's why I had to do the flowers yesterday. To make a good impression.' She watched as Moxon tried to untangle this stream of information.

'The ones in the foyer look gorgeous,' said Bonnie, irrelevantly. 'I noticed them particularly, just now.'

Moxon had gone pink. 'This sounds extremely interesting,' he said. 'I'm sure somebody will have spoken to this woman, and got a name. We'll have to check through all the bookings.'

'I've just thought of something,' said Bonnie excitedly. 'There *is* a clue, after all.' And before they could stop her she was running across the car park, dodging vehicles and heading towards the church.

Chapter Fourteen

There would be people in Hawkshead who never quite forgot the scene of three women and a man chasing madly across the main car park and over the street in pursuit of a flaxen-haired girl. It was a distance of perhaps two hundred yards at the very most, but it made quite an impact.

Bonnie came to a stop in front of the old school-

180

house, now a museum, which William Wordsworth and his brothers had attended. 'School!' she panted.

Her elders surrounded her, braced for a renewed chase. 'For God's sake,' panted Corinne. 'What the hell do you think you're doing?'

Helen was holding both hands to a visibly agonising hip. 'I can't run,' she moaned. 'Don't make me run again.'

'The school,' Bonnie repeated. 'That's the clue. The note written on a page from a schoolbook. Ben must have told the person to do that, deliberately.'

'For heaven's sake,' said Corinne again. 'Why not just say "Go to the school"? Why make things so complicated?'

'Because he didn't dare. If the woman heard him, he'd be in deep trouble.'

Simmy interrupted. 'If she heard him saying *anything* to a passing schoolboy, it would be just as bad. Don't you think? I mean – if he could speak to someone, then the sensible thing would be to tell them where he was being kept, and who by. All these clues and games are just ridiculous.'

Bonnie looked hurt. 'They're not,' she said.

Moxon adopted a deeply severe expression. 'There is a thing called "wasting police time", you know. If you and young Mr Harkness are simply enacting parts of your game, without any danger to either of you, that would qualify. In that case, you would be in considerable trouble.'

'A man's *dead*,' Helen reminded him.

'Yes, he is. And your boy was at the scene. That much is understood. But beyond that is all conjecture. I'm wondering whether Ben took it upon himself to play detective, and has been following the killer or killers ever since. This message, "Ben says he's okay" would fit that scenario only too well. In so many ways,' he concluded wearily.

'He wouldn't leave his mobile behind,' Helen objected.

'He might,' Bonnie corrected her with a worried glance at Moxon. 'Having a phone would make everything too easy. And he probably wants us to see the photos on it.'

'Ah, yes. The photos.' Moxon nodded to himself. 'I forgot about the photos.'

'You're forgetting rather a lot these days,' said Simmy, thinking of how she herself had been overlooked the previous day.

'Simmy!' Helen gave her a horrified look. Her deference to the police was unexpected, given how bold her son was. Then Simmy realised that not everybody was like her own mother, who showed deference to nobody. Helen might have produced a boy who saw no reason to treat anyone as his superior, but all her other children were of ordinary talent and attitude. The courage and spirit Helen had shown so far that day might well be the result of Ben's influence on her and not a central element of her character.

Moxon took it better, but was still not happy. 'I think I might be forgiven,' he said. 'There's a lot to think about.' He wriggled his shoulders. 'And I should be at the hotel thinking about it, not here with everyone who knows and loves young Ben. I'll take this' – he waved the sheet of paper – 'and get forensics to look at it. And I'll send a couple of men up here to have a look round.' His eye fell on Bonnie. 'I don't understand the bit about the school.'

They were standing on a path that led steeply up to the church. To their right was the museum, with its door standing half-open. It was a perfectly preserved eighteenth-century schoolroom, magically enhanced by the ghostly fact of young Wordsworth's bottom having graced the seats and his elbows the desktops. A simple scrap of history, which a minority of tourists found tempting. Simmy herself had never been inside it.

'It's in our game,' said Bonnie.

'So...?'

'I don't know. I could have got it wrong.'

'It seems pretty tenuous to me,' said Helen.

Simmy became aware that Corinne had drifted back towards the street. 'My car expires in a couple of minutes,' she said, to nobody in particular. 'And I did have something I was meant to do this afternoon.'

'Go,' said Bonnie. 'I can get a ride with Simmy and ... Mrs Harkness.' She looked at Moxon. 'Can we drop the Kendal thing for now?'

He gave an old-fashioned little bow, while smiling at the adults. 'I think so,' he said.

Helen didn't correct Bonnie or suggest the use of her first name. After all, the girl was only seventeen: still a child in the eyes of the law. And in the eyes of anyone casually encountering her, thought Simmy. A volatile child, passionately in love with Ben Harkness, open to anything he might suggest to her and rendered delirious by his attentions.

183

She would tell lies for him, break every rule, climb every mountain. Either she would find him when nobody else stood a chance, or she would ruin any hope of the police getting a result. Moxon obviously found her at least as baffling as he did Ben. As far as Simmy could ascertain, there were no Moxon offspring, which might suggest an ignorance as well as a failure of imagination when it came to grasping the nature of teenagers.

Then a boy of perhaps fourteen emerged from the museum, followed by a man, woman and small girl. He assessed the group standing obstructively between them and the street, and looked meaningfully at the sheet of paper still in Moxon's hand.

'You found it, then,' he said carelessly.

Nobody reacted. Double and treble takes at his words made every face comical. Moxon looked at the paper, then at the boy, then at Corinne. Simmy looked at Bonnie. Helen was the first to regain her wits. 'It was you? You saw Ben? Did you?'

'Early this morning. He was with a woman.' The words emerged flatly, as if learnt by heart. Which they had been, of course.

'Who are you?' Bonnie demanded. 'Do you know Ben? Where do you go to school? Did he give you the paper to write on? How *was* he?'

'Who are these people, Barnaby?' asked the woman.

'Dunno,' he shrugged. But his eyes were on Bonnie, his mind on her questions.

'We're looking for my son,' said Helen. 'And it seems he spoke to this young man – presumably *your* son? This man is a police detective.'

184

'What?' The father of the family spoke up. 'Police?'

Moxon did his best to take charge. 'Could I ask your lad a few questions, sir? There's no need to worry, he's not in any trouble. But he is an important witness. We do need to know just what was said earlier today. Perhaps we could find somewhere...' He looked around. The group had grown uncomfortably large, and not one of them had any intention of missing what happened next.

'We're on holiday,' said Barnaby's mother. 'We don't know anybody here.'

Moxon focused on the boy. 'Were you alone when you met Ben? Or with your family?'

'I was on my own. We're staying at Ann Tyson's House, and I went out to get a paper for Dad, and some milk. There was a guy in the shop, bit older than me. He whispered to me what he wanted me to do. There was a woman–'

'Was she holding onto him?' Helen interrupted. 'If not, why didn't he just run away from her? He's a fast runner when he tries.'

'Who *was* she?' Corinne said. 'Was she old or young?'

Moxon cleared his throat. 'If *I* might be allowed to ask the questions,' he said ponderously.

Barnaby stood tall, enjoying the attention. 'She wasn't holding onto him, and he didn't look as if he wanted to run away. She wasn't very near him, actually. He told me to watch out for an old blue car, and if I saw it, to put a note on it saying he's okay. W456 OBY. Easy to remember. I got the right one, then?'

185

'What were you doing in the car park?' Moxon wondered.

Barnaby flung out his arms in frustration. 'No, no. We were in our car when I saw it first. We went to Coniston, but then decided to come back here for a bit. We can *never* decide what to do.' He threw an accusing look at his father, who did have an indecisive sort of manner. 'Anyway, I thought it looked as if it was going to the car park, so when we parked there as well, I had a look and found it.'

'Ri-i-i-i-ght,' said Moxon slowly. 'Lucky for young Ben, then.' He frowned at Corinne. 'How could he possibly know you'd be in Hawkshead today?'

'He'd know *I* would be,' said Bonnie. 'That I'd be searching for him. And it's the obvious car I'd use to get here.'

Moxon nodded doubtfully. Bonnie turned impatiently to Barnaby. 'Did he give you the paper to write on?'

'No, but he said to use something from school, if I had it.'

'And did you?' She stared at him in wonderment. 'What year are you?'

'Year Ten. I only had an old maths workbook, with a few pages left at the back. Dad was going to help me with some stuff.'

'Year Ten hasn't broken up yet. You – and your sister – should still be in school. What year's she?'

'Five. We always have holidays in term time. It's way cheaper, even with the fine.'

'So this woman in the shop – she didn't hear what Ben was saying to you?' Moxon persisted.

Barnaby shook his head.

'But he could have got away from her without any trouble?'

'If he'd wanted to, yeah. *He* was watching *her*, see. Not the other way around.'

'Did she know he was? I mean, did she even know he was there in the shop?'

'Not sure. Might not have done.' He puzzled over this question a bit more. 'Could be she didn't.'

Helen was clearly losing patience. 'So he wasn't with her, after all? What you said in the note isn't definite, is it? He's just playing some idiotic game and causing us all sorts of worry in the process.'

'He's trying to catch a murderer,' said Bonnie staunchly. She still hadn't all the answers she wanted. 'How did he look?' she demanded of Barnaby.

'All right. A bit muddy round his feet and the bottom of his trousers.'

'I still think he was forcibly taken yesterday,' said Simmy, who was starting to realise that of all the people present, she had the least claim to be there. Moxon was battling a noisy collection of women, struggling to get coherent answers to his questions, and she for one could help by getting out of his way. 'And that means he almost certainly knows who killed Dan. So he's in danger, even if he managed to get free this morning.'

Moxon looked unaccountably upset at this contribution. Bonnie spoke for him. 'You're not supposed to mention killing in front of his mother – or strangers,' she said. Then she pulled Simmy away a little and whispered, 'For all we know these people did it.'

187

'No!' How could a family of holidaymakers possibly be suspected of committing murder and kidnap? 'Don't be ridiculous.'

Moxon suddenly cracked. He made a jerky fretful motion with his arms and uttered a huffing sound. 'This is a complete waste of time. I'm leaving you all to it.' Then some core of professionalism asserted itself. 'Let me have your names and contact numbers,' he said to the bemused father of Barnaby, 'and then get on with your day. I very much doubt that we'll need you again.'

'No!' wailed Bonnie. 'You've got it all wrong.'

He cut her off with a sharp motion and focused on the family man. Stubbornly Bonnie approached the boy and handed him her phone. 'Put yours in,' she said. 'I'll do the same.'

They exchanged numbers and then the group disintegrated. Helen and Simmy had been on the edge for a while. Corinne had been fruitlessly trying to restrain Bonnie and chivvy her back to the expiring car, in fear of a parking fine.

Moxon literally ran to his vehicle, looking more like a junior office administrator than a police detective. From behind, Simmy observed, he was rounder, with meaty shoulders and buttocks. He ran with short strides, self-conscious and awkward. But when a woman with a baby buggy obstructed him, he dodged her with a neatness Simmy found almost balletic. Poor old Moxo, she thought fondly. Things never went smoothly for him.

Bonnie was still enraged. 'The *fool!*' she snarled. 'He's going to be very sorry about this.'

Helen was pale and quiet. 'If Ben really is just

188

playing a game, he'll be in serious trouble when we find him.'

'Not if he catches the killer,' said Bonnie. 'Then everybody will be all over him. He'll be a hero. He must be shadowing that woman because he knows she's the one.'

'A woman couldn't have lifted Dan over that fence and into the lake,' said Simmy. 'Not by herself.'

'Well, half the gang or whatever it is, is very much better than nothing.' She watched the family drift away, heads close together as they discussed the bizarre goings-on in Hawkshead. 'They're staying at Ann Tyson's House. That's a coincidence for a start.'

Corinne snorted. 'It's one of the best places for a family to do self-catering. There's a flat at the back where they can come and go as they like.'

'It's still a coincidence,' Bonnie insisted, and Simmy felt inclined to agree with her.

'So what *is* this game?' she asked. 'Moxon seemed quite impressed by it.'

'It's difficult to explain. It's based on Wordsworth when he was a boy. He lived here – went to this school, and stayed in Ann Tyson's House. They moved to Colthouse, and I went there for a look today. I found evidence that Ben had been there yesterday.' She waited for the reaction.

'What?' said Helen.

'Yes, but it doesn't help. It'll have been before all the drama kicked off. In fact, I think it might be a big red herring.' She grimaced. 'I *knew* I shouldn't tell the police about it. They'll never understand.'

189

'Who can blame them?' said Corinne. 'Now come on. I've got to move the car or I'll get a fine. There's the man, look. Quick, Bon. It's thirty quid or more.'

Simmy watched as Bonnie hesitated and then reluctantly did as instructed. She was left with Helen, at a loss as to what to do next. It had to be well after one o'clock, and her neglected shop was nagging at her. If Ben really was all right and conducting his own maverick investigation, there was much less need to be in Hawkshead. The idea of the boy acting out an episode of *Spooks* combined with the Famous Five was both annoying and amusing. 'He'll be fine,' she said aloud, more to herself than Helen. 'He might even get a result.'

'I'll kill him,' said Helen through gritted teeth. 'He'll wish he really had been kidnapped when I've finished with him.'

'I ought to get back.' She was very aware that she depended on Helen for transport. 'Can you bear to take me?'

'Gladly. Do you think they'll take that liaison woman away now? That would be a plus, anyway.'

Simmy shrugged. 'Don't ask me.'

They drove back, hardly speaking. 'We never had lunch,' Helen remembered. 'The Elleray's probably open, if you fancy something.'

Simmy resisted the temptation. 'I have to open the shop, and see if there are any new orders. If I lose business, that'll just add insult to injury. And I suppose there's a chance that Ben could call me there.'

Helen blinked. 'At the shop? Why?'

'Oh, I don't know. Maybe because I didn't answer the mobile yesterday. Although, after that, I don't imagine I'm anywhere on his list of useful people.'

'What was all that with Bonnie and photos on his phone?'

Again Simmy said, 'Don't ask me. I've completely lost the plot now.'

'Come on – don't give me that. You can read his mind better than any of us.'

'What?' She was genuinely amazed. 'Better than Bonnie? Or Melanie? That's not true at all, Helen.'

'Think about it. Clear away all the police stuff and those people just now. Get back to yesterday and that phone message. What does your gut tell you happened?'

'At the time I was convinced he was in trouble. But now I can easily see that he could have decided to play detective. He could have run away from the killers and hidden somewhere, watching them. Then he'd follow them somehow ... although, if they had a car, I don't really see how.'

'It was all very close to the hotel, right? And there are all sorts of outbuildings and small rooms and cellars where someone could hide. What if he's been there all along?'

'Impossible,' said Simmy firmly. 'Somebody would see him. The police must have searched the whole property. They've got a huge team there, with an incident room and everything. It's crawling with them.'

Helen sighed. 'Well, here we are in Windermere again. I'm going home. Corinne's got to get that

191

exhaust fixed. Bonnie isn't likely to escape back to Hawkshead for a third time, is she? You should keep her in the shop with you. Give her some work to do.'

Simmy resented the implication, but had to concede that it merited consideration. 'I'm worried about Melanie,' she admitted. 'She didn't sound like her usual self at all when I phoned her.'

'That Moxon man is a bit limp, isn't he? Seems completely out of his depth. If Ben really were in danger, I'd be very unhappy to be relying on him to save him.'

Simmy's unease was growing. 'I won't be satisfied until I've got Ben right here in front of me.'

Helen laughed. 'You sound more like his mother than I do. I've decided not to worry about him any more. When the girls get back from school I'll tell them he's all right. After all, that's what his message said, isn't it?'

'Yes,' Simmy agreed. 'That's what it said.' But she had no illusions as to Helen's true feelings. Her words might have been courageous, but they were far from convincing.

Chapter Fifteen

Ben might be okay, but Melanie definitely was not. Simmy had spent barely an hour in her belatedly opened shop before her worries about the girl got the better of her. She had hoped that Bonnie might materialise and take over, but there was no sign of her. One customer had been in and bought half a dozen yellow roses, and two orders for the weekend had popped up on the computer. The intervening silence gave her far too much opportunity for anxious reflection.

At half past three, she phoned Melanie again. 'Simmy – what now?' came the instant response.

'Just wondering if anything's happening,' said Simmy. 'Sorry if I'm a bother.'

'No, you're not. I didn't mean it the way it sounded. I'm trying to get back to the hotel, but the car isn't here. And I don't really know if I should. Nobody can tell me whether I'm needed or not.'

'Would this be one of your days, normally?'

'Yes. But they're probably not taking any new guests while all this police stuff is going on. The ones who *are* there are most likely wanting to leave, now their holidays have been spoilt. It'd be just my luck if the whole place went bust because of this.'

And mine, thought Simmy, with the flowers in mind. 'But you're mainly upset about Dan,' she said. 'Do you want to tell me about him?'

'Not really. There's hardly anything to tell. I'd only had two nights with him. I wasn't madly in love or anything. I don't want you to think that. It was more a matter of convenience, if I'm honest.'

Her voice sounded hollow, as if she had hammered this approach into her own head, as the one she would find easiest to live with. Simmy had little difficulty in seeing through it. 'It was still a terrible thing, finding him like that. You might need someone who can talk you through it, better

193

than I can.'

'Yeah, I've got PTSD, or whatever it is. I don't mind admitting it. I still can't breathe properly.'

'It's only one day ago, Mel. Are you still at home?'

'No. I came out. It's nice and sunny. I'm watching the swans and eating an ice cream, in front of the Belsfield. Just getting myself straight, you know?'

'Come up here then and we can have a chat.'

'I don't want to talk, Simmy. There's nothing to say.' Then she belied her own words by bursting out, 'I can't believe I'll never see him again – that some total waste of space has wiped him out for no reason, and ruined everything in my life. I know the police think I had something to do with it. It's only Moxon who's speaking up for me, and he'll cave in if they pressure him. Nobody's going to give me a job after this. It'll be like a horrible stink following me around for ever.'

At least she was talking, Simmy told herself. But she shouldn't be out there in the streets of Bowness, pouring it all into a mobile phone. What comfort could there be in that?

'You sound pretty bad,' she said baldly. 'Let me get my car and drive you back to Hawkshead, if that's what you want.'

'No, no. I don't. I just want it all to be over with. I just wish I'd never said anything to you or Dan about flowers. If you hadn't been there with Ben, none of this would have happened.'

Simmy went cold. 'What on earth do you mean? That's absolute rubbish, Melanie. We didn't have anything to do with Dan being killed.'

'No, but I wouldn't have been the one to find him, would I? And they wouldn't have dumped him in the lake if Ben hadn't come across his body. He'd have been in the woods, and somebody else would have found him, probably one of the guests, and most likely after I'd gone home.'

'I'm not sure what difference that would make, in the long run.' Simmy wrestled with a rage that was out of all proportion. Melanie didn't know what she was saying, and couldn't be blamed for the effect of her words. 'You sound awfully selfish.'

'Maybe I do, but it's how I feel. You wanted to know, didn't you? You wanted me to talk? Well, that's it. I try to do you a good turn and this is how it ends up.'

'Okay. I understand. I can even see that it could look like that. But it's not going to help to cast blame. The only people who should be blamed for anything are the ones who killed Dan. And don't forget about *Ben,*' she finished angrily.

'I bet he's perfectly okay. He'll be playing some weird game, you see.'

'We still have to find him.' She devoted a couple of minutes to filling Melanie in on what had happened in Hawkshead. 'And he probably isn't half as safe as he thinks he is.'

'That's all so typical,' said Melanie crossly, and finished the call.

Simmy was left with a sense of everybody isolated from everybody else. All of them were alone, or with people who could offer no real help. Herself, Bonnie, Melanie, Ben – they had always worked together before this. They had bounced ideas around and shared their various talents, and caused DI Moxon all kinds of exasperation in the process. This time, the centre of the action was at an uncomfortable distance, and the most vital member of the team was missing. The demands of her business were a distraction, too.

Then she had a visitor who only served to confuse things further.

'Hiya!' chirped Ninian Tripp, as if he was the one person in the world she most hoped and expected to see. He was even carrying a bulky canvas bag, which he set down with great care on an empty piece of floor. 'Brought you some new pots. Sorry it's taken me so long.'

It had taken him several months. Simmy had long ago given up hope that it would ever happen. 'Let's see,' she said, without enthusiasm.

He peeled back the fabric to reveal three large vases. One was terracotta, one glazed in a lustrous shade of blue, and the last a deep orange. 'I wanted them all to be different,' he explained. 'I like to think they represent Europe, Asia and Africa.' He tapped each one in turn.

'Why is Asia blue?' she wondered.

'I thought the Himalayas. The icy summit of Everest, sort of notion.' The pot was roughly triangular, the colour darker at the base. Its mouth was barely two inches across. Simmy tried to visualise the most appropriate flowers for it.

'I see,' she said.

'And the terracotta could equally well be Africa, I know, but I was thinking of Thrace, maybe. Some ancient meeting point, where cultures

196

clashed.' He indicated the curlicues he had cut into the rim, which was folded back on itself in an elegant line that then flowed inwards and out again, giving the pot an almost female shape, with waist and hips. The orange one was plain, with a matt finish and a crude design in black to suggest a river or snake.

'They're too good for this place,' she said. 'They're worth more than my customers would pay. They're works of art.'

'Sweet of you to say, but if I could just get people to look at them, I'll be happy. They can make a talking point, maybe.'

'They'll do that, all right.'

'Are you okay? Have I done something? Or *not* done something, most likely.'

She made a face. 'Normally I might have had a robust answer to that, but just at the moment, there's too much else to worry about. Didn't you hear what happened in Hawkshead yesterday?' Silly question, she realised. Ninian never listened to the news. He was a latter-day hermit, shut away in a small cottage on the side of a little fell near Bowness.

'I did not,' he said. 'I was hoping there wouldn't be any more of these happenings that you seem to get yourself drawn into.'

'I hoped the same thing. But a man was killed up at a hotel there, and Ben's disappeared. We think he's doing some sort of idiotic detective work. Moxon's furious with him, and Bonnie doesn't know what to believe. Melanie blames me and I just want to get on with my work.'

'Whoa!' Ninian put up his hands in a familiar

gesture. Unlike Simmy, he was expert at not get-ting involved in anything unpleasant. Something about him said, Don't ask me, I'm useless, and people acted accordingly.

'Never mind,' she sighed. 'What price should I put on the vases, then? Or aren't they for sale?'

'Eighty quid, twenty-five per cent for you,' he said promptly.

'Okay.' She had no expectations that they would sell, but they would enhance the effect of her flowers, especially if Bonnie was given full rein to arrange them. 'Is there anything else?'

'Don't be like that.' His boyish smile was sweetly seductive, but her immunity levels had risen considerably in recent weeks. 'I thought you might want to come over at the weekend.'

'I don't think I will,' she said firmly.

'My appeal wore off, did it? That's a pity. We weren't so bad together, were we?'

'We were fine, as far as it went.'

He cocked his head at her. 'Had a better offer?'

The rage that Melanie had engendered was still swirling. 'Shut up,' she snapped. 'Don't be so *trivial*.'

'Uh-oh,' he said. 'You've got me to rights, as they say. The thing is, my love, life *is* trivial. That's the great secret of existence. But if it helps, I should perhaps tell you that I thought I saw young Mr Harkness in the back of a car with a man, last night. It may not have been him, of course,' he finished airily.

'Where? What time was it?'

'I was on the bus, coming back from Grasmere. It must have been about nine, I guess. The car

198

was going the opposite way from the bus. I don't remember the exact spot. There was a woman driving, and I thought it a bit funny that nobody was in the front with her. I couldn't see very well. It was all over in two seconds. But it *did* look like him. And he did not look happy.'

'What sort of car?'

'I have no idea.'

'You'll have to tell the police.' She felt almost as unhappy about this as she supposed he did. 'It throws everything into question all over again. What if he really *has* been kidnapped? That's what we thought at first. And why would they be going towards Grasmere, of all places?'

'Kidnapped?'

She explained as briefly as she could, but Ninian asked a lot of very basic questions, which was annoying. When she'd finished, he simply said, 'It probably wasn't him, anyway.'

She studied him doubtfully. His information was both unwelcome and unreliable. She would have to do something with it – or force Ninian to do it himself. 'I expect it was,' she sighed. 'Not many people look like Ben.'

'I might even have dreamt it,' he said, infuriatingly. 'I was dozing on and off. You know how you do in buses. It's a conditioned reflex or something.'

'You didn't dream it, Ninian. Be sensible.'

'I don't altogether follow this message thing in Hawkshead. But you all ended up thinking Ben was okay – is that right?'

'Moxon did, anyway. He was cross about it, wasting police time when he's meant to be investigating a murder. And we all know Ben – he *would* do that sort of thing. Bonnie believed it, which convinced the rest of us, including his mother, pretty much.'

Ninian nodded, with a little frown. 'If the baddies are driving around in plain sight, other people might have seen them, then. It seems a bit unlikely, really, that it *was* Ben in the car. He'd have been banging on the window or trying to open the door, if they'd kidnapped him. Golly Moses, it's a real muddle, isn't it,' he finished.

'If there was a man in the back with him, he was probably not able to do anything like that. He might even have had his hands tied.'

'Mm.'

'We'll have to tell Moxon,' Simmy said, with a sinking feeling. 'And that'll start everything up again. Poor Helen!'

'Helen?'

'Mrs Harkness. Ben's mother. She won't know what to think.'

'How is that different? Surely nobody knows anyway? After all, the boy's still missing from home, whether I saw him or not.'

She picked up the landline phone. 'Call the police,' she ordered. 'I've got Moxon's number here, look.' She extracted a rather crumpled card from a little pile next to the till. It had been used quite a lot over the past few months. She had thought of throwing it away, several times, but that had felt like tempting fate. Fate evidently wasn't interested in such minor details. There was no escaping Moxon, with or without his card.

Ninian flinched away from the phone. 'You do

it,' he whined. 'You know him much better than I do.'

She'd expected this. 'I'm not doing any of the talking. Stand still until I'm through to him.'

But she didn't get through. The call went to voicemail. 'Hello, this is Simmy Brown,' she dictated. 'I'm with Ninian Tripp, who thinks he saw Ben in a car last night, between Grasmere and Ambleside. He was with a man and a woman. He doesn't remember anything about the car. We're at the shop, but I'll be closing at five.'

'Saved by the wonders of technology,' Ninian said. 'Thanks, Sim. I know I'm a wimp. You're much better off without me.'

They were back to the earlier topic, she realised miserably. Ninian was offering her uncomplicated sex, which ought to be enough for a woman of her age and situation. She ought to jump at the chance, according to most people she knew. She could hear her mother expressing amazement at her lack of enthusiasm. In the sixties, nobody would ever turn down an offer of going to bed with a healthy, good-natured man like Ninian. Or so Angie claimed. Simmy had never quite believed it had ever been as easy as that. For herself, it was impossible to avoid thinking ahead. She knew she would end up feeling grubby and very slightly ashamed at the meaningless encounter. Nothing was ever going to come of it. She and Ninian were not in love. They were never going to live together and have babies. The sex they had thus far engaged in was friendly enough, but nothing special. While she knew that her attitude and expectations were almost entirely created by the culture of romance and couplehood that persisted all around her, this did nothing to change them. If she couldn't have a complete relationship with a man who took an obvious delight in her whole self, with prospects for the future and a thorough mutual trust, she was never really going to be interested.

She gave a little wriggle of her shoulders, and dodged the subject. 'Do you remember *anything* about the woman who was driving the car?' she asked.

'Let me think. You do realise I never imagined it was important. It was just a glimpse, and only now when you tell me there's a problem with the boy have I even given it a thought. She was just a woman driving a car. Normal sort of size and shape. Lightish hair, possibly. But look, Sim, I could be making it all up. You read about how totally wrong eyewitnesses usually are. If you were to tell me the chief suspect has purple hair and enormous spectacles, I could probably square that with the person I saw. And even worse with the man in the back. I'd say he was fairly large, clean-shaven and not very young. But I wouldn't swear to any of it.'

'Would you know them in an identity parade?'

'I doubt it.'

'But you're fairly sure it really was Ben.' She felt a growing desperation at this elusive clue. With anybody but Ninian, the testimony would be more reliable than his vague uncertainties.

'I was sure at the time. Sure-ish, anyway. I said to myself, "That's young Ben Harkness. Wonder what he's up to now." That's exactly what I thought. Then I remembered he's finished school

202

for the summer, and could have aunts or some-thing who'd be glad to take him for a nice drive up to Grasmere. It didn't seem unusual, except for the man with him in the back. That was what made me look a bit more closely than I'd have done otherwise.'

Simmy could see that he was trying his best to co-operate. He wanted to please her, and that made her feel warmer towards him than she'd done for some time. After all, who could remain cross with sweet Ninian Tripp? She was tempted to give him a hug, just for being there and taking things seriously. 'Thanks,' she said. 'It's going to be helpful. I mean – if you saw him, others might have done as well. The police can put out a call for any other witnesses.'

'Maybe they can hypnotise me into remem-bering what sort of car it was.'

'Yeah,' she laughed. Ben would say of course they *could*, but there was no chance that they *would*, because it cost too much, and any results wouldn't justify the expense. Unless Ninian could come up with the number plate, of course. And from the window of a bus, he was unlikely even to have seen that.

'Melanie's blaming me,' she said suddenly. Something about Ninian's softness; the way he was simply standing there so patient and accepting made her want to splurge the most acute of her worries. 'If I hadn't taken Ben to the hotel and let him go down to the lake, then she and I would not have been the ones to find Dan's dead body. It's true, but he'd still be just as dead without any of us being there. She sat there in the water with him on her lap. I suppose that's going to haunt her now for the rest of her life. I sort of expected her to be tougher than that. Silly, I know.'

'She's tough enough,' he said. 'It's my guess that she feels guilty about something she said and did, and she's projecting it onto you.'

Ninian had been through rocky emotional times himself, with years of therapy. As a result he could sometimes come up with surprisingly accurate insights about people's inner workings. Simmy had seen him with Bonnie Lawson, recognising elements the two had in common.

'Oh,' she said. 'Do you think so?'

'How well did she know this Dan person?'

'She's spent the night with him, twice, I think. She insisted there was no great love between them, but she seemed terribly fond of him when she discovered he was dead.'

'Dead,' Ninian repeated gently. 'That's a pretty big thing, you know, even when it happens to a total stranger. If you've got his head in your lap, you can't really avoid the enormity of it, can you?'

Simmy was assailed by a tormenting image of her own stillborn daughter lying in her lap, cold and silent and unmoving. 'No,' she whispered. 'Poor old Mel.'

'Right. So go easy on her, okay? She'll be fine after a bit, but for now her world is probably upside down, and she has no idea how to deal with it. Just because she's grown up in a family of losers doesn't equip her for something like this.'

'Thanks.' She gave him a watery smile.

Then – as happened so uncomfortably often – an unexpected figure came into the shop.

Chapter Sixteen

'Dad?' Simmy stared at her father as if at a ghost. 'Are you all right?'

There was no immediate reason for such a question. He was tidily dressed, his hair brushed, no wild look in his eye. And yet there was definitely something wrong.

'I can't find your mother,' he said, with an apologetic smile.

Simmy took a breath. This was the sort of thing a senile old person would do – but the fact that Russell had found the flower shop on his own, and was in a presentable condition, gave credence to his words. 'Didn't she say where she was going?'

'If she did, I didn't hear her. The thing is, that girl who works here came to the house wanting her. When I went to look for her, she was nowhere to be found.'

'Girl? Bonnie, you mean?'

'I'm not sure that's her name. Big lass. Dark hair. Lovely skin.'

'Melanie! That's Melanie.'

'Yes,' he said, with evident relief. 'Of course.'

'Why isn't she with you? Where is she now?'

'Who? The girl?'

'Yes. And Mum. Oh, for heaven's sake, this isn't making any sense at all.'

'That's what I said.' His very mildness was

alarming. 'The girl went away. But before that she said maybe I should come and ask you, because Angie might be here. Or you might know where she's gone.'

'Well I don't.' She gazed at her father in perplexity. Only three months ago he had been absolutely normal, fully functioning in every way. Was it feasible that dementia could set in so rapidly? It was no longer possible to ignore his deterioration; a doctor must be consulted as a matter of urgency. But first they had to find Angie.

'I bet she left a note,' said Ninian cheerily. 'Why don't we all go back for a look?'

Russell gave him a long, considering look. 'All right,' he agreed at last. 'That's a sensible idea. Good man.'

It wasn't apparent to Simmy that he knew who Ninian was, despite several encounters. Her friend had even spent Christmas Day with the family only seven months earlier.

'I'll lock up, then,' she said. 'It's almost closing time, anyway.' Thinking back over the long day, she felt suddenly exhausted. Far too much had happened for a scant eight or nine hours. On balance, nothing at all was any better than it had been the previous day. Ben's whereabouts and state of mind were still a complete blank. Dan Yates was still just as dead, his killer still evading detection. Bonnie, Melanie and Helen were all frightened and miserable. And she herself was saddled with a parent who was losing his wits and another who'd emulated Ben Harkness and gone absent without leave.

Her car was a few streets away, and as always she

had to think hard to remember where she'd left it. With tired, dragging feet she led the two men southwards towards the network of small roads where parking was unrestricted. 'P'Simmon!' came a welcome voice from a side street just behind them. 'What are you doing?'

'Mum.' She turned and almost fell into her mother's arms, so great was her relief. 'Dad came to the shop, saying he'd lost you.'

Behind her, she heard the clearing of a male throat. 'Um...' said Ninian. 'You won't need me any more, then. Everything should be all right now, by the looks of it.'

Simmy let the exaggeration pass. She refrained from listing all the things that remained very far from all right. All she said was, 'Thanks, Ninian. But don't forget the police are going to want to talk to you about last night.'

He made a rueful face, like a schoolboy threatened with an interview with the Head. 'They know where to find me,' he said. Simmy wasn't entirely sure that this was true, but she merely nodded.

'See you, then,' he smiled, and turned back towards the main street. Intending to catch a bus down to the further end of Bowness, she supposed, where he would have to walk home up Brant Fell.

'Why do the police want him?' asked Angie, after leaving a moment for Ninian to get out of earshot.

'I'll tell you later. Let's get Dad home. Where were you?'

'Shopping.'

'Oh. Well, Melanie's been looking for you, for some reason. She got Dad all agitated, and he came out to try to find you. At least, that's what he said.'

'I suppose you want to talk about *that* later as well.' Angie gave an angry little snort to indicate how trying people were being. 'And why in the world would Melanie Todd want me? She hardly knows me.'

'I have no idea. I spoke to her less than an hour ago and she was in Bowness feeling miserable. Perhaps she was just hoping for a cup of tea and a shoulder to cry on.'

'I hardly think she'd choose *me* for that.'

They were walking briskly, Russell flanked by his two women, forced to maintain the pace. 'What's the rush?' he asked at one point.

'We've got people coming,' said Angie. 'They'll be annoyed if there's nobody to meet them.'

For the hundredth time, Simmy was made aware of the restrictions imposed by running a Bed and Breakfast. Not only the mornings relentlessly spent preparing large breakfasts, seven days a week, but the afternoons, where people were liable to arrive at any time after three o'clock – and sometimes earlier than that. One or other of her parents needed to be there to receive them. During the summer there was never a free day; the resulting pressure difficult to imagine. Had this, then, been a factor in sending her father into his tailspin, in addition to the violence and danger that his daughter had been exposed to?

'I'm not staying,' she said, when they got to Beck View in Lake Road. 'It's been a pretty awful day.'

208

Angie faced her with a thunderous expression. 'And what about *my* day?' she demanded. 'And every other day for the past umpteen weeks?' She gave her husband a little push. 'Go and put the kettle on,' she ordered him. 'I'm desperate for a cup of tea.' Again, she waited until the subject of her remarks was beyond earshot. 'I haven't been shopping at all,' she hissed. 'I went to the doctor.'

'About Dad?'

'About both of us. I can't sleep. I can't get a minute's peace, day or night. Nobody gives a button for how I'm feeling, with all their own troubles. And I include you in that. It all got more than I could stand, so I went to the bloody doctor.'

The rage was complicated, but Simmy was quite aware that the mere fact of consulting a doctor was enough to make her mother angry. In her world-view a doctor was strictly for vaccinations and transitory injuries. To seek help with anything more nebulous, hinting at emotional difficulties, indicated real desperation. 'So what did he – she – say?'

'She. It ended up with me talking about your father, since he's the reason I'm in such a state. She wants him to have a scan, because she thought it sounded as if he could have had a stroke, or aneurysm or some sort of "episode" and there's treatment for all that kind of thing. If he was getting Alzheimer's, it would be more gradual, she thinks. To see her face, you'd assume she was giving me good news.'

Angie's own face was a picture of scorn.

'Well, if there's treatment...' said Simmy cautiously.

'Right. A lifetime of drugs that'll keep him practically comatose, or give him ghastly side effects. Honestly – am I the only one who thinks we're living in a totalitarian state governed by medics and pharmaceutical companies?'

'Probably,' said Simmy. 'They're only trying to help, after all.' She knew she ought to keep quiet, that her mother was in a mood for passionate diatribing and the quickest way to stop her was to say nothing. But she saw no way to avoid replying, so she squared her shoulders and said firmly, 'I'm sorry, Mum. Go and have your tea and forget it for now. I'm going home. If Melanie comes back, tell her you've got too much to do to talk to her this evening.'

'What's come over you?' Angie's rage had mutated into reproachful disbelief. 'So hard and self-absorbed all of a sudden?'

'I'm not.' The accusation was piercingly unfair. 'It's just that I'm as tired as you are. The weather doesn't help. We all need an early night, so we can start sorting it all out in the morning.'

'"Sorting it all out"?' Angie repeated with hurtful contempt. 'And how do you think we'll do that?' She paused. 'What possible reason can Melanie have for wanting me? What use can *I* be to her?'

Simmy gave no reply. Resentment was flaring warmly, not just towards her mother, but the whole business at Hawkshead. Once again she had been drawn into something that did not concern her in the least. People she didn't know had killed and been killed, for reasons she could not begin to guess. She was the still centre of a

210

swirling mass of overwrought people, all of them wanting something from her. If Melanie wanted Angie, that was one weight off her – Simmy's – back.

They were still barely inside the house, facing each other in the hallway. From the kitchen came the sound of a whistling kettle. For a moment, Simmy was tempted to sit over a mug of tea and give herself up to the needs of her parents. It was what she would normally do, without a second thought.

But this was not a normal evening. Her only wish was to escape to the peace and solitude of her own cottage in Troutbeck. So, steeling herself against pangs of guilt at her heartless behaviour, she did exactly that.

She took the easternmost road to her village – the one that carried on to Kirkstone Pass and Ullswater once it had passed Troutbeck. In summer it was well used by visitors in cars or hiking, with a few on horseback for good measure. To her right rose fells and crags which she had yet to properly explore. Paths led up and over the top, then down into Kentmere, which was also little known to her. By road it was a long and tortuous distance away. On foot it was an easy hike. She and her father had resolved to do it one summer weekend but all such plans were on hold until his state of health could be ascertained. A better map reader than she was, he needed to be in full possession of his wits before such a venture could be attempted. She would never dare to go by herself.

She returned to her cottage with a mixture of

relief and self-reproach. It was disgraceful of her to walk away from so many distressed and needy people, for no reason other than that she had had enough. Ben was still missing – that was the most stark fact of all. His claim to be 'okay' was decreasingly reassuring as night approached. Where was he? What was he doing? Where would he sleep? Had he had anything to eat? These maternal anxieties made her think of Helen and how much more acute they must be for her. There was a high chance that he was no longer okay, of course. If he was shadowing people he knew to be capable of murder, then he was obviously in real danger. And yet Moxon had seemed to drop all concern for the boy, once he heard the tale of the note on the windscreen.

A concern that would surely revive once he got the message about Ninian's sighting. Again, Simmy felt guilty. She should have made a better effort to contact the detective, trying different numbers, making it seem more urgent. But then – why should *she* be the one to do it? It was Ninian's sighting, not hers.

Because she cared intensely about Ben, of course. Because principled jibbing at doing Ninian's work for him could lead to resulting harm for the boy. Ben was worth a hundred Ninians. Even Ninian himself would agree to that.

But there really was nothing more she could do that evening. She scrambled three eggs for herself, and ate them quickly. Her phone was switched off, a deliberate refusal to participate any further in the convolutions centred on Hawkshead. She would go to bed insanely early and hope for better news in the morning. 'I'll be far more use after a good night's sleep,' she muttered to herself. Sometimes she wished she had a cat to talk to. It would make her feel less crazy. But cats killed too many things, and were really not ideal as companions. She drifted off to sleep thinking sadly that cats and dogs were all basically substitutes for wholesome human relationships. And she did not want an animal to remind her of how defective she was in that department.

Chapter Seventeen

Bonnie felt tight with frustration. Her skin was stretched with it. Her breath came shallow and quick. Nobody – not even Ben's mother – understood how serious and urgent everything was. First, she absolutely had to see Ben's photos, even though she could no longer be sure of their usefulness. Could a picture prove anything more to her than it did to the police? And if there was, by some miracle, a shot of the killer with or without an accomplice, then Moxon and his mates would have homed in on it and be sending out appeals for help in catching the person concerned. Which was not happening, because she had just spent twenty minutes simultaneously watching the TV news channel and listening to the local radio. Corinne was keeping a close watch on her, saying almost nothing.

It was five o'clock when this surveillance eased

up a bit. 'Better get something on for supper,' said Corinne. 'Is there anything you fancy?'

She instantly saw her chance. 'Is cottage pie too much to ask?'

'It'll take a while. I'll have to start from scratch. Wouldn't you rather have something from the freezer?' Against all appearances, Corinne was a very good and generous cook. Catering for her multifarious foster children had been one of her greatest strengths. 'Give them some decent grub and you're halfway there,' she said to the social workers when they marvelled at her creations.

'I can wait,' said Bonnie, with a fleeting pang of shame.

'Okay, then.'

It was her own fault, thought Bonnie. Corinne ought to know by now how essential it was to watch her oldest charge. Bonnie had run away before, several times, though not for a few years now. The others had all been too young to contemplate an escape – and none of them wanted to leave anyway. Bonnie had no problems with Corinne, either. It was just that she needed to be somewhere else and this need outweighed her loyalty to her carer. *I'm seventeen,* she thought fiercely. *Old enough to do as I like.* A sentiment that Corinne generally agreed with.

She waited five minutes and then slipped quietly out of the house, and began trotting southwards towards the police station. It was a zigzag route through streets of houses, before emerging onto the main road leading down to Bowness. Moxon probably wouldn't be there, she knew, and the whole place could have already closed up for the evening, but she had to try. It was unfair of them to ignore her the way they had. She was determined to make a nuisance of herself until they were forced to take notice. What, after all, did she have to lose? Until she had Ben right there in front of her, she wouldn't be able to rest.

The police station was open. The desk was manned by a buxom female constable Bonnie had never seen before. Her hair was wound into a lump at the back of her neck, and her skin looked as if she'd been unwisely exposing it to the sun. 'I'm Bonnie Lawson,' she said firmly. 'I'm helping with the business in Hawkshead. I think Inspector Moxon wants to see me. Is he here?'

The woman was unimpressed. 'You *think* he wants to see you? How does that work, then?'

'He might have forgotten to send a car for me. We have to look at some photos together.' She stood as tall as she could, but was still humiliatingly small. At least her voice emerged clear and loud. She had always been able to use her voice to good effect.

'What's your address?' asked the desk person.

Bonnie gave it. 'I believe Mr Moxon lives quite close to us, actually,' she added. It was mischief, she knew. Not just the *Mr*, but the implication that there was a social connection between them.

Doubt flickered gratifyingly in the officer's eye. 'Wait a minute,' she said, and disappeared through a door behind her into realms that Bonnie had never entered. She was gone for over five minutes, which was a long time to hover in a reception area that was depressing in its efforts to provide information and reassurance.

When the woman came back, she was nicer. Her wide face had softened and she was holding a sheet of paper. 'Okay,' she said. 'Now I understand who you are.' She consulted the paper. 'Your boyfriend's the one who's gone missing. DI Moxon did leave a message about you, as it happens.'

So why wasn't it here on the desk, in case I came in? Bonnie wanted to ask. This was a murder investigation, after all. Vital testimony could be lost unless every member of the team was completely up to speed with who was who. She could organise the whole business better herself, she was sure. And with Ben at her side, the two of them could probably solve every crime in Cumbria, given the resources the police had access to.

'Yes?' she said. 'What's the message?'

'Listen – it's not meant for you directly. It's just that your name's here amongst a lot of other stuff. He says he's coming back here around five-thirty, and will catch up with you then. He's been in Hawkshead all day, at the hotel there.'

'I know he has,' said Bonnie patiently. 'I was with him for some of the time.'

'Yes, well, there's a whole lot going on. They've cancelled our leave this week.' A flash of resentment told Bonnie that this WPC had been personally inconvenienced by the Hawkshead business. 'The incident room up there is being wound up tomorrow and everything's coming back here. It'll be easier, then.'

'Will it?' Bonnie had a strong sense that it ought to be the other way around – every police officer should be taken to Hawkshead, where they could search harder for Ben. 'I don't see how.'

The woman sniffed, as if to say, *Well, I don't intend to explain it to a slip of a thing like you.*

'It's five-thirty now,' she said. 'I'll wait for him.' And she sat down on a moulded plastic chair under a noticeboard full of well-intentioned homilies about locking up your possessions, or marking them with SmartWater. The impression this gave, which was much discussed by Corinne's friends and relations, was that the police were devoting considerably more effort to persuading people to protect their property from theft than to tracking down objects that had actually been stolen. Once it was gone, that was that. It didn't make for friendly relations.

But when someone was violently murdered, they had to step up and activate whatever detection skills they possessed. Ben, Simmy and Melanie had been involved in no fewer than four murder investigations over the past year, with Ben's resulting opinion of the police a confused mixture of fascination and contempt. He could do better, he insisted. Not only that, but he *would.* He was going to devote his life to the science of solving crimes, especially murder.

But Ben's interests ranged wider than that, hence the 1780 game and all its ramifications. It was, she knew, partly intended as diversion and education for her. Something the two of them could engage in together, a special project just for them. And as a bonus, if it were to be finished, it might raise some income. There was a big market for video games, and although amateurs seldom succeeded in breaking into the commercial side, if anybody could, it was Ben Harkness.

Her hunches of that morning were still sustainable, she believed. Ben had been focused on the game when he went to Colthouse. And while he definitely had discovered Dan Yates's body, and very likely stumbled upon the killer or killers, he might well be intending to weave his observations into the game somehow. But here she floundered. Would he really put her and his family through such anguished worry for such a reason? Surely not! He was much more likely to be exercising his civic duty as he saw it, by following the criminals and gathering evidence against them.

Then Moxon arrived and interrupted her swirling repetitive thoughts. He came in with another man, ushering him with that firm manner that the police adopted. It combined respect with a clear assertion of authority. The man was familiar to Bonnie, but she could not immediately place him. Tall, quite old, with a neat grey beard and old-fashioned clothes. She gazed up at him from her chair, until the memory clicked into place. He was one of the guests from the hotel who had been on the lawn that morning.

'Miss Lawson,' Moxon greeted her without surprise. Somebody must have phoned to tell him she was there, she supposed. 'Can you give me ten more minutes, while I take Mr Ferguson through? It's quite important.'

She shrugged and smiled, mainly for the benefit of the woman on the desk. 'No problem,' she said. 'Except Corinne might be worrying about me, I suppose. I didn't tell her where I was going.'

'Call her then.' He scanned her hands for the expected phone, raising his eyebrows when it was

218

not in evidence. 'Where's your phone?'

'Here.' She took it from the pocket of her jacket. 'I'll tell her you want to talk to me. How long do you think we'll be?'

He said nothing, but tilted his head and uttered a little laugh. She had seen him do the same thing with Ben. It indicated amused exasperation at their cheek, while at the same time taking them rather more seriously than most senior policemen would.

She let him go, wondering about Mr Ferguson. Had *he* killed the under-manager? It seemed highly unlikely. Easier to believe that he had glimpsed some shadowy figure amongst the trees on the edge of Esthwaite and come forward to offer a vague statement. Or overheard some suspicious-sounding conversation that had only now come to mind. Whatever it was, Moxon wasn't going to tell her – unless the old bloke was arrested and charged and the whole thing solved by bedtime.

At last, she was seated in front of a laptop looking at the pictures from Ben's phone. A computer techie in Kendal had captured eight images from the memory and had added times and dates to them before transmitting them to the laptop in Windermere. There was the tied-up clump of ferns in the burial ground, timed at 11.26. Then pictures of the burial ground itself with its plain stone grave markers; the stone trough in the farmyard with the ancient black pump placed above it; a granite rock on the side of a grassy track followed a few minutes later. She peered closely,

219

wondering about its significance. There were faint letters scratched onto it. 'That's F and C, isn't it?' she asked Moxon.

He had obviously not seen the letters before. 'Looks like it,' he agreed. 'Does that mean anything to you?'

'Fletcher Christian,' she said promptly. 'He's in our game. He was at school with Wordsworth, you know. But not in Hawkshead.' She frowned. 'It's just another picture we can use at some point. All the animation's going to be based on what's really there, you see. It's much more multilayered than ordinary games. You can take it to the actual places. I mean – you *will* be able to. It's going to be awesome,' she sighed.

Moxon sighed even more loudly. 'I didn't understand a word of that.'

'Never mind. It's nothing to do with the murder. The time's still before he called Simmy, look.'

But then the next picture jumped fifteen minutes and was unavoidably relevant. It showed a man lying prostrate on the ground with shadows from overhead trees making patches across his torso. His face was turned sideways, but easy to recognise. Moxon was plainly uneasy at letting Bonnie see it. 'This is the one we're most interested in,' he told her. 'Although it doesn't show anything immediately helpful.' He cleared his throat. 'Except, of course, that we never saw him in this position. He was in the lake when your friends found him.'

'Typical Ben, taking a picture,' she said, feeling somewhat light-headed. 'Before he called Simmy, I suppose.'

'Two minutes before. Which seems rather a long time, wouldn't you say?'

Bonnie looked up at him, where he stood at her shoulder. 'What are you thinking?'

'Look at the next picture.'

It showed a more distant view of the body, with trees behind it. Ben had evidently retreated a short distance away from the woods for this picture. 'There's a rough field between the trees and the road,' Moxon said. 'With a path that runs up to the hotel.'

'Yes, I know.' She brought to mind the terrain she had covered that morning. 'You've got it all taped off now.'

The next picture was almost exactly the same, but the one after that seemed to be much closer to what she and Moxon had been looking for. Tilted at a crazy angle, it was a smudgy shot of a pair of human legs encased in trousers and wearing sturdy brown walking shoes. 'Wow!' she breathed. 'That must be the killer! Those are men's shoes and trousers, aren't they?' She leant closer to the screen. 'You can tinker with it and get the colour and material, can't you?'

'The trousers are some sort of cotton. Not denim,' he said. 'And the shoes are fairly distinctive.'

'Quite smart, then. Likely to be one of the guests at the hotel.' She paused, trying to think. 'Is that why you've brought Mr Ferguson in? To compare his clothes with the picture?'

'Quite definitely not,' said Moxon firmly. 'He came of his own accord.'

'I hope he's told you something useful.' She

221

looked up hopefully, but Moxon's face remained bland, and he said nothing. She sighed and looked back at the pictures. 'That's the last one, then? So when did he call Simmy and leave that message? You can't take a picture and talk on the phone at the same time.'

He nodded. 'The call comes between the last two pictures. He must have acted very quickly to get this final shot.'

'So we know there was some sort of struggle, do we? Doesn't this picture prove it? And if there was, we can't be sure that he is okay, after all.' A twist inside her made her gasp. 'They might even have *killed* him by now.'

Moxon merely watched her, with a patient sort of sympathy.

Her head was buzzing. 'Ben's not okay,' she said flatly. 'I never really thought he was. I can *feel* it. He's in real trouble.'

The detective was being oddly calm. She wanted to smack him, make him react more urgently. He moved away from her and glanced at his watch. 'I don't know,' he said quietly. 'I really don't know.'

'It's a lot more than twenty-four hours now,' she insisted. 'Isn't that when you start to take this sort of thing more seriously?'

'This is no "sort of thing" I've dealt with before. He's not a missing person as such.' He rubbed his cheek, like somebody trying to wake himself up. 'Trust your Ben to land us with something new. We're not at all sure what the best procedure might be.'

She stared at him. Was he admitting weakness? Even failure? 'He's a hostage,' she said. 'Isn't he?'

'In a way, perhaps. We have absolutely no way of telling whether he's acting independently, or whether he's under duress. But there's been no ransom demand. No threats. Just that strange little note on your mother's car in Hawkshead.'

Normally Bonnie would have said, *She's not my mother*, but she let it pass. Corinne was the closest she was ever going to get to a maternal presence in her life, anyway. Moxon knew that. He probably said it deliberately.

'Right,' she said. 'And that *must* have come from Ben. Who else could it have been?'

'I agree. But he might have been forced to do it.'

'That's not the way that Barnaby boy made it sound. I can't work it out. The photos don't really help, either.' She had turned on the chair, sitting sideways and looking at him. She felt like a proper adult, taken into the confidence of a senior police officer. It was an extension of the way Ben made her feel. They both treated her like a serious person with important things to say. It was intoxicating. She felt ready for anything. For some reason it made her think of Melanie Todd, who had not shown herself half as strong when events turned nasty.

'There's been another development,' he said suddenly. 'I wasn't sure I ought to tell you.'

'What?'

'You know a man called Ninian Tripp?'

'Of course. He's a mate of Corinne's. And Simmy has a thing with him. Everybody knows Ninian.'

'Okay. Well Mrs Brown left me a voicemail a

little while ago, to say Mr Tripp thinks he saw Ben in a car last night. With a man and a woman. Somewhere towards Grasmere.'

'Simmy told you? Why didn't Ninian do it himself?'

'Why, indeed. Do you think that's significant?'

'Not really. Just typical.'

They exchanged smiles full of the shared knowledge that Ninian was not a very worthy person when it came to the things that mattered. A bit like Melanie, thought Bonnie unkindly. 'Is he sure it was Ben?' Interesting, she noted, that her instant reaction had been that of course it wasn't Ben. Ninian was too dreamy to provide reliable evidence. 'What would that mean – if it was him?'

'God knows.'

'A man and a woman. What else does he remember?'

'I've got somebody with him now, trying to find out.' He made a tetchy little click with his tongue. 'I don't have to do *everything* myself, you know.'

'I never said you did. It's just – it mostly *is* you, though, isn't it? That's what Simmy would say.'

He inhaled deeply and worked his shoulders. 'Go home,' he said. 'We can't do any more this evening. I mean – you can't. I'm trusting you not to go off again on your own, all right?'

'I won't go anywhere today,' she compromised. 'Corinne's made a cottage pie.'

'Nice.'

Bonnie's history of disordered eating, involving a lot of missed schooling and periods in hospital, made any reference to food hazardous. Even Moxon, only vaguely aware of the story, clearly felt himself on shaky ground.

'I'm over all that,' she assured him. 'Ben's straightened me out. I owe everything to Ben,' she finished with a wild look. 'That's why he's got to be all right. Do you see?'

'I do, indeed. His mother would no doubt say the same.' It was a gentle reproof that Ben himself would appreciate. 'First thing in the morning, we'll be pulling out every stop to find him. That's a promise.' He put a hand on his heart like a man from an earlier age. 'A solemn promise.'

Bonnie was only slightly impressed. 'Thanks,' she said. 'I'll be off, then.' She was back in the low evening light of the lakeside street before he could say any more.

But the day was not quite done yet. Corinne was uncharacteristically annoyed when she got back. 'Sneaking off like that – again,' she accused. 'What am I supposed to think? You did it deliberately, making sure I was busy in the kitchen, you little beast.'

'I called you,' Bonnie defended.

'Right. About an hour after you'd gone. What good was that supposed to do?'

'It wasn't an hour. Nothing like.'

'Just don't do it again. I'm on your side, you little idiot. Why do you think you have to lie and play games with me? That's what I don't understand.'

Bonnie sighed. She didn't entirely understand it herself. It seemed to be engrained in her bones, the need to outwit and escape. People were so often in her way, blocking her path, threatening to confine her somehow or other. It had produced an instinct to go her own way whenever she could. 'Sorry,' she said. 'Is the cottage pie ready?'

'Dried up by now.'

'It'll be fine with some ketchup. I want *lots*.' It was a shabby trick, she knew, but one she could not resist using. Any hint of appetite earned a high degree of favour, even from Corinne, who knew the score better than most.

'That's good.' Corinne smiled forgivingly.

Then the doorbell rang, and Bonnie left her foster mother to answer it, while she tucked into a moderate helping of the food. It was delicious, she had to admit. Corinne added mushrooms and herbs and soy sauce, besides grating celeriac into the mashed potato. There was no better cottage pie in the world. That was unarguable.

'Visitor for you,' Corinne announced, three minutes later. Bonnie looked up to see a person she had no reason to expect to see that evening. A person she had not thought kindly of over the past few hours.

Chapter Eighteen

'Don't stop,' said Melanie, indicating the plate of food. 'I'll talk while you eat.' Her voice was husky and there were grey smudges under her eyes.

Bonnie obeyed, more to make a point than anything else. Her curiosity was raging, along with a rising excitement. It was barely possible to force the meat and potatoes down her throat. But she was wary of letting her friend see any of this. Melanie's role in the disappearance of Ben was obscure, and probably peripheral, but in Bonnie's mind there was an uneasy association.

'So, listen. I'm going to talk about Dan. I need to get it straight in my head, and there's nobody else I can find to help. I tried to find Simmy's mum just now. She's always been incredibly sensible. But she wasn't there. It was a stupid idea, anyway.'

'Why not Simmy? Isn't she good at that stuff?'

Melanie pulled a face. 'I think I've annoyed her. She was quite off earlier on, when she called me. She thinks I've gone all self-pity and helplessness. And I wasn't very nice to her, either.'

'I thought so too,' said Bonnie. 'To be honest. You should have been with us today.'

'Yeah, well...' Melanie wiped a finger below her good eye. 'It got to me, finding him like that. I couldn't even *think*. I just kept feeling his head, all wet and heavy on my legs. I'm going to feel it for the rest of my life.'

'You won't,' said Bonnie, through a full mouth. 'It just seems like that now.'

'Maybe. This afternoon I sort of woke up a bit and started to put my mind more to who might have done it. And I remembered a few things from the past week or two, in the hotel. Things that might have something to do with it.'

'So tell the police,' Bonnie urged her. 'They need all the help they can get, if they're going to find Ben.'

'I thought Ben was okay.'

'He probably isn't,' said Bonnie miserably. 'If he was, he'd have come home by now. The important thing is, if the police can get some idea of who killed Dan, they'll know who's taken Ben, as well. Same people. See?'

Melanie pulled out a chair and sat at right angles to Bonnie, drawing idle circles on the plastic-coated cloth. 'I don't know. I mean, about telling the police. It could get the hotel closed down. I have to think of my job, references, and all that. And if there's really something going on, they'll find it out without my help. They probably know it already, anyway. There's a woman who turned up yesterday. They'll have clocked her by now. She's been before.'

'Who is she?'

'I'm not sure, but she had something going on with Dan. Not *that* sort of thing. Business. Something dodgy. He pushed me out of the room before he'd talk to her.'

'When?'

'Last week. I thought she was making a booking for rooms or a party, but then I wondered if she was an inspector of some sort. You know – health and safety or food hygiene or something. Or even an Egon Ronay spy. But none of that really fitted. There was some understanding between them that they wanted kept secret.'

'I saw two men there today, who looked real villains.'

Melanie tossed her head impatiently. 'They're nothing to do with it. They'll be the Americans Dan was so worried about. They're in the hospitality industry, and I got the feeling they might be thinking about buying the hotel outright. Everybody was drilled in advance, making sure we impressed them.' She gave a hollow laugh. 'That turned out well, didn't it.'

Bonnie gave up trying to eat. 'They didn't look like that. More like Mafia bosses.'

'Well, they'd hardly hang around looking like that if they'd just killed Dan, would they? Trust me, they're not important.'

'I don't know how you can be so sure. They might be bluffing it out. That'd be the clever way to do it.' Bonnie heard Ben silently applauding her observations. It was exactly what he would think himself. 'And what about the other guests? That Mr Ferguson – the tall old chap – was at the police station just now with Moxo.'

'Was he? He's a sweetie, in his way. Just wants some peace and quiet. His wife died. He told me all about it on Monday. I didn't like him at first. He complained a lot when he arrived. But then he settled down and seemed happier. He even mellowed towards Gentian. Gave her a toffee.'

Bonnie's antennae quivered. 'Isn't that a bit ... you know? Old man giving little girl sweets.' She waggled her head meaningfully.

'No, no. My God! Gentian's not the sort of kid anybody could feel like that about. She'd scream the place down, for a start. And she probably knows exactly where to kick a man. She's a horrible kid, basically. Out of control, with a vicious streak. Likes to cause trouble. Ask Simmy – she saw what she was capable of, on Monday.'

Bonnie closed her eyes for a moment, wondering what had gone wrong for young Gentian to

229

earn her such a character analysis.

'Then there's the Lillywhites,' Melanie went on. 'He's a bully and she's a doormat. She won't even *breathe* until she's sure it's okay with him. I've never seen anything like it. Their room is weird, as well. Rila – she's one of the chambermaids – took me for a look. Everything was absolutely pristine. They'd made their bed, wiped down the bathroom, put everything straight. It was just the same as when they'd arrived, except the towels were damp. We didn't know what to make of it.'

'Force of habit, maybe,' Bonnie suggested. 'She's a boring little housewife who cleans everything every day. Even on holiday, she can't stop herself.'

'Mentally ill, if you ask me,' said Melanie.

'And the staff. What about the staff? Isn't it most likely that one of them had a grievance against Dan and took it to the extreme? Moxon says Ninian saw Ben in a car with a man and a woman. Could that have been the manager and his wife, maybe?'

'What?'

'Yes. Last night. Somewhere up Grasmere way, I think. Of course, Ninian's an idiot, so it's probably not right. If it is, then it's hard to square with the windscreen note and all that.'

Melanie smacked the table. 'Yes, Simmy said something about a note. You'll have to explain what it means.'

Bonnie gave a full account of the events in Hawkshead, except that she omitted any mention of Ben's game.

Melanie repeated part of it. 'So – he was in a shop with a woman, but she wasn't really keeping him there. The boy who wrote the note thought Ben was perhaps following her, without her realising?'

Bonnie rubbed her nose. 'He didn't quite say that. That was just what I thought might be going on.'

'It would make sense, though. So then maybe she caught him and was driving him somewhere. If Ninian can be believed, that is. Which he probably can't.'

Bonnie groaned. 'It's so awful not knowing where he is,' she burst out. 'I just want to go out there and find him.'

'He'll be all right,' Melanie said with certainty. 'It's all completely typical of him. Ninian saw some totally other boy in that car. How big a coincidence would it be, if it really *had* been him? That wouldn't happen. But he should come home tonight, all the same. It's not fair on his mother.'

'Or me!'

'Or you.'

Bonnie could see that Melanie was making a big effort to be thoughtful and considerate, biting back some sharper remarks. 'I know it's not the same, Mel,' she said. 'What happened to your Dan is as bad as it can get. But I can't help being scared for Ben. And I *want* him. I want to know I can phone him. There's just a horrible great gap where he's supposed to be.'

'What are the police doing to find him?'

'Bugger all. They haven't got a *clue*. They don't

231

even know if he really is missing, that's the trouble. Moxon seems to be half-asleep, and snappy with it. I don't think he's up to the job, really. He said himself he didn't know whether Ben's a hostage or what. They've asked everybody at the hotel a thousand questions and crawled around in the woods, and that's mostly it, I reckon. I mean – what else is there to do, when you think about it?'

'But Mr Ferguson was here at the station? Is that what you said? Why him?' Melanie frowned. 'Maybe he saw something yesterday. Maybe he overheard something.' She brightened slightly. 'He *is* always hanging about, listening to people. Lonely, you see. Nobody much bothers with him, poor old bloke.'

'I don't know,' sighed Bonnie. 'I didn't even remember who he was when he first came in with Moxo.'

'Why would you?'

'I told you – I was at the hotel today. I saw them all. Even that Gentian and her mother. Seems rather a hard-faced cow. The kid was behaving all right, though. Bored out of her skull, obviously.'

'How was it? At the hotel, I mean.' There was something wistful in Melanie's question. 'I've been thinking about it all day.'

'The guests were out on the lawn and the police were inside. They've got an incident room where they ask all the questions. I think that's just for today, though. They're all coming back here with the paperwork in the morning.'

'They'll be wanting to know everything about Dan's life. Don't they always do that when a person's murdered?'

Bonnie wrinkled her nose. 'Don't ask me. Why – does he have a wife tucked away somewhere? How old was he, anyway?'

'Thirty-one. He said he was married for a year or two and then divorced. The job took up practically all his time. A wife wouldn't see much of him.'

'Didn't stop him having one, though. You told us on Monday that he was smarmy. That's the word you used. Smarmy.'

'I know. Everybody's going to keep reminding me of that. It was just an act, all that. Really he was great. Really nice, you know?' Tears escaped down her cheek. The false eye, to Bonnie's fascination, appeared to lack the equipment for crying. 'I can't stop crying, every time I think about him,' Melanie sniffed. 'I *never* cry. It's ridiculous.'

'Don't mind me.'

The older girl laughed through the tears. 'I should have been there with you all today. I knew I should – but I couldn't make myself get there. It would be just like going to work, but absolutely different at the same time. I just kept hearing *Dan's dead, Dan's dead* in my head, on and on. And the way some of those cops looked at me yesterday wasn't nice. There I was, soaking wet and shivering, and nobody really bothered to see if I was okay. I hated the whole lot of them. I wanted a bomb to drop on the hotel and kill everybody in it. Even Simmy.'

Bonnie's heart lurched. 'Why, what did Simmy do?'

'Not much. Not for a while, anyhow. She just hung about, getting in the way. Once they'd got

Ben's message off her phone, they didn't need her any more, but she kept on sticking around looking tragic. I mean – it really isn't anything to do with her, is it?'

'She took Ben there in the first place.' Bonnie eyed Melanie carefully as she said this, aware that she was repeating something Simmy had said.

'Right. I told her it was all her fault, because of that.'

'You didn't really mean it. It's not so terrible.'

'She didn't like it.'

'I know. But she can be annoying. Sounds as if you think the same. Like a mother one minute, and just one of us the next. Why doesn't she get a life?'

'We *are* her life,' said Melanie. 'That's the trouble.'

Corinne interrupted their rather hollow laughter, opening the door and saying, 'Time to break it up, girls. I need to get in here.' She threw a frustrated glance at Bonnie's half-eaten cottage pie. 'Something wrong with it?' she demanded.

'Of course not.' Bonnie gave her a look that warned her not to play such a tired old game. 'It was scrumptious.'

'Right. Well, there's a whole lot more we can have warmed up tomorrow. And probably the next day as well.'

'Can't wait,' said Bonnie, thinking that the crispy edges of warmed-up cottage pie were really very appetising. People always thought that a person with anorexia took no pleasure in the flavours and textures of food, but they were wrong. Plenty of things got her saliva flowing. It was all the stuff that came with it that caused the difficulties.

'Going to the shop tomorrow, are you?' Corinne asked. Then she looked at Melanie. 'And the hotel? Or has normal life ceased altogether?'

Both girls went blank. It was a question neither of them had yet addressed.

'I see it has,' observed Corinne. 'Well, that won't do, will it?'

'You're as worried about Ben as we are,' Bonnie told her. 'So you can stop pretending.'

'All I want is for you to stay where I can see you. That's enough for me to worry about, just at the moment.' Corinne made a playful pretend cuff at Bonnie's head, successfully lightening the atmosphere as she did it.

'I'll go,' said Melanie. 'Sorry I put you off your supper.'

'Phone me tomorrow, then. We'll go and see Simmy and work out a plan.'

Melanie got up and Corinne groaned theatrically. 'And what's poor old Moxon going to think about that?' she asked.

Bonnie slept badly, dropping into tangled dreams for short spells and then surfacing to find that reality was no better. She could find no logical thread to follow, nothing that prompted her to explore a particular place, or approach a particular person. The previous day had been a model of clarity by comparison. All she could think of was that she should phone Melanie, and they would go together to the shop and try to construct a credible theory. That's what Ben would do. He

235

would draw a diagram with circles and arrows and neat remarks. He would list every known fact, and every individual involved. She recited some of these facts to herself – mysterious, smart woman at the hotel, with some link to Dan. Possible sighting by Ninian. No, no – that wasn't a fact, she told herself. That was a useless diversion, taking them away from the proper path.

Her next dream included trees and police tape that was tied around the ankle of the Gentian child. Somewhere behind her she could feel Ben, but something was preventing her from turning round to look. It was a rope made of plaited rushes, wound around her legs. The other end was in the middle of Esthwaite, anchored by something heavy that she knew would be horrific if she managed to drag it out of the water. When she pulled, the tape attached to Gentian tightened and the little girl screamed.

At last it was morning, sunshine streaming through her window, and the hoped-for enlightenment was as far away as ever.

Over breakfast, she tried to convince Corinne that she would keep her informed of every move she made. 'I'll be at the shop all day, anyway,' she said. 'You don't have to worry.'

Corinne merely sighed.

The shop was unlocked when she arrived shortly before nine. Simmy was in the back room constructing a colourful spray of flowers. 'Got to take these to Newby Bridge in a minute,' she said. 'It's for Moxon's mother-in-law. Can you hold the fort till I get back? I'll only be about forty minutes.'

'Okay.' It felt strange the way Simmy was carrying on as usual. 'No news about Ben, then?' she couldn't resist adding.

'Haven't heard a word.'

'So they haven't found him.' Again, the tightness, the inability to breathe, had her in its grip. He had been gone for two nights now. 'Where *is* he? What's *happened* to him?'

Simmy closed her eyes and said nothing. It was the most terrifying thing Bonnie had seen for ages.

'You think he's been killed?' she said, in a choked whisper. 'You do, don't you?'

'I don't think anything. My mind's paralysed. There's nothing we can do, except just wait. So let's get on with our jobs, and see what happens.'

Bonnie stared at her. 'You're joking, aren't you? You can't mean you're just going to carry on as usual and hope something turns up? That's like giving up altogether.'

'I just don't see—'

'Well, I do. Melanie agrees with me, as well. We've got to sit down and make a list of every single little thing, all the facts, and the people, the times and *everything*. We might see a pattern, or a clue or something. It's what Ben would do,' she concluded fiercely.

'You've spoken to Melanie?'

'She came round last night. She said she'd tried your mum, but she wasn't in. I don't know what good that would've done, anyhow.'

'None at all,' agreed Simmy listlessly.

There was a silence, before Simmy returned to her flowers. She glanced out of the small window,

237

looking onto the yard behind the shop. 'At least it's another warm day. He won't be feeling cold.'

'What? Why should he?'

'Well, he was hardly wearing anything. Shorts and a T-shirt. He left his rucksack in my van.'

Bonnie's head turned hot. 'Shorts?'

'Yes. His legs are quite brown, although he said some of it was dirt.'

'No, no. That Barnaby said he had trousers. They were wet around the bottom. You heard him.'

'Did I? I didn't notice.'

'Where would he get trousers from?'

Simmy was unbearably slow. 'I have no idea.'

'It *must* mean he was kidnapped. The people changed his clothes, in case the police were looking for someone in shorts. Did you tell them what he was wearing?'

'I don't think they ever asked.'

'This is *important*, Simmy. It's a massive great clue.'

'It could be, I suppose. So phone Moxon. I've got to go. They want the flowers by ten o'clock.'

Bonnie lost it. 'Go on, then. Can't risk losing any business. Can't let an old lady down. It's only my boyfriend who might be dead. What does that matter, compared to a bunch of flowers?'

Simmy pretended not to hear. She lifted the finished spray, wrapped cellophane around it, raised her chin and walked out of the back door without a word. Bonnie watched her employer climb stiffly into the van, and then dug in her pocket for her phone. Her hands were shaking, as she realised she had no idea of Moxon's number.

Melanie knew it, though. And Melanie arrived five minutes after Simmy left. 'It's here, look,' she said, riffling through Simmy's stack of business cards. 'You must have seen her using it by now.'

Bonnie shrugged. 'If I have, I forgot.' She grabbed the scrappy object from Melanie and started keying in the number. 'Oh bummer. My battery's going. Can I use your phone instead?'

'Why do you want to call him?' Melanie wanted to know, handing over her phone. Bonnie merely flapped at her to stay silent. Melanie efficiently produced a charger and connected Bonnie's phone to a power socket. 'Never know when you'll need it,' she muttered.

'Hello? Is that Inspector Moxon?' the younger girl asked, making an effort to sound calm and responsible. 'Good. It's Bonnie Lawson. Um ... I think I've found some evidence that Ben really has been kidnapped. That boy at the old school place yesterday said something about trousers. But Simmy says she's certain Ben was wearing *shorts*.'

She pulled a handful of her frizzy hair in frustration, as she listened to his reply. 'No, but *how* could he? He didn't have any other clothes. He wouldn't have bought some, would he?' More listening, but little more speaking, before she finished the call. 'He's not very impressed,' she said. 'Don't you think the man's a fool?'

'He's probably just trying to stop you going up there again and interrupting things.'

'Hmm,' said Bonnie.

Melanie didn't stay very long. 'I need to call old

239

Bodgett and find out where I stand. He might want me to go in today, if the police are packing up. Then I have to get the car off my idiot brother, before he takes it to Carlisle or Lancaster or somewhere. He's always doing that without telling me.'

A customer gave Melanie her opportunity to depart. Bonnie called after her, 'It was hardly worth coming, was it? Why'd you bother?'

The customer – a middle-aged man buying red roses, his face almost the same colour as the flowers – gave her a worried look. 'Oh, don't mind me,' she snapped. 'Do you want me to wrap some fancy ribbon round these?'

'No, thank you,' said the customer, almost throwing money at her.

She was tempted to throw it back, so foul had her temper suddenly become. What was the matter with the police that they could ignore such a clunking great piece of evidence? Moxon had sounded as if he was in a crowd of people all talking at once. His impatience with her had been offensive. She fumed for a further ten minutes, alone in the shop, before bringing her rage under a degree of control.

Her only hope was to go back to square one and think everything through all over again. Whatever his situation, Ben would try to send her a message. Or he would rely on her to work it all out from the facts available. The photos had to be significant. The anonymous legs encased in trousers, perhaps? But surely that picture had been taken during a struggle, not deliberately aimed? And before that, Ben could not have known he would be captured, chased, challenged – whatever it was that had happened to him. So in fact the pictures on his phone meant nothing. They told the police how and where Dan's body had been lying, but said not a thing about Ben himself.

Which left the bizarre events in the middle of Hawkshead. Here she really got into the momentum of her enquiry into the most likely explanation. With Simmy due back in ten minutes, she forced herself to think quickly. Her fingers twitched as she made mental notes, ticking off facts and suppositions, moving on to assumptions. Ben had taught her how this should be done. They had practised, laughing together, inventing little scenarios for each other.

And thus it all clicked into place, from one second to the next. All thanks to a second look at the assumptions everyone had been making.

Chapter Nineteen

Simmy, too, had time for some calmer reflection that Thursday morning, as she drove down to Newby Bridge with the flowers for Sue Moxon's mother. She had woken feeling depressed and useless. While expecting that she would be told if Ben was found, she could think of nobody she could phone for news. Not Helen, anyway. It would be a dreadful intrusion. When Bonnie arrived at work looking so wan and droopy, it was obvious that nothing good had happened.

Her advice about waiting passively for some-

241

thing to develop had been intended as mature and reasonable. Instead it came across as heartless and defeatist. No wonder Bonnie had been so angry with her. It was as if she had already written Ben off as gone for ever. How truly stupid she had been. When she got back, she would make amends.

The eighty-year-old looked closer to sixty, flinging the door wide and welcoming the flowers as if they were the one thing she had really wanted all her life. 'How absolutely *lovely* they are,' she cried. 'Thank you ever so much. Did you do them yourself? What a talent you have!'

The accolade went a long way to putting some backbone into her again. She had no reason to give up. She had all kinds of abilities and characteristics that had helped in past situations to identify killers. Why was she being so pathetic now?

She drove as fast as she dared back up to Windermere. Bowness was as usual thronged with holidaymakers, coaches, bicycles, straggling families with tiny toddlers. It was not possible to speed through Bowness. But she got through more quickly than usual and was into her little backyard again by five minutes to ten.

'Bonnie,' she called. 'I'm back. I want to say I'm sorry for what I said earlier on.'

But Bonnie wasn't there. The shop was coldly, implacably empty. A note was propped on the cash register.

'Gone to look for Ben. Don't worry about me.'

Simmy's immediate reaction was to distance herself. Let Bonnie do what she liked. The thwarted intention to apologise and try harder mutated into indifference. She had learnt before that anxiety and fear were self-limiting emotions, at least for her. The apparent permanency of her father's condition had been a surprise. Was it possible to sustain a worry for weeks on end? She couldn't see how. And fear was even more transitory. Fear for Ben's welfare had started as an acute and overwhelming state of mind. Now, only two days later, it was a much duller sensation. Was this a defect in her, then? Bonnie evidently thought so.

She reviewed earlier occasions where she had blundered into hazardous situations involving malice and physical injury. None of them had required deliberate independent action from Simmy. She had been told what to do by others, or been on some innocent project that turned nasty. If she had been given any choice, what would she have done? There had been moments when she had put another person's welfare before her own – moments she recalled with some relief. But she had seldom been decisive or shown much initiative. She was no eager amateur sleuth, as Ben very much was.

But Ben and Bonnie were little more than children. They were blundering about in a world of aggressive and unpredictable adults, where nobody knew for sure who might do something terrible. Detective Inspector Moxon himself appeared to be unprepared for what might happen. He did not feel like an adequate protector of vulnerable youngsters. In fact there was a definite suggestion

243

that he regarded these youngsters as part of the problem.

Nobody came into the shop for the next hour. That gave her a great deal of time for reflection along these lines. She was aware of a persistent vision of herself inside a bubble, idling in a flower shop while in the world outside there were people dying and hating and kidnapping, playing games and feeling several strong and painful emotions. She was increasingly sure that this was a culpable detachment on her part. But she was at the same time being ignored by everyone. They had pushed her to the sidelines, and given her no sort of role. Even Ninian was more involved than she was, with his dubious sighting of Ben. And her mother had been sought out by Melanie as a confidante, rather than Simmy herself. Corinne was probably driving Bonnie back to Hawkshead and Helen Harkness would be hassling the police to find her boy. They were all *doing* something, while she remained in her lonely, floral tower.

Why had Bonnie been so excited by the detail of Ben's clothes, she wondered. There were all kinds of explanation, surely, other than a sinister one. He might have friends in the area who'd lend him something warmer and agree to remain silent about seeing him. He might have encountered a walker on the fells and swopped his shorts for trousers. Anything was possible.

And yet, Bonnie knew Ben very well indeed. She was attuned to nuances and hints that nobody else could see. She had spent whole days with him since they first got together, and virtually every evening since Ben's exams had finished. In the enforced separations, they texted and phoned and almost seemed to commune by telepathy. If anybody could find Ben it was Bonnie. And perhaps the fact that his clothes had changed was all the inducement she needed to get started.

At eleven o'clock she was rescued from increasingly tangled and self-reproachful thoughts by Melanie, who came bursting through the door in just the same fashion as she had on Monday. It was déjà vu, in fact. It made Simmy smile, and for a moment persuade herself that it was indeed Monday, when there was nothing to worry about, rather than this increasingly unsettling Thursday.

'Can you drive me to Hawkshead?' Melanie panted. 'I can't get my car. Gary's gone off somewhere and isn't answering his phone.'

'Not really,' said Simmy. 'I'm here on my own. I can't just close the shop.'

'Yes you can. You've *got* to. Where's Bonnie?'

'Looking for Ben. Where do you think?'

Melanie pushed her fingers through her thick, dark hair. It was a gesture Simmy had not observed before. It indicated an unusually fraught frame of mind. 'It's a nightmare, Sim. He's been gone two days now. What if he's ... you know ... *dead?*'

'He's not. Of course he's not.' Again, Simmy felt old and tired and peripheral.

'He might be. Dan is, remember? It can happen.'

Simmy said nothing. It had all been said already.

'Anyway, I have to get to the hotel. Bodgett insists I turn up, unless I get a doctor's note to say I'm too ill.'

245

'They can't say that. That's not how it works these days.'

'Tell him that. He's going mad up there, from the sound of it. A group booking just came in. They're arriving tomorrow. Eight people.'

Simmy blinked. 'And you had all those rooms available? In July? At short notice?'

'People cancelled when they heard what had happened.'

'Did they? You'd think they'd be curious to see the place where there'd been a murder. Aren't the general public meant to be ghouls about that sort of thing?'

'Some are. But Mrs Bodgett had to phone them all and explain the situation, and some of them took the refund and bailed out. Mind you, they won't find anywhere else up here. They'll have to go to Norfolk or … Milton Keynes, instead.'

'And then they'll be sorry.'

'I doubt if they will. It's going to be pretty weird in Hawkshead. Somebody from an agency will have to do Dan's stuff, and that's going to be horrible, for a start. There'll be mistakes. Penny's never the most balanced person at the best of times. Any little thing can set her off.'

'She's the skeletal receptionist,' Simmy reminded herself. 'She did look rather flaky. If that's the word. Ditzy? Volatile?'

'She's amazingly good at the job, most of the time. Makes people feel special. I'm supposed to be learning from her how to do it.'

'I thought Dan was pretty good at it, too.' She remembered how subtly the man had dealt with the complaining guest, offering him a free drink.

'Although I did wonder whether the chap ended up feeling a bit of a fool.'

'What chap?'

'The husband of that couple. I forget their names. They're on the ground floor.'

'Lillywhite,' said Melanie. 'So – are you going to take me, or what?'

'Isn't there anybody else?'

'Who, for instance?'

'What about the bus? There's a perfectly good bus that goes every hour. Or the ferry. Why not use the ferry?'

'I just missed the bus. And the ferry takes ages. I can't face all that hassle.'

Simmy sighed. 'I suppose I'll have to take you, then. You'll never speak to me again if I don't.'

'Believe me, I wouldn't ask if I could avoid it. You've been really off, this past day or so, you know that? Anyone would think you didn't care about any of this stuff.'

'What stuff?'

'Dan and Ben, of course. See? That's what I mean. You act as if nothing's happened.'

'Stop it, will you. I can't take any more unfair criticism, when there's absolutely nothing I can do. I don't understand what people *expect*.'

Melanie was halfway out of the door. 'Where's your car?' she demanded. 'Where did you leave it this time?'

'By the library, I think.' Every morning Simmy had to find a space for her car in one of Windermere's streets, and every evening she had to try to recall exactly which street it had been.

'People expect you to care,' said Melanie as they

walked briskly along the main street. 'They want you to take an interest and share in their feelings.'

'I've done that. I've done it religiously since Tuesday. I'm worn out with it, because it doesn't seem to be helping anything.'

'I think you're tired because of the effort to keep a lid on it,' said Melanie. 'We all know how much you love Ben. I think you're scared stiff that he's been hurt or worse. So you just shut it all off, and try to carry on as usual.'

'Thanks very much,' Simmy muttered, fighting against tears. 'I didn't realise I needed a psychiatrist.'

'Don't be stupid. Just don't pretend everything's okay. It's not fooling anybody. It looks cowardly to me, if you want the truth.'

'Who said I wanted the truth? Look, there it is.' She pointed ahead, over the busy Lake Road, to a small white car just visible in a side street. 'I knew it was near the library.'

They drove in near silence, Simmy wrestling with a mass of wounded feelings and confusions. Melanie was right, of course. Reared in a family where emotions were all too readily expressed, where nothing felt safe and nobody could be relied upon, the girl had acquired a wisdom that Simmy could barely aspire to. Hadn't Ninian assured her that Melanie was essentially tough? Her traumatic encounter with a dead body might have rocked her back for a day or so, but it hadn't flattened her.

'You know, I'm more concerned about my job than anything else,' Melanie confessed, shortly before they reached Hawkshead. 'That makes me cold-blooded and selfish. So I'm not saying you're any worse than me. I didn't even mean to criticise. I just thought you were fooling yourself. Okay?'

'Yeah, it's okay. I am a coward. I know I am. I always have been.'

'You've got a right to be. After your baby died, I would think any danger of something terrible like that happening again would be scary. Terrifying. And Ben's a bit like your kid sometimes, isn't he? So that would count. If you see what I mean. It'd be like putting your hand into a fire, knowing already how much it'd hurt.'

'I do love Ben,' Simmy said huskily. 'But there are people with much more claim to him than I have.'

'It's not about claim, is it? That's not how it works. You're allowed to love him as much as you want. And you can be as panicked about him as the rest. They'll be glad if you are. It makes them feel better.'

'And what about you and Dan?'

'That's different,' said Melanie quickly. 'Absolutely different. The main thing about Dan is that if they catch his killer, they'll most likely find Ben at the same time.'

'I know. So I have to pull myself together and see if I can be of any use in catching the killer, then. Not that I see much scope for that. Whoever did it has probably left the area completely by now.'

'I doubt it. I doubt it very much. That'd be like confessing to it. And if they've got Ben, that'll just make it more difficult. Unless the people Ninian saw really were them, of course.'

'In that case, they were driving northwards on Tuesday evening. They could be in Inverness by now. Or anywhere.'

'So why would Bonnie be looking for him here?'

'Wishful thinking. Or maybe they were just taking him somewhere discreet to buy him a pair of trousers.'

'What?'

Simmy told the story, along with some of her theories as to how it might be significant. 'Bonnie got very excited about it,' she concluded.

'It can't have been him in the car, then,' said Melanie after such a long pause that they were driving up to the hotel before she spoke. 'Because he was in Hawkshead yesterday.'

'Doesn't follow. They might have brought him back again. Here you are, then. Should I come in with you, do you think?'

'Oh!' Melanie gave a startled laugh. 'I never gave that a thought. How will I get back again, if you leave me here?'

'Get the bus, like I said before. They run all evening.'

'Yeah,' said Melanie without enthusiasm.

'Or make Gary come for you.'

'Not likely. I'm not having him coming here the way he looks. Have you seen him lately? He's got a nose stud that went septic. His face is like a horror movie.'

'Yuk!'

'Yuk's not the word. He might have to have a whole piece cut out if it doesn't clear up soon. He'll be way weirder to look at than me, at that rate.'

Simmy knew better than to offer glib reassurance, even though Melanie's eye was not weird. Most people barely even noticed it.

'I'll hang about then, I suppose,' she offered. 'How long will you be? You're not here for a full shift, are you?'

'Well ... I might be. Let me go and ask. If I'm on until the evening, could you come back for me after work, maybe?'

'Try to find someone to take you to the ferry. That's the easiest way.'

'There won't be anybody.' The girl forced a smile. 'That's why it was so simple just to stay over with Dan.'

'I'll wait while you go and see what they want you to do,' she said. 'No rush.' She tried not to think of people trying the door of the shop and finding it locked. The lost business would be minimal, she assured herself. It was a warm, dry day. They'd all be walking up Wansfell and Kirkstone and the Old Man of Coniston. Nobody would want to buy flowers on a day like this.

Without thinking, she got out of the car along with Melanie. It would be too warm to sit inside the vehicle for long. 'I'll just potter about in the garden,' she said.

It was forty-eight hours since she had last been there, or a bit less. Moxon had kept her waiting for much of Tuesday afternoon, she remembered. Her time had been wasted. Her presence had been overlooked and forgotten. The only person to refer to her part in what had happened was Bonnie, and she probably blamed Simmy for taking Ben there in the first place. It was little

251

wonder she felt so remote from everything. It was obviously everyone else's opinion as well. Melanie was using her as a free taxi, and nobody else was thinking about her at all.

The day was turning very warm, which was sure to get people talking in terms of a heatwave. Three nice days in a row was something to be celebrated. Meandering around the side of the hotel she got a panoramic view of Esthwaite and the dozen or so small boats strewn upon the surface. The water looked utterly calm, more like a pond than a lake. The idea that the most extreme act of violence had been committed on its banks was almost inconceivable.

'Doesn't seem possible, does it?' said a man behind her.

She turned to face the bearded hotel guest she had first seen on Tuesday. 'Ferguson,' he said. 'Forgive me if I startled you.'

It was a line from a bygone time, probably before even this elderly gent was born. It made her smile. 'Persimmon Brown,' she replied. 'I'm the florist. I saw you earlier in the week.'

'I remember. And you found the body of the unfortunate Mr Yates. It surprises me to see you here again, when the place must hold such unpleasant associations. But of course, life goes on, and there will be more flowers to arrange.'

There was a slight foreignness to his accent and something strange about his tone. 'You've stayed on, then,' she said. 'I gather quite a lot of people left early, and others have cancelled their stay here.'

'I believe in getting my money's worth,' he said

252

gravely. 'And I have not found myself particularly incommoded by the dramatic events. In fact, I have been a model citizen and conveyed to the police what I hope has been useful information.'

'Really?'

He made a rueful face. 'It seems I blundered a little. I reported a conversation I overheard between two guests, which appeared to suggest suspicious behaviour. On closer examination, it turns out that I was mistaken.'

'I'm sure they were grateful to you, all the same.'

'I doubt if they were. They were obliged to bring me back here from Windermere, after my interview, and that was inconvenient.'

'So why not interview you here? Wasn't there an incident room set up for that very purpose?'

'They did not wish to draw attention to the fact that I was giving information. I like to think that was due to a concern for my safety.' He shook his head. 'The whole experience was profoundly interesting, I must say.'

Simmy was confused. It seemed to her that Moxon could easily have asked this man to repeat the overheard conversation as part of routine interviewing of staff and guests. Taking him away in a police car, and then bringing him back the same way, would surely attract considerably more attention. She could hear Ben's ghostly voice, hypothesising that this had been Moxon's intention all along. 'Flushing them out,' he would say. 'Making them nervous that old Fergy had seen something he shouldn't.'

'Who were the two guests?' she asked him. 'The ones you overheard.'

253

'Two men, who have American accents, but look Hispanic to me. That is, of Mexican or Central American origin. They were staying here, looking very conspicuous, but this morning I hear they've gone again.' He worked his shoulders irritably. 'I only wish everyone else would do the same. That Appleyard woman and her child are a constant aggravation, and the Lillywhite couple show no signs of enjoying themselves at all. They stay out all day long, and then come back with stony faces, not saying a word. Definitely not my idea of a holiday.'

'Did that smart woman come back? The one who was here on Tuesday – do you remember? She was in a bad mood because nobody was attending to her.'

Mr Ferguson brightened. 'Oh yes! She comes every day, but doesn't stay. Her name is Sheila. I think she's trying to organise some event in the big room on the first floor. The one with balconies overlooking the mere. And nobody ever has time to discuss it with her. I have her down as some kind of businesswoman, offering seminars in how to be more successful, hoping to hire the room over the winter.'

'But it would have been Dan Yates's job to sort it all out with her?'

'So it would seem. And Miss Todd has been absent, too. I imagine she might have managed to agree some details.'

'How do you know all this?' she blurted.

'Simply by sitting behind a newspaper in the lounge for an hour every morning. I have heard a great many conversations that way.'

She laughed. 'No wonder Inspector Moxon wanted to talk to you,' she said. 'He must think you're very useful.'

'And I disappointed him,' sighed the old man. 'It was ever thus.'

'What do you think of Penny, the receptionist?' Simmy asked, after a quick glance around. It belatedly occurred to her that it could be embarrassing if this conversation were to be overheard.

'Far too thin for comfort,' he responded. 'But much less unbalanced than she appears at first sight. All she wants is to ensure the guests have their needs met, and she does a sterling job in that respect. I have learnt very little about her personal life, but I detect a severe degree of trouble.'

'She must have anorexia, surely,' said Simmy, thinking of Bonnie.

'I fancy not. I have an impression of a physical disorder. In fact, I should not be surprised if she has a lethal tumour, and knows her time is limited.'

'Heavens! Would she still be working if that was the case?'

'If that *were* the case, then she might well welcome the distraction from her woes,' he said, reminding Simmy powerfully of her father's insistence on the correct use of the subjunctive case.

'Do you think she's in pain?' The idea was growing increasingly alarming. 'How sure are you about this?'

He waved a hand, sweeping her questions aside. 'Pure supposition,' he said. 'Think no more about it.'

What an annoying man, she thought. Eavesdropping, gossiping, jumping to conclusions. Sneaking up on her the way he had, and forcing her to talk to him. Thinking about it, she wasn't sure she could believe a word he'd said.

'Well, I must get on,' she said firmly. 'I just came over here for a look at the view.'

He bowed his head and gave her a look that suggested he was unconvinced of her veracity. She wished she could find Moxon and ask him for his opinion of Mr Ferguson. Something about him was decidedly disconcerting. Perhaps he knew who had killed Dan – even the whereabouts of the missing Ben.

Perhaps, she thought wildly, he was a murderer and a kidnapper, posing as a harmless old holiday-maker.

Chapter Twenty

Melanie was coming out of the front entrance when Simmy returned to her car. 'It's okay,' the girl called. 'You can go. I'll be here until nine this evening. He wants me to do some extra time, to make up for yesterday.' Simmy waited for the resentment that this would surely occasion, but it never came. 'It's fair enough, I suppose,' came the surprising comment.

'Hardly,' she protested. 'You were in a state of shock.'

'I could have worked if I'd wanted to. Anyway, it's okay now. I'll have plenty to do.'

'I've been talking to Mr Ferguson. He's a very odd man, don't you think?'

Melanie looked blank. 'Not that I've noticed. What did he say?'

'Lots of things. That woman in the suit – did you see her on Tuesday? Apparently she's trying to arrange some sort of weekend in the big room upstairs. Maybe you can do that for her? She's annoyed, he says, because there was nobody to deal with her.'

Melanie's blankness deepened. 'What smart woman? I have no idea what you're talking about.'

'Maybe you didn't see her. She was trying to get some attention on reception in the middle of all the chaos after we found Dan. He said she's been back every day, and still hasn't got any satisfaction. You wouldn't think it could be all that difficult,' she finished.

'It might, if she wants rooms and food and equipment. Somebody would have to sit down with her and go through every detail, with costs and so forth. That room holds a hundred people. If they all want feeding, that's a big deal.'

'He thinks she's some sort of businesswoman, wanting to run seminars.'

Melanie frowned. 'What did she look like?'

'Very well groomed and uptight. She had high heels and a dazzlingly white blouse under a blue jacket. A bit like an accountant, I thought. Or an insurance assessor.'

'Oh, her. I know who you mean. She's been coming in and out, talking to Dan about something confidential, for a while now. Fancy you seeing her as well. She's called Sheila something.'

257

'Yes.'

'Well, she can't be important, if she keeps coming back like that. Ben would call her a red herring.'

Simmy smiled. 'He would,' she agreed. 'So I can go, then, can I? You'll be able to get the bus back, I assume.'

Melanie's expression was resigned. 'If I have to.' Then she frowned. 'Why didn't Ben get the bus back to Bowness on Tuesday, instead of asking you to fetch him? If he'd done that, we'd have none of this business now. Or less of it, anyway,' she added with a flinch at her own forgetfulness. 'I mean, Dan would still be...'

'Ben said there was some problem with the bus. They'd cancelled the next one, for some reason. And I was coming here anyway, so it all worked nicely. Or we thought it did.'

Without warning, the banked-up anxiety about the boy's fate came flooding through. 'Oh, Mel – what can possibly have happened to him? After all this time – where on earth *is* he? We're just carrying on, when he might be hurt or even...'

'Dead. We've got to say the word. Dead, dead, dead. It sounds better if you keep saying it. Like cancer. It's daft to be afraid of a word.'

Melanie was crying. Simmy's throat was thick. They clasped each other in an instinctive hug, like schoolgirls on the TV news after losing one of their classmates. Simmy hoped it was making them both feel better.

Then Melanie pushed them apart. 'I've got to *work*,' she said. 'The hotel's got to get itself back on track, and without Dan nobody's sure what to

258

do. I know I've only been here a month, but I have my uses. Oh – and can you do some more flowers tomorrow?'

'What? Did the manager tell you to say that?'

'I asked him and he said of course. We can't let standards drop now. He wants the weekend to really make a splash. I've got a list of websites to contact, to offer some special deals. I'm doing Facebook and Twitter and the rest, as well. We're really fighting back.'

'Even before they know who killed Dan,' murmured Simmy. 'Seems a bit hasty.'

'It's *business*, Sim. If you drop the ball, you never get it back again.'

It was good to see Melanie so energised, Simmy told herself. All her talents were firing up again, after the single day of apathy and self-pity. Hadn't Ninian predicted something of the sort? And yet there was something heartless about it, too. Dan would be replaced, the evidence of his death covered over and forgotten. Unless, perhaps, it turned out that a prominent and trusted member of the hotel staff had killed him, she thought sourly. Then they might have a much harder struggle before they could redeem themselves.

'All right. I'll go and open the shop again,' she said, feeling heavy and reluctant. 'And order more flowers for tomorrow.'

'I'll call you about that,' said Melanie. 'Thanks for the lift.'

Simmy drove slowly down the winding driveway and onto the road into Hawkshead. There were groups of cheerful holidaymakers everywhere she

259

looked. Bare arms and legs, stout walking boots, floppy hats and eager dogs. There was a sense that all these people had been released from a long, cloudy wait, poised to leap outside the moment the sun appeared. They had snatched up their flimsiest clothes and rushed outdoors to make the most of it, because it could surely not last more than another few days. To Simmy's eyes, there was something faintly grim about it.

The prospect of returning to the empty shop with no Ben dropping in, no customers, no urgent tasks, was unappealing. Bonnie was off on her own wild adventure; her parents were struggling with troubles that she could not really help with and Moxon had forgotten her. Loneliness had been a lurking enemy ever since her baby died and deprived her of the reliable company she had expected to enjoy for the rest of her life. Her husband had somehow faded away, along with little Edith. The cowardly, almost shameful, return to the bosom of her parents had been an escape from the anguish of that fatally ruined life as a wife and potential mother.

But she had no wish to go into Hawkshead again, either. What good would that do? She didn't know anybody there, and was in no mood to sit eating a solitary lunch at one of the cafés. They were probably all full, anyway. She would skirt the little town along its southern edge and retrace her route via the outskirts of Ambleside to Windermere. Except she found herself mistakenly heading southwards again, on the wrong side of Lake Windermere, the signs indicating the Sawreys. Crossly she pulled onto a grass verge and tried to work out where she'd gone wrong. The area was such a maze of little roads, none of them direct. Hawkshead was on an ancient crossroads where you could head for Coniston, Furness, Ambleside and the Sawreys – none of them quite where a novice might expect them to be. No straight lines or level plains. Settlements scattered at random, with the bodies of water forcing lengthy detours – it all led to confusion. She knew she should have acquired a satnav long ago, but somehow it felt like a weakness. She could read a map – but the map was in her van. She could follow directions and work out the points of the compass from the position of the sun. But in the middle of the day this was not so easy. For a painful moment she very badly wanted her father and his competent good sense.

The only thing to do was to turn round and try again. There would be a sign to Ambleside that she had missed.

She awkwardly turned in the little road and started back. Then, glancing through a gateway she noticed two people sitting on a large granite rock close to a tree, in earnest conversation. One had a very distinctive halo of the palest blonde hair. And the other, for a heart-stopping moment, might have been Ben Harkness. With a lurch, she braked and took a closer look. It was certainly Bonnie, but her companion was a younger, smaller boy than Ben. It was, in fact, the boy who had acted as Ben's messenger the previous day.

Without even thinking, she was out of the car and pushing at the closed gate in seconds. 'Bonnie!' she called. 'What are you doing?'

The girl looked up slowly, her expression hard to read at such a distance. She did not stand up, and with a gesture, kept the boy where he was, too. 'Leave me alone,' she called. 'I'm perfectly all right. Stop following me.'

Simmy hesitated. She had no right to force herself onto the girl. She showed no sign of distress and there wasn't the slightest hint of danger. But neither could she simply drive away and leave her. Something dangerous might well be about to happen. If she was searching for Ben, then she could get involved with violent and frightening people.

'I can't just go and leave you,' she shouted back.

'Yes you can. How did you find me, anyway?'

It was too complicated to explain at top volume across half a field. She pushed again at the gate, which was firmly chained shut.

'No!' yelled Bonnie. 'I don't want you now. Go away, Simmy. There's nothing useful you can do. I'll phone you later on.'

'Well, make sure you do,' yelled Simmy, and went back to her car.

She found she was shaking when she tried to start the ignition. The shock of seeing Bonnie and then being rejected so uncompromisingly had been severe. The indecision as to what, if anything, she ought to do; the fear that Bonnie was walking into a situation she couldn't hope to manage, all combined to render her helpless. Perhaps she should call Corinne, as a first step. She would have a better idea of what Bonnie might do and the best way to keep her safe. It would be a sensible way to pass the buck, at the very least.

But she did not have Corinne's number in her phone. Somewhere at the shop it was noted down, but she'd never had to use it.

She fought hard to think logically. Bonnie knew Ben best. She had been resourceful enough to ensure she had the Barnaby boy's number as well as giving him hers. She had once again got herself to Hawkshead from Windermere – most probably on the bus that Melanie had missed, unless she'd hitched again like the day before. The bus took almost an hour, where a vehicle could do it in a third of the time. Part of Simmy was repeating *Good luck to her, then.* Let her do everything she could to find her beloved, because it didn't seem as if anybody else would manage it.

But she, Simmy, could not persuade herself to simply drive away and leave these youngsters to their fate. If Bonnie wanted her to go away, she would remove herself from sight. But she would not leave Hawkshead. She would perhaps find an inconspicuous spot to park and walk quietly back to keep a protective eye on them. Only then did she think to wonder where Barnaby's family was.

Chapter Twenty-One

Most of Simmy's guesswork had been accurate, as far as it went. Bonnie had flown out of the shop at ten minutes to ten, with the intention of catching the Hawkshead bus. What it lacked in speed, it made up for in reliability and anonymity. That was, if it hadn't been cancelled, as sometimes happened.

It was not cancelled, and the moment she was safely tucked down in a seat near the back, she made the phone call, hoping it had enough charge for what she needed.

'I need your help. Can you meet me somewhere?' she asked, after introducing herself. 'How about outside the National Trust shop in forty-five minutes?'

'My parents want us to walk up the Furness Fells,' he objected. 'I'll never be able to get out of it.'

'What time?'

'About two minutes from now.'

'Are you walking from the village or driving some of the way?'

'Driving, they finally decided after about two hours' discussion. They're making a detour around Esthwaite, luckily, and then heading for some car park in a wood, halfway down the lake on the other side.'

'Bugger it,' said Bonnie. Fortunately there were no other passengers within earshot, who might remember a pretty young girl using unladylike language. She did not want to be remembered. She thought hard for a few seconds. 'Listen. There's a place called Colthouse, which would be on the way – I think. Can you somehow get them to stop there, for a look at the old Quaker Meeting House and its burial ground? Say it's for a school project or something. You could even try looking for Priest Pot – though you won't find it.'

'What's Priest Pot?'

264

'A pond. Say you heard it's got rare newts in it. Are you doing biology?'

'Not really. It's all part of science.'

'Never mind. They won't know, will they? You'll think of something. There's a house that Ann Tyson lived in – ask your B&B woman about it. It'll be interesting.'

'Yeah, I might manage that. Tomorrow's the last day, so we're trying to catch up with everything we've missed so far. My mum's quite into the historical stuff.'

'Good. Well, I'll be there as soon as I can. Call me in half an hour and tell me where you are. Stall them, okay. Go for a long crap or something. Isn't that what boys do?'

His response was a comical snort of embarrassed admiration. He was only fourteen, Bonnie reminded herself. You couldn't say anything without causing embarrassment. But he'd be hooked by this time, intrigued and flattered at being needed by a girl so much older than himself. She had to talk to him, preferably face to face. But if it came to it, she could get the essentials over the phone. The main thing was to be in Hawkshead and take it all from there.

The bus was prompt and she descended into a sunny spot between the two big car parks. The Old School where she had met Barnaby was close by. Across the road to the south were the campsites and water meadows that led to Esthwaite. The chances of actually catching up with the boy and his parents were obviously slender, but his phone call, made at the precise moment she had requested, had brought good news. 'It worked like

265

magic,' he said. 'Mum's suddenly into Wordsworth big time, and the story about him staying in a house down here got her going. We're there now, and she's googling like crazy, trying to work it all out. Dad's gone into a coma, he's so bored.'

'What about your sister?'

'She's looking for caterpillars. She's always looking for caterpillars.'

'Tell her there are rare ones by the pond. Have you found the pond yet?'

'It's the other side of the road somewhere, according to the map, but we can't see it. Dad says it's all an illusion.'

'Where's the car?'

'Beside the Quaker place, top end of a farmyard. There's nowhere else to park, but I'm not sure it's allowed to leave it there.'

'Okay. Give me ten minutes and I might catch you. I'll phone when I'm close.'

'Great.'

Now she almost ran along the road towards Colthouse, holding the image of how it all fitted together in her head. All you had to do from Hawkshead was take the road to the Wrays, and then veer off to the minimal settlement of Colthouse. It was no distance at all.

There was a derelict Dutch barn that she hadn't noticed the day before, but everything else was as she remembered. At the upper end of the farmyard, she saw a white car, parked all alone by a stone wall. She phoned the boy again and he answered instantly.

'I'm here,' she said. 'I can see your car.'

'We're coming back to it now. Dad put his foot

down and said we were wasting time. What do you want me to do?' She heard an adult female voice speaking sharply, asking the boy who he was speaking to. 'It's the girl from yesterday, Mum. She wants to ask me something.'

'No!' Bonnie cried. 'Don't say it's me.'

'Too late.'

'Well, don't say I'm here, okay. Can you get away for a bit?'

'How?'

She realised his parents were now listening to every word he said. 'How's your gut today? Not loose at all?'

The sound he gave was familiar. 'You're obsessed,' he accused her.

'No, I'm not. But say you've got to disappear behind a tree and you'll catch them up. No need to worry, but it's pretty desperate. That sort of thing.'

'They won't believe me. I never have any bother in that department.'

'There's always a first time. Look, there's a gate right here and a field with some rocks and a lot of rushes in it. I'm climbing over the gate, and waiting for you. Just do your best, okay?'

She waited barely five minutes, before sighting him vaulting the gate in a manner very far from that of a boy in the throes of gastroenteritis. His family were nowhere in sight. He cantered across the grass towards her, grinning broadly. 'Tasha found a painted lady or something, and wants to take it home. She's having one of her meltdowns.'

'Did you put her up to it?'

'Sort of. She got the idea I needed to get away.

267

She can be quite good like that – sometimes.' He shook his head in wonderment at the idea that a small sister might have her uses.

'So, let's make this quick. That boy in the shop yesterday. Describe him. Every detail. Clothes, hair, accent. Everything. Plus exactly what he said to you.'

'Okay. Wait a minute.' He closed his eyes unselfconsciously, and Bonnie had a fleeting thought that he and Ben would very likely get along famously together. 'Light-brown hair, and bluey-coloured eyes. No glasses. Ordinary accent. Thin sort of lips. Must have been sixteen, maybe. Not very tall. Jeans, with mud on them. Don't remember his shirt. Something with sleeves. He didn't say much – just that he had a hunch his girlfriend might be in the town, in a blue Citroën, and if I could find it, would I put a note on it to say he's okay.'

'That's great,' she said, trying to force a smile. 'It wasn't Ben,' she added. 'No way is that Ben Harkness. Ben would have added something about Wordsworth or a certain date, to make sure I knew it was him. If there was nothing like that, then I know for sure it was somebody else. Sent by his kidnappers,' she concluded with an expression of pain.

'Wow! So where's your Ben, then?'

'That's the big question. The boy you saw must have known where Ben is, and who's got him. They must have extracted my name and car number from him. Unless they're people who know us already.' She frowned. 'And that can't be right.'

'I don't understand what's going on,' he complained. 'Can't you tell me?'

'Have you got time?'

He shrugged. 'They'll have to wait for me, won't they?'

'It hit me this morning,' she explained all over again, repeating it more for her own benefit than his. 'That note you wrote. If it really had been Ben you saw, he would have found some way to give me a proper message. As it was, it didn't say anything that meant anything. And then Simmy said he was wearing shorts, and Ninian said he saw him in a car – and I knew for sure it was some other person altogether. Someone *pretending* to be Ben, to stop the police searching for him. I mean – how clever was that! It almost worked.' She gave him a look, partly apologetic. 'At first, I thought you'd made it all up, because you were working with the kidnappers. But the people you were with were obviously your real family, and they'd never let themselves be seen if they were part of a gang. And then I called the number you gave me, and it was really you, so that clinched it. You were just an innocent pawn.'

'Pawns can be useful,' he said. 'But I still don't get what's happening. Has he really been kidnapped? For absolute real?'

'It's the only explanation. If he was tracking the killers, or doing his own investigation, he'd have contacted me by now. So he can't. He's a prisoner... Oh, damn it.'

She'd seen Simmy Brown standing at the gate, and Simmy Brown had obviously seen her. 'I'll make her go away,' she muttered to Barnaby and proceeded to do exactly that. It gave her a pang to watch her friend and employer leave in confusion, but there was no time for conscience. 'Now,' she pressed on. 'The woman. What did she look like? How do we know whether she really was connected to the boy, or just an innocent shopper?'

He closed his eyes again. 'He seemed nervous of her. He kept looking at her to see if she was watching us. She was quite old, but not *ancient*. Bit older than my mum, maybe. Trousers and a sort of greeny-coloured top, I think. She had a shopping bag. Sorry – that's all I can remember.'

'That's okay. You've been really great. I hope you won't get into trouble. You'd better go now. Your car's just over there.'

'Yes, I know,' he said with dignity.

'Okay. So, I'll call you later, let you know how it's going. If you like,' she added.

He got up from the uncomfortable stone perch. 'Don't forget that pawns can be useful,' he said again.

'You've been really useful already. Thanks, Barnaby.'

He beamed at her. 'You're great, you know. Clever. Brave. He's a lucky bloke, your Ben.'

'Thanks,' she muttered through clenched teeth. It would be stupid to start crying now, she told herself fiercely.

She needed to *think*. Ben had done a lot to teach her how this could be most constructively accomplished. Go back to first principles. Start with known facts, putting them together to make a firm picture. Add some hypotheses and test them. Do not make assumptions. Do not believe witnesses unless they have proof. Memory is faulty and people have their own motives for saying what they do.

This led her back to the hotel and the killing of Dan Yates. She sat on the cold granite and checked her thinking off on her fingers, step by step. Firstly, from Melanie's description of the hotel, the staff were all decent people, working cheerfully as a team, sharing in the fruits of the place's success. While this might not be entirely reliable, it produced a strong impression that the people to focus on were much more likely to be guests, rather than staff.

Next, there had to be at least two of them involved. It took two to lift Dan's body over that fence. Anybody could see that. It would almost certainly take two to spirit Ben away without his being able to leave a clue or raise a rumpus. He wasn't especially strong, but he was agile and resourceful and he knew some useful judo moves. He would have realised instantly that his attackers had already killed Dan, and be fully aware of the danger he was in. Here, she quailed. Ben had never before found himself in direct jeopardy, even though he had been face to face with people capable of murder in Coniston. Would he lose his nerve, collapsing into jelly and begging for mercy? Not impossible, she had to admit. If fear paralysed him, then she might not be able to rely on his brainpower. It might explain the total silence since Tuesday. It made it all the more desperately urgent to find and rescue him.

She had seen some of the hotel guests for herself, the previous day. The harassed mother of

271

young Gentian, for a start. Did she perhaps have a husband and son as well? A husband to help her lift the dead Dan into the lake, and a son to masquerade as Ben? It would be good cover, pretending to be a single mother of a demanding girl child, when really there was far more going on.

That led her to the question of motive. Why would any of the guests have any reason to kill Dan in the first place? *Impossible to know at this stage,* she heard Ben's ghostly voice admonishing her. Motive was not a useful element, he had told her, until much later on.

So, what about the bizarre business with the note on the car? How had the three-link chain of Ben/boy in muddy jeans/Barnaby ever come to be? How had Barnaby been selected for the task of leaving the note? It seemed an incredibly long shot, even to guess that Bonnie and Corinne would be in Hawkshead just at the right time. There had to be inside knowledge, somebody spying on her and passing information to Ben's captors. She thought again about the guests. That Mr Ferguson, for one. He had been taken to Windermere police station, which suggested he was of some significance. Could he have told the criminals that she was in Hawkshead? And what about the weird couple with the stupidly tidy room? And the two foreign-looking men who had shown up so suddenly? Could the whole lot of them be in it together? Did they want to take over the hotel, and decided a nasty murder in the grounds would be just the thing to reduce the value of the business?

Motive again, she chastised herself. Stick to observable facts. Like that big room with the balcony. She had seen someone there, hadn't she? Someone who gave an impression of furtiveness. What *was* that room? Why wasn't it used more regularly? What was in it? She should ask Melanie, check there was nothing important she ought to know about it. She'd intended to do that already, but never got the chance.

She continued with her internal catechism. Where would Ben have been taken? If the kidnappers wanted to carry on as normal, in the eyes of the world, they'd have to tie him up and leave him alone for long periods of time, while they went about as usual. Especially if they were registered as guests in a hotel. That meant it would need to be somewhere close by. Somewhere they could come and go without being conspicuous.

She could feel herself inching towards a theory. Better than a hypothesis, according to Ben, a theory made use of known facts and constructed a viable picture that could be tested. She went over it carefully, finding new details to support it.

She had to speak to Melanie. Then she had to go into Hawkshead and summon all the courage and quick-thinking she could manage. She must be prepared for anything. And she had to do it all by herself.

Chapter Twenty-Two

Melanie answered after several long moments. 'Yes? Bonnie? What do you want?'

'Three questions. It won't take long.'

'Where are you? What are you doing?'

'Never mind. Where are *you?*'

'At work. Busy.'

'Okay. Listen. First – what's that big room at the hotel used for? The one upstairs.'

'Groups. It's kept clear, with just chairs and the equipment for presentations. People rent it at weekends mostly, in the winter. We can do banquets in there if we have to, as well. There's a shiatsu woman who does special sessions in there sometimes. She brings lots of mattresses and cushions.'

'Is it fully booked for this winter?'

'No way. In fact, nobody's used it for the last month. Dan was trying to get somebody for October, but I don't know who.'

'Thanks. Second question – is the front door locked at night? What happens if a guest comes back at midnight? Is the reception desk manned round the clock?'

'No, it's not. There's a keypad by the door and we give them the code. They can let themselves in and out, as they want.'

'Right. And what happens after breakfast? I mean – do they have to go out so the room can be cleaned, or can they stay in all day if they want?'

'God, Bonnie – haven't you ever stayed in a hotel? They put a "Do Not Disturb" sign on the door and nobody goes in. They've paid for the room – they can do what they like, when they like.'

'I haven't, actually,' said Bonnie quietly.

'Sorry. Is that everything, then? Am I allowed to ask what this is all about?'

'Not yet. Just one more thing – are there any rooms on the ground floor? Guest rooms, I mean.'

'Yes. Two. The Lillywhites have got one, and the other's empty at the moment.'

'Thanks, Mel. That's great. Bye now.'

'No, but–' Too late. Bonnie had ended the call with a decisive press of her thumb.

None of Mel's answers had done anything to dent her theory, but neither had they confirmed it in any concrete way. The rest was up to her. With a deep breath she stood up and went back to the gate. Climbing over it was easy enough, although she wobbled slightly at the top. She had never been good at gymnastics or athletics or any of the sporty stuff they forced you to do at school. She generally ended up bruised and sore and resentful.

It took six minutes to walk back to the centre of Hawkshead, trying her best to look purposeful and old enough to have business to attend to. With every step, she had a new thought, ranging from a recitation of virtually everything Ben had ever said to her, to an awareness that there were no school-age children anywhere to be seen. Barnaby and his family must have stood out a mile, taking their kids away in term time. If the muddy-jeans guy had been on the lookout for a schoolboy, he would have had very slim pickings. And who else but a younger boy would have done as he asked? No adult would have gone along with it. What would he have done if no suitable kid came along?

Do it himself, of course. So why hadn't he, anyway? Yet again, she rehearsed the whole peculiar scenario. Maybe that had been the plan, but the appearance of Barnaby had given him a new idea. If he was the son or brother of the kidnappers, he'd want to stay in the shadows, doing nothing worthy of notice. Had he assumed that the holidaying family would disappear before anyone could question them? Was it a major glitch in the plot that Bonnie had actually spoken to the boy? Surely it must be. She was merely intended to read the note and stop worrying about Ben. So did they *know* she'd met Barnaby? Had they been watching? Was that even possible? The idea made her shudder.

She was passing the upmarket gift shop with its pricy china, and taking a left turn into the crooked little square at the heart of the town. The National Trust shop was one of the few things she remembered from her last visit to this part of Hawkshead, some years earlier. She looked around, trying to work out directions and landmarks that she and Ben had used in the game. Everything had been on paper, gleaned from Google Earth and maps. The buildings were accurately positioned, but the reality was unsettlingly different. Everything was much closer together than she had realised. The road surfaces, the sounds from the pub, the way the shadows fell on this sunny July day – none of them had been factored into their embryonic storyboard. Ben had talked about the need to make an actual film of the place when it came to the final stages. He had admitted to a lack of detailed knowledge as to how that was done, airily dismissing it as a technical issue that could be delegated to somebody else when the time came. Bonnie had been more than happy to go along with that approach. For her, the interest was in the history and the secret messages and the way the whole thing fitted together.

The very heart of the village was comprised of a big, oddly shaped three-storey building that was actually two separate establishments. They were connected by a single wall, and one was an abandoned bookshop. Its windows were blank and the two doors firmly rendered impassable with padlocks and stout chain. It did nothing for the look of the place and she found herself fantasising about opening some sort of shop there herself. Something artistic, brightly coloured and enticing. Like Persimmon Petals in Windermere, but far larger and more ambitious. And in keeping with the rest of Hawkshead, she thought ruefully, as she recognised two art galleries close by. There were people sitting at tables on the pavements, just a few feet away, laughing and boasting about their good sense in coming here when the sun was shining.

She crossed the square and examined the shop again from a different angle. The upstairs windows were grimy. It must have been empty for ages. What a waste. She meandered a little way along the pavement, in front of the well-remembered National Trust shop, until another face of the empty shop was visible and tilted her head back to look at the upper windows. She saw it immediately. Etched into the grease and dust of a high window were four numerals. Impossible to miss; impossible to mistake their import.

1780

It stood bright and clear in the sunny July day. And only one person in the entire universe would have written those numbers in that way.

'I've found him!' she muttered aloud, scanning the window feverishly for any sign of life. Then she turned cold and still at the thought that someone might be in there watching her, realising what she was thinking, plotting how to escape again. And if they could not escape safely with their hostage, they might murder him, just as they'd murdered Dan Yates.

Her options were essentially twofold. She could slip away out of sight and call the police, telling Moxon what she had seen and assuring him that Ben either was in the shop now or had been very recently. She could almost trust the trained officers to break down the door, surge up the stairs with guns drawn, and grab Ben from his captors before they could inflict any harm on him. It would probably work. There would be no advantage, at that point, to killing Ben. But then, neither would there be any worse outcome than could already be expected as penalty for killing Dan.

They had nothing to lose.

And, of course, they might not be in there, anyway. Her beloved might be lying in a dusty corner, trussed and starving, barely conscious, just waiting to be released from his bonds. All the police would need to do was to walk in and collect him. But they would not do that – because they'd be expecting a trap, an ambush. A bomb rigged to go off, perhaps, or a gun that would fire when a door was opened. They would go through a whole rigmarole of safety checks before they could place any of their team at risk. If they thought someone could be in there with a weapon, the rigmarole would be tenfold.

So there really was only one option. Bonnie herself had to get into the building, dodge any traps and bring Ben out again, without the kidnappers ever knowing it had happened.

He must be upstairs. She walked all around the three accessible sides of the shop, counting doors and windows, wracking her brains for any scrappy little hint she might have picked up from Ben in their discussions about crime and chases and how to solve a mystery. They had watched every single episode of *Spooks* together, with its innumerable tricks for following people and blending into the landscape. They had stolen a few ideas for their game, building on them until they'd made them their own.

How had the kidnappers got in? If they'd done it during the day, in full view of people in the streets, they must have some tricks of their own. All the local shopkeepers would know the building was empty and unlikely to be visited by two adults and a teenaged boy. So what had they done? She walked around it again, trying to look as if she was waiting for a friend who was late. She pretended to make a call on her mobile, and then spent two full minutes admiring the window display in one of the art galleries. Inside she was growing increasingly distraught. Ben might be dying, just a few feet away. And here she was dithering about, wondering how to get into a disused shop. How tight was the security going to be? There was nothing in there to steal. There must be loose window catches or a forgotten back entrance. It was an old building, probably with a cellar. That might have its own entry.

Architecture was another new subject that Ben had begun to teach her. Not because his mother was an architect, but because buildings played such a vital role in human life. He had a special interest in the way that doors opened – inwards or outwards, and which side the hinges were placed. 'Just take note,' he'd told her, 'and see if you can work out why they've been placed as they are. Sometimes you can see it's been done all wrong.' They'd made a note for their game, to include some unwisely designed doors that would impede the player's progress.

Oh Ben, she howled inwardly. In the short time she'd known him, he had filled her with inspiration and confidence and a whole new view of the world. If there was anything at all she could do to save him, then she must do it. And quickly. No more hanging around, agonising about it. A dawning sensation of being watched was nagging at her, too, as she stood there. Was there someone inside that building, monitoring her movements and getting ready to hit her if she caused trouble? Never mind if there was. She had absolutely no choice in the matter. She *had* to act.

She was afraid she would be noticed if she took yet another walk around the same route. So she crossed the street away from the shop and made a crooked path through another small street containing a pub and one or two houses. Everything was suddenly in a different time zone, with cobbles underfoot and only a handful of parked motor vehicles in sight. Ahead the street fizzled out into a country lane, which climbed up into the higher ground that eventually became Hawkshead Hill.

There were alleyways between the houses, leading back into the town square. There were square openings designed for a horse and carriage to go through. Many of the streets were too narrow for a modern car to pass along. Very probably there were underground tunnels connecting them all up, but she had no way of knowing that. All she knew was that the core of the town dated back well over five hundred years and during that time a lot of politics and conflict had happened. If there weren't tunnels, there certainly *ought* to be.

Too much thinking, she chastised herself, and too little action. She'd been ten minutes faffing about, probably making herself stupidly conspicuous and putting Ben in even more danger. She knew, really, what she was going to have to do. She had done it before, though unwillingly. Kicking and screaming, in fact. It was the one part of her early years that she had not yet fully confided to

Ben. It was almost always kept shut away and ignored. But now it came roaring out, filling her head with panic.

Because she had seen outside the abandoned shop the only possible way in. It was close enough to a childhood experience to bring back all the terror of being forced into a space leading to a dark, stifling cellar. She knew she had to do it, while at the same time knowing she could not.

She knew because she had once been pushed down a filthy, dark coal chute into a cellar by a drunken immature boyfriend of her mother's, who thought it would make a good game.

Chapter Twenty-Three

Simmy had seated herself near a window in the Queen's Head pub, with a glass of wine and a ploughman's. Her view of the street was patchy, and there was no way she could be sure of Bonnie's movements from there, but she was content for the moment to be close enough to be of some use if there was trouble. In a few minutes she would phone the girl and ask if she was all right, without revealing how nearby she was. It was a poor compromise, she supposed, but better than nothing.

Her car was in the main car park, which was full to bursting with visitors' vehicles. It seemed they routinely left the car there and went off in all directions on foot. A great many of them were in the town, messing about in the shops and pubs instead of climbing the fells as might be expected.

Bonnie had leapt ahead of her in the search for Ben, putting her to shame for her lethargy and hopelessness. She must have discovered something from that Barnaby boy which sent her into the middle of Hawkshead, because Simmy had seen the girl walking the quarter-mile from Colthouse into the village, and felt a pang of frustrated remorse that she wasn't at least driving her. She had been told to go away, it was true, but she ought not to have obeyed the order. Bonnie was little more than a child, unable to grasp the real danger she would be in if she tried to tackle the unknown murderers.

Simmy drained her glass, thinking she ought to indulge in wine a bit more often. It made her feel relaxed and optimistic. The ploughman's included the nicest chutney she'd had for ages, and there was a very pretty girl behind the bar. In the midst of violence and worry, she found herself in a momentary oasis of calm. It was her nature to do so, she supposed. Never tempted to see herself as a rescuer, she was content to be the bringer of delight in the form of flowers. And even though the occasion was not always a happy one, the flowers themselves gave pleasure.

Then she saw people she recognised outside. It was the couple from the hotel, the Lillywhites, walking briskly along the pavement towards the village centre. The wife was in front, which seemed at odds with the relationship Simmy had observed on Tuesday. She was throwing remarks over her shoulder at the husband, who looked mutinous, but not nearly as domineering as Simmy remembered. They certainly did not look like carefree holidaymakers.

She watched them out of sight, wondering whether she ought to follow. The idea was both exciting and ridiculous. They would see her in no time, because she was tall and unskilled and Hawkshead was a very small place. That would be embarrassing. So she finished the last of her cheese and sat back for a moment, asking herself exactly what she thought she was doing.

Then another familiar figure passed by the window. This time it was the smart woman in high heels, head held high and tight skirt emphasising the curves of her posterior. The word *streetwalker* flashed disconcertingly into Simmy's head. The wiggling walk was provocative, and quite out of place amongst these wholesome fell walkers and their friends. Except, she supposed, nobody was altogether wholesome. In ordinary life, they were quite likely to be addicted to gambling or online pornography or be cruel to animals, or conducting dishonest transactions of one kind or another. Bad people went on holiday just as much as good ones – possibly even more, spending their ill-gotten profits.

The woman teetered away, the heels of her shoes surely lethal on the cobbled streets.

And this time, Simmy got up and followed.

Afterwards, she could not properly account for the way time telescoped. Events felt to be passing in a flash, from that moment when she left the pub,

284

even though there were long minutes in which nothing happened and she felt mad with frustration and indecision. The little procession proceeded the few yards into the centre of Hawkshead, where there were cafés, galleries and a big abandoned bookshop. Simmy loitered uncomfortably, keeping the dark figure of the high-heeled woman in view and hoping not to be noticed herself. The woman went around the disused shop, where there was an open area in front of the King's Arms pub. A shop selling fancy jams and cheeses was the main attraction. A steeper street led up to the church. Simmy wondered if she could walk briskly past as if going up there, without being recognised. It would give her a useful vantage point. So she gave it a try, rounding the corner and trying not to catch the eye of any of her three quarries gathered together outside the bigger and more handsome building attached to the empty one. The two women were speaking, while the man stood a little distance away.

Clumsily, Simmy walked by. A large man was walking towards her, and she stepped around him, so he would hide her from sight. Then a woman pushing a baby buggy provided a similar screen. By the time she dared take another look, the trio had closed up and were apparently heading back the way they'd just come.

This was stupid, Simmy told herself. The people were just chatting. She ought to call Bonnie to check she was all right and then get back to work. Nothing here would help to find Ben or catch Dan's killers. She got her phone out and turned it on. It felt good to have the means to connect to a friendly voice. Perhaps she'd call her mother, or Ninian or even Helen Harkness, before Bonnie. Ninian never answered his phone, though. It had surprised Simmy to learn that he even had one. Helen might not be in any mood to chat, and her mother was likely to have nothing but depressing things to report about her father.

She looked up again, thinking about her options, her gaze on the big picture window of the empty shop. Something inside moved. Something light-coloured, barely visible against the sunny glare of the street. It was impossible to be sure what it was, but the way it moved indicated a person, darting unnaturally fast across the open space. When she blinked, it had gone, and none of the handful of people close by showed any sign of having seen the same thing.

No longer caring about remaining concealed or conducting her idiotic shadowing of the hotel guests, she went to the window and peered in. There was a dusty blue carpet on the floor and a door was open in a corner. Nothing moved. There was every reason to think she'd imagined the ghostly figure that had looked so worryingly like Bonnie Lawson. And even if she had seen something, how could it possibly be of any significance? No reason, and yet she knew in her guts that something climactic was happening. Then her phone rang.

'Simmy? It's Bonnie. Where are you?'

'Standing outside a big empty shop in the middle of Hawkshead.'

'I thought I saw you just now. I'm inside it.'

'Oh.'

'Listen. You'll have to call the police for me. Call Moxon – I haven't got his number, and my battery's almost flat. We've got to go carefully, or they'll get away. Do you see? Tell him ... tell him...' Her voice broke and there were no more words for a moment. Simmy peered desperately through the dusty window, forgetting the Lilly-whites and the smart woman just the other side of the building.

'Bonnie? What's the matter?'

'Ben's here. He's almost unconscious. But he won't let me call an ambulance until the criminals are caught. Do you understand? We have to have evidence, and catch them now, before they get away.'

'That sounds like Ben,' said Simmy, still not fully convinced of the reality of the situation.

'Right.' The voice choked again. 'He's got to have water,' she said. 'Can you get some to us some-how?'

'How?'

'Put a bottle through the broken window, round the back. Low down behind a parked car. Just drop it in.'

'All right. Yes. I'll do that first.'

'Thanks.'

'I don't know what else we can do, though. Moxon's not going to just arrest them on my say-so, is he? They're right here, right now. They must be coming in. They must have a key or some-thing. How did *you* get in?'

'Don't ask.' Bonnie sounded faint and weak. 'How many of them?'

'Three.'

'Okay. Let them come in. I'll hide. They might be bringing water for Ben. He hasn't had any for ages. He thinks they meant to leave him for dead, but maybe they've changed their minds about that. Or they might be planning to take him somewhere else. We need to keep them here until the police come.'

'Oh, Bonnie. That's not going to happen, is it?'

'You can help. It's great you're here. You can lock them in. Or create a diversion or something.'

Simmy felt useless and wholly lacking in any sort of initiative. She couldn't see the three apparent criminals, so had no idea what they were doing. They might even have moved away, never to be seen again. If they had spotted her, they might have guessed she was following them. 'How will they get in?' she whispered. 'All the doors are padlocked.'

'They've got a key to one of the padlocks. They must have scammed it off the agent or something. They've been walking in and out as if they owned the place, Ben says.'

'So he's all right? Talking and everything? Just thirsty – is that it?'

'He's not all right,' said Bonnie, also in a whisper. 'Not at all. He can only say a few words at a time.'

'How long have you been in there?'

'Never mind that now. You have to *do* something. We're trapped in here until you do.'

'All right. Hang on. Leave it to me.' She had no idea what made her say that, but it sounded reassuring, and Bonnie most definitely needed reassurance.

'Wait,' came Bonnie's small voice. 'Don't call me, okay? If the phone goes off, it might give me away, if I'm hiding. Do you understand?'

That little detail had to have come from Ben, thought Simmy. Even in a state of delirium, his brain was functioning better than hers. 'Got it,' she said. 'Bye for now.' She almost ran round to the Co-op on a parallel street and bought their biggest bottle of water. This was the shop, of course, where that Barnaby boy had met Ben. But ... that made no sense, if Ben had been tied up inside that building since Tuesday. She shook her head, and went to find the broken window.

It took a little while to see it. Was this how Bonnie had got inside, then? It looked dreadfully small and tight. What a brave girl she must be! And when she bent over and peered in, the floor looked a long way down. Wouldn't the bottle crack when she dropped it, spilling the precious water?

But she could see no other alternative but to do as Bonnie had asked. Glancing around, seeing that nobody was watching, she pushed her arm through and let go. It sounded all right, as it landed, just a plastic thud, with no suggestion of cracking. She wanted to wait and speak to Bonnie, down there in the gloom, but she had other tasks to perform, and it was foolish to linger near the window, risking giving away what Bonnie had done.

Before she could start keying in Moxon's number, she wanted to rehearse what she should say for the best effect. She knew so little about what the police would do, once they were told where

289

Ben was. There had to be procedures for rescuing kidnap victims, and those procedures had to be trusted.

She would keep it simple, then. Just that she'd spoken to Bonnie who was hiding inside the empty shop with Ben, afraid that his captors would return and be dangerous.

Her thumb was actually on the first key when the phone tinkled in her hand, indicating an incoming call. The screen told her it was Melanie.

'Mel? Sorry, can you wait a bit? I've got to call Moxon.' She glanced around, wary of observation or even attack, if the Lillywhites and their friend really were the criminals. Why hadn't she asked Bonnie to confirm their identities when she'd had the chance? But of course, they must be. Why else would they be there, just the other side of a wall from the suffering Ben?

'Why're you calling him?'

'I can't explain now, but we've found Ben.'

'What? Wow – that's brilliant!'

'Yes, but–'

'And I've got news for Moxon, as well. I think there's something dodgy being planned for the upstairs room. I can't work out what exactly, but it's to do with that Sheila woman you told me about...'

Simmy went cold. How could she tackle the people she'd been following when she had no idea which, if any, had evil intentions? 'Thanks, Mel,' she said. 'I'll get back to you the minute I've made this call. I promise I will. But I've got to go now.'

What were the three people *doing,* she wondered. It seemed unlikely that they would stay in the doorway attracting attention to themselves for no good reason. Warily, she walked back around the corner for a look. They *were* still there, but the body language had changed dramatically. The woman in the tight skirt was plainly angry, stabbing a finger at Mr Lillywhite and glaring into his face. Mrs Lillywhite had her arms folded, feet planted firmly on the pavement, the image of an immovable object.

Crazily, Simmy saw this as an opportunity. Suddenly decisive, she walked up to them and smiled. 'Hello!' she chirped. 'Remember me?'

It seemed for a moment to have been an inspired thing to do. The three shifted awkwardly and glanced at each other. 'Um...' said Mrs Lillywhite.

'You know – the florist at the hotel. I found Dan Yates's body on Tuesday, with Melanie Todd. It was terribly traumatic for her, you know. And me, of course. A dreadful thing.' She prattled confidingly, throwing random smiles at them in turn.

'Of course,' said the man. 'You poor thing.'

'Yes. Well, nice to see you. I'd better get on. Things to do.' She looked up at the blank window beside them. 'Time they got someone to take this place on, don't you think? It spoils the look of the village like this.' She tilted her head in a poor show of ingenuousness. 'Or are you thinking of taking it on yourselves? Are you in business?'

It was too much; far too much. All three gave her strange looks. But they did start to move away from the building, which struck Simmy as a positive development, even if it contravened Bonnie's order that the kidnappers not be allowed to escape.

'Bye, then,' she said, and gave a fatuous little wave. This reminded her that the phone was still in her hand, and she was still supposed to call DI Moxon as a matter of extreme urgency. How many minutes had she wasted already?

The Lillywhites and the second woman were still in earshot. There was a frozen aspect to the situation, everyone apparently waiting for someone else to move. If this was a dramatic climax, unfolding to a spectacular denouement, there was no outward sign of it. People were passing by, chatting and laughing, entirely unaware that anything interesting was going on before their eyes. Their very presence was a rock-solid protection, Simmy realised. Not just for her, but for Ben and Bonnie inside the shop. And yet the urgency remained. Crossing the road again, she stood close by the display on the pavement outside the National Trust shop, and made her call.

Thankfully, Moxon answered almost instantly, with his habitual, 'Mrs Brown? How can I help you now?'

'I'm in Hawkshead,' she gabbled. 'We've found Ben. He's inside the big empty shop, in the middle of the town. Bonnie's in there with him. The people who kidnapped him are here as well. She says they mustn't escape, so you shouldn't all rush here and frighten them away.'

His response was impressive. 'Who are they?' he asked.

'Mr and Mrs Lillywhite, guests at the hotel. And another woman. Sheila something. Melanie thinks she might have found out what it's all about. She called me just now.'

'I see. And is Ben all right?'

'Not really. Very dehydrated and not fully conscious.'

'We'll need medics, then.'

'And I'm not sure Bonnie's okay, either.'

'Where are the Lillywhites now?'

She looked round. 'They've gone. Oh, no, they're still here – it looks as if they're going into the shop, through the door at this end. Oh, my God. You'll have to get here quickly. They've got a key to the padlock. I never thought they'd do it. I thought I'd frightened them off. Oh, please – please send someone as quick as you can.'

'Five minutes,' he said. 'Stay where you are.'

But of course, there was no way she could do that.

Chapter Twenty-Four

Bonnie had not exactly found a hatch leading to a coal chute. Instead there was a low window opening onto the pavement, in a shadowy angle between two high walls. The pavement must have been built up over the years to half-cover the opening. There was about eight inches of glass pane, grimy and barely noticeable. A black car was usefully parked between it and the street, shielding her almost entirely from sight.

She could almost certainly wriggle through there

293

if she could remove the glass. It was divided into three sections, each probably nine inches wide. She might even kick away the wooden dividers, making a hole over two feet long by eight inches high. That would be plenty. But her scalp tingled and her skin crawled at the thought. What was on the other side? Some small, cramped cellar, with a locked door and no light? There'd be light from outside, she reminded herself. It wouldn't be so bad. It might be a massive cellar, with an easy access into the rest of the building.

She had to do it, right away. Standing with her back to the wall, holding her phone and gazing intently at it, she kicked backwards as hard as she could, wishing that traffic was allowed into Hawkshead, to provide some covering noise. As it was, the place was entirely too quiet for comfort. But the tinkling glass was blessedly subdued, and although two or three people looked up, none of them spotted her, tucked behind the car.

She kicked again, trying to choose moments when nobody was close by. The brittle old glass fell into the cellar, and the wooden struts soon followed. It was done in a minute. She turned and looked at her handiwork. There were still some jagged spikes of glass, which she quickly disposed of, the resulting aperture quite big enough to admit her.

Again, her scalp reacted, the hair follicles be-having like a threatened dog's. She could feel all her hairs rising, in an atavistic attempt to make her look more alarming. An old memory had her in its grip, of being pushed into a filthy, airless little space and left there. This, she assured

294

herself, was altogether different. This was going to be easy. And the reward at the end would be immense. She was going to save Ben, because Ben mattered more than anything.

Waiting for a moment when nobody was walking close by, she dropped to the ground and pushed herself head first through the broken window. Head first had not been her primary choice. There was a lot to be said for going in backwards, stomach to the ground, feet and legs leading the way. Sideways would have been ideal, but there was nowhere near enough space for that. But she could not summon the courage to go blindly into the unknown. She had a horrible image of her feet being grasped and pulled by some monstrous entity waiting for her on the floor. She had to *see*. So she dived through, head, shoulders, arms, catching herself on her hands as she tumbled from a height of five or six feet, cutting her right palm on broken glass and spraining her left wrist. At least there was no monster. Nothing but a lot of dust and cobwebs, and a flight of steps just visible across the open space.

The sprained wrist shot a painful jolt through her when she tried to lever herself to a vertical position, but she ignored it. The steps were in semi-darkness, made of stone and leading nowhere. She peered upwards in disbelief. Why wasn't there a door? She tried to think of cellars she had seen in films, and slowly concluded that there must be a hinged hatch, set into the floor of the room above. It would open upwards, pulled by some sort of knob or handle and propped open. Or else pushed from below. It would have to be operable from below, she insisted to herself. What if it swung closed by accident while somebody was in the cellar? They'd have to be able to open it. There had been a film she'd seen not long ago with Corinne, a western, where there was just that sort of arrangement. This must be the same.

The light coming in through the broken window was not reaching the top of the steps. Her eyes were still adjusting to the gloom, she told herself. Soon she'd be able to see everything much more clearly. She looked back across the dirty floor, seeing her own footprints as darker smudges. There was no way she could get out again without assistance. Only by shouting for help to passers-by in the street could she leave the way she'd come. And that was not an option until she knew what was happening to Ben, and what danger he was in.

So she climbed the steps, soon being forced to crouch in the dwindling space between the upper steps and the floor overhead. Which side would the hinge be, she asked herself, trying to work out the structure. Most likely above the top step, she concluded – otherwise the flap would have to be opened back across the floor of the room above, occupying excessive space, and being difficult to prop. This meant that she should push at the other edge, hoping desperately that there was nothing heavy on top of it, and no bolt or catch fastening it.

Her active brain was doing its best to subdue the physical reactions that her body was independently undergoing. Her legs trembled, her heart raced and she was very cold. Small whimpers came involuntarily to her lips, before she could bite them back. While there were definitely spiders on all sides, there could also be bats, mice, wood-lice, and a whole lot more. Bonnie Lawson was not afraid of any of these things individually, but the idea of an accumulation of them was horrible. Much more horrible, however, was the *dirt*. Bonnie was very frightened of being dirty. She could feel sticky black stuff on her hair already. Her hands were not just injured, but foul from the grime on the floor. The shivering was totally out of control by this point, fuelled by disgust and horror at what was touching her.

Because that was the permanent legacy of the stupid prank played on her when she was little. Stuffed into a tight tunnel, she had soon tumbled free onto a forgotten heap of coal. But then she had come away blackened by the dust. Her tears had welded it to her face. Her mother had screamed at the sight of her, and pushed her roughly away. She had used words like *filthy* and *disgusting*. From that day, Bonnie had needed to be very clean at all times. Otherwise, nobody would ever love her. At its worst, when she was thirteen and her body suddenly chose to develop its own special monthly dirt, she translated the associations via blood into food itself. Meat was dirty. Tomatoes and beetroot, butter and potatoes – they each had their particular revolting elements. Slime, crust, crumbs, seeds, juice – it was all im-possibly vile.

Therapy had finally managed to dispel these extreme connections, and she was almost okay again about food. But dirt itself remained insupportable. And blood was hardly any better.

And now, in this neglected cellar, she was really quite dreadfully dirty, as well as bloody.

But Ben needed her, somewhere in a room above her. She was going to have to put her back against the hatch and heave away until it opened. Little Bonnie Lawson, barely six stone in weight, would have to become a lever, raising the heavy wooden flap and pushing it back far enough to climb through.

So she did it, for love of Ben as well as from a knowledge that there was no alternative. She had come this far, solving the mystery when nobody else could, and to go back now would be shameful. Even though nobody would expect a fragile woman-child with a sprained wrist to perform such a feat, she expected it of herself.

She crawled onto the top step, and on her knees she bent over and set her back against the wooden slats above her. Then she pushed, expecting to have to push repeatedly until she dropped.

But it gave instantly. It moved willingly, rising an inch or so as she pushed, the whole thing balancing on her spine. It took a moment to understand that there was no hinge. It was also much smaller than she'd expected. It was almost *flimsy*, she realised with a thrill. It was impeded slightly by a floor covering, but when she pushed it gave readily. She raised both hands, and again ignoring the double pain, heaved the thing sideways, and pushed her head through the opening. The carpet on the floor of the shop did not come to the very edge of the room. Only a narrow band had been covering the hatch. Wonderingly, she

298

hauled herself up and into the empty room.

It had been easy! Euphoria flooded through her. She was a hero! All she had to do now was find Ben and rescue him.

She crossed the room, which must have been the main part of the shop, once filled with books. It had a large window looking onto the town square. People would see her when she crossed it to the door at the back. So she moved in a great rush, thinking she'd make the merest flash to anybody outside. Glancing out, she saw a tall woman on the opposite pavement. Could it be Simmy? She didn't wait to stare any harder, but the thought that there was a friend just outside gave her strength. Indeed, the whole cheerful scene, just a sheet of glass away, made everything feel much less terrifying.

There was a door, and a staircase and an up-stairs and then another flight to a higher level, where she found a nasty little room containing a bucket and a blanket and a huddled figure with hands and feet all tied up.

'Ben! Hey, Ben!' She shook his shoulder. 'It's me.'

He groaned, but did not open his eyes. His lips were cracked and his skin damp to the touch. There was a bruise on his forehead. His breath came loud and fast. Bonnie had never encountered anything like this before.

'Ben!' she shouted at him. 'Wake up!'

One eye opened fractionally. Then it focused and widened and its mate joined in. 'Ak,' said Ben.

Bonnie leant back, bracing herself for the *filthy*

and *disgusting* reaction. He couldn't possibly love her any more, the way she looked. Then the dry mouth kinked and the tied hands behind his back twitched in an automatic attempt to reach her. 'Bonnie,' he breathed. 'Oh.'

Where to start, she wondered. Untie his hands. Find him some water. Reassure him. Cuddle him. *Love* him. The first looked impossible. The second was insuperably difficult, unless there was still a water supply to the building, which she doubted. So she began with the others. 'It's okay now,' she crooned. 'I'll get you out.'

'How?' The voice was painful in its aridity. 'Knife?' He wriggled to indicate the urgency of cutting the bonds that kept his arms painfully behind his back.

She shook her head, causing a small shower of black detritus to fall on his face. 'Sorry,' she said, and brushed it away. Then she rolled him over and inspected the tie around his wrists. It was black, plastic and tight. One of those things with ratchets that only went one way. 'I could bite it, maybe,' she suggested, and bent over to give it a go.

Her front teeth were sharp, but she couldn't get a proper purchase without nipping his skin. Then she found a quarter-inch between his two wrists and set to work. Her jaws were aching within seconds from the pressure she was exerting, but it worked. The plastic separated and Ben's arms did the same. 'Ak!' he groaned again. Bonnie badly wanted to massage his damaged skin, but her own hands were so sore and dirty that she refrained. Instead she looked at his legs, taking great satis-

'faction from the fact that they were bare.

'I knew it,' she muttered. Aloud, she said, 'Shall I try to do your feet as well?'

He gave her a look, full of gratitude and concern and unspoken questions. 'Water?' he asked hopelessly.

'Sorry.' She grimaced at this unforgivable oversight. 'What a fool I am. I never thought.'

He frowned, as if this presented a considerable difficulty – which it probably did. She had a small cotton bag with her containing phone, tissues and a tube of Supermints. 'Isn't there a tap in here somewhere?' she demanded.

He shook his head.

She was ready to open a vein to let him drink, if only she had a knife. Perhaps she could bite herself deeply enough to get some blood flowing. But that wouldn't help. Blood was too salty to be of much use. Urine might be better, but she was fairly sure she couldn't manage that, either.

Just outside, there were shops full of bottled water, juice, Coke. It was crazy to let Ben die of dehydration in the middle of a busy summer town. 'I'll have to go and get you something,' she said, dreading a return through the cellar, and entirely unsure of the consequences of shouting for help from random passers-by. They wouldn't react well to a blackened girl emerging from a broken window at ankle level. They would bundle her into an ambulance without listening, or turn and head the other way, trying to pretend she was a hallucination.

'No.' He was emphatic. 'Don't go. Phone.'
'Who?'

'Simmy. People might come back.' Fear was plain in his bloodshot eyes. 'They want me to die.'

'How do they get in?'

'Padlock. Key.'

She nodded. 'They don't want you to die, Ben. They'd have done it by now and thrown you into one of the lakes. They might bring you some water any time now. Do they come in and out every day?'

He shook his head, less in a negative than confusion. 'Don't know. In and out.'

'Is there a loo here?' Where there was a lavatory, there'd be water. 'What do you do, if not?'

His lips twitched again. 'No water, no pee,' he croaked.

'Okay.' There would be time enough later for all the questions. She focused on her phone and called Simmy.

More questions, more answers. 'Call Moxon,' she urged. And, 'He's got to have some water.' The news that Ben's captors were right outside came as a very nasty shock. 'I'll hide,' she decided. But they would see that Ben's wrist tie was severed, unless he lay on his back, hiding the evidence. Although he had said nothing directly, she knew how much it mattered that the criminals be caught. She knew that Ben would always feel his suffering had been for nothing, if he was merely rescued, without a proper end to the whole business. They must be arrested, charged and convicted for what they'd done. She felt it as strongly as he did. She finished the call, not daring to feel reassured, but hopeful all the same.

'I saw your sign at Colthouse,' she told him. 'The ferns tied with rushes.'

He frowned in puzzlement. 'The game,' she reminded him. Then, 'When did you put the date on the window? *How* did you? That was what showed me you were here. Brilliant.'

He tried to speak, but only managed a syllable before his throat dried up too much for speech. She had been silently counting minutes, at the back of her mind. Simmy had almost had time to fetch water and drop it into the cellar. 'I'm going down,' said Bonnie. 'It's all going to be fine, you see.'

She stroked his clammy brow and forced herself back down the stairs, through the hole in the floor and down into the cobwebs and dust of the cellar.

The bottle was there, catching the light and gleaming like treasure. It had not suffered from its fall, and it was wonderfully big. She would pour it all into Ben and save his life. And she would never go anywhere ever again without a bottle of water.

Back upstairs, she pulled off the cap and pulled Ben more upright. In her absence, his eyes had closed again, and his breathing was even louder. He was lying on his side, curled up, his face turned towards the floor, his hands between his thighs.

'Come on,' she urged. 'Drink this.' She tried to apply the mouth of the bottle to his lips, but the angle was wrong and it spilt onto the floor. 'Ben! Wake up. I've got water for you.'

But he did not respond. Desperately she poured a small trickle onto his face, hoping to shock him awake. But nothing happened. She pulled at him, rolling him onto his back and then trying to prop him against the wall, but only managed to crumple him awkwardly, so his chin rested on his chest. The bottle got knocked, and she caught it just in time. Could he swallow, she wondered. Lifting his head, she made another try at introducing some water.

She gave him too much, so he coughed it out again. At least the coughing was a sign of life, she thought, as she started again more gently. This time, he did swallow – she was sure he did. His lips closed around the plastic, like a sucking baby.

They continued in that way for a while, with Bonnie refusing to think of anything but trickling water into Ben's body, reviving him from the terrifying slump he was in. So when she heard footsteps and voices coming up the bare wooden stairs, she was paralysed. There was nowhere to hide, no choice but to stay where she was and face the people who might well want her boyfriend dead, in spite of her assurances a few minutes earlier.

Chapter Twenty-Five

Simmy was acutely aware of people's stares, as she ran around the empty shop, peering through its windows, curving her hands around her face to shut out the dazzling sunlight. It was so weird to think that a room somewhere above that big space

– so easily visible to the shoppers and sightseers outside – was hosting a scene of violence and horror. She briefly entertained a notion of standing there and screaming for help. She would gather a crowd of fifty people who would storm the building and save Ben and Bonnie from the Lillywhites. People power would prevail. Why not?

Then a very obvious thought belatedly came to her. If the kidnappers had opened the padlock and gone in, the door must surely have been left open behind them. There was no way they could padlock it from the inside. At best they would have to ram it shut with some sort of object. Which door had they used? She had been a fool to go off and let them disappear. But she'd had no choice – Ben needed the water more urgently than anything else. Her thoughts tangled and leapt from one detail to the next as she ran round again, checking the padlocks.

She found it within seconds. The chain that had connected the door to its frame was dangling loose, the padlock nowhere to be seen. But it wouldn't open when she pushed it. Like the door of her own neglected shop, there was an ordinary lock, operated with an ordinary key, and that was keeping her out. So why the padlock, she wondered crossly.

Her phone broke into her helpless frustration and she snatched it eagerly from her bag, hoping it was Bonnie with good news. *How could it be?* asked a sceptical inner voice. Bonnie was trapped as much as Ben was. Her best hope was probably to huddle in a corner of the cellar and wait for someone to pull her out through the disconcertingly small window.

It was Melanie. 'You didn't call me back,' she accused. 'What are you doing? Where are you?'

'Almost exactly where I was last time, as it happens. It's all going wrong. The police haven't come.' She couldn't remember what she'd told Melanie the first time she called. Any complex doubts as to who knew what had long been discarded. She couldn't even remember the last time she and Bonnie and Melanie had all been in the same place at the same time.

'But Ben's okay, right? That's what you said. What about the kidnappers? Have you seen them?'

'Yes, I think so. I'm sorry, Mel. It's all happening, right here. But I can't get in and I'm petrified they'll be hurting Bonnie and Ben. They don't know I've called the police. They'll think they can do what they like.'

'That woman – with the tight skirt and heels. She's called Sheila. She's some sort of estate agent. She sells and rents out commercial properties. I found some of her emails to Dan. She wanted to sell something to the Lillywhite couple, apparently, but that wasn't her reason for coming to the hotel. She's trying to arrange a fair, with a whole lot of shops and things all being advertised at once. It'd be in our big room here. She's desperate to get everything organised in time for September.'

'How does that link to what's going on here?' Simmy's impatience had reached screaming pitch. 'What does it matter?'

'At the very least it means she's innocent. She's got no reason to kill or kidnap anybody.'

'But–' Then Simmy saw a figure who had so

306

often before been at hand when events became unbearable. Except, not always, she remembered. He was improving, then. Or she was mellowing, because she didn't think she had ever in her life been so glad to see anyone. She abruptly ended the call with Melanie.

Although he appeared to be alone, she was confident that there was a whole team of sturdy officers tucked around the corner somewhere. She almost ran towards him, resisting the urge to hug him with the greatest difficulty. 'Oh, thank you for coming,' she gasped. 'They're all in there now. You can catch them easily.'

He wiped a hand across his brow, rubbing at a spot between his eyes, as if working out the best way to convey terrible news. 'I think you've got the whole thing wrong,' he said. 'It's not your fault. Those kids have been messing you about. We've just heard from Mrs Harkness. She says Ben's perfectly safe, with his brother. It's all over and done with now. Apart from making an arrest for the murder of Mr Yates, of course.'

'No!' She stared at him, her mouth open. 'Has Helen *seen* him? Has Wilf? Somebody's playing a trick on them. Ben's in there. I *know* he is.' She waved an unrestrained arm at the empty shop. 'So's Bonnie, and three – two – I don't know ... criminals.'

'She's quite certain about it. I'm not sure of the details, but the brother – Wilf – was called to a place in Ambleside, where Ben was waiting for him. They phoned their mother from the car. They'll be home by now.'

'It isn't possible,' she said flatly. 'It can't have

307

been Wilf. Did Helen speak to Ben himself?'

Moxon shook his shoulders irritably. 'I don't know.' He looked up at the shop. 'How do you know anybody's in there? It looks deserted to me.'

'I saw Bonnie right there in that big room. Then she phoned me. Then I gave them some water. Then the Lillywhites and Sheila Something went in. At least, I didn't see them going in, but the padlock's undone, and they disappeared, so that must be where they went. Haven't you got any backup, then?' She almost wailed. 'How can I make you believe me?'

'It was Wilf's phone. It was his voice. I have to take what his mother told me as right.'

'No, you don't, because I *saw* Bonnie. I saw the window she broke to get in. I *know* she and Ben are in there.'

'Window? Show me.'

But before she could lead him around to the back of the shop, they were both frozen in place by a piercing scream, which came from the upper floor of the building beside them. It was followed by a crash of breaking glass, and a shower of shards falling onto the pavement close to where they stood.

'See,' said Simmy, both relieved and appalled. The scream had sounded terrible. 'Now will you do something?'

Moxon's face was a mixture of alarm and confusion. 'There's only me,' he said. 'I can't force an entry on my own.'

'Coward!' she spat at him. Hadn't there been a time when he'd have had a police whistle, which summoned miraculous hordes of burly officers moments after being blown? Now he seemed incapable of any decisive action. 'So call somebody,' she urged.

Another scream put some fire in his belly and he began to set the process into motion. From Simmy's point of view it was laborious and inefficient. She went to stand directly below the source of the broken glass and shouted, 'Bonnie? Are you okay?'

There was no response. Or if there was, she couldn't hear it, because a fair-sized crowd had already gathered and several people were talking loudly. Shopkeepers were leaving their posts behind their counters and coming out to see what was happening. They all stared up at the broken window. 'Can't have been double glazed,' said a man. 'They're almost impossible to break.'

'Somebody screamed,' said a woman. 'Who's in there, then?'

It was the realisation of Simmy's mad scheme, at least in part. She could very probably mobilise them into a rescue team, catching the wicked Lillywhites in the process. 'There's a boy in there, who's been kidnapped,' she shouted. 'His girlfriend's gone to rescue him, but his captors must be attacking her. It was her who screamed. Will somebody help me break in?'

Nobody moved. British people did not readily violate the rules to the extent of breaking down doors. They looked at her suspiciously, plainly doubting her credibility, if not her very sanity. It was, after all, a highly unlikely tale she was telling them. She remembered that the fact of Ben's abduction had been kept out of the news. Nobody knew there was a missing boy.

'Come *on*,' she yelled at them. 'You heard that scream.'

That was true. At least a few of them had heard it. And they could all see the shattered window. 'All right, then,' said a large man. 'If you're sure.'

'Yes! That door – see the chain's been unlocked. It's just a Yale now. And the frame's not very thick. I bet it'll give quite easily.'

He gave her a considering look. 'I'm not doing it with my shoulder,' he said. 'I need some sort of lever, like a crowbar.'

'No, no,' came Moxon's voice. 'I'm a police officer. I've called for backup. Leave it to us.'

More confusion as the people stared from him to Simmy and back, unable to draw any rational conclusions from the few facts they could see for themselves. One or two plainly thought Moxon as unreliable as Simmy, if not more so. 'You're never a policeman,' said a young woman. 'Where's your badge, then?'

With only a shred of dignity, he produced it. Simmy had not been sure that detectives carried such things, but supposed there must be times like this when credentials were required.

She tried to think. Inside the building there were three criminals and two young innocent victims. The noise outside must surely have got through to them by now, which meant they knew they couldn't hope to escape. So what would they do? Who had broken the window, and why? Were they planning to burn the whole place down, with Ben and Bonnie inside? Or to leap from the upper window, in a desperate effort to get away?

Why had they gone in there, anyway? Had they left possessions there that had to be retrieved?

Questions flocked through her mind, each one wilder than the one before. And then it struck her that she need no longer hesitate in phoning Bonnie. There was no possibility that the girl was hiding quietly in a cupboard. Her phone was still in her hand, and she activated it quickly.

By a miracle, Bonnie answered. More than a miracle – a sort of madness, in the midst of such chaos. It almost made Simmy laugh. 'What's happening?' she asked. 'Was that you who screamed?'

The girl's voice was impossibly calm. 'It's nearly all over now,' she said. 'I can come down to let you all in. We need an ambulance for Ben. And me, I suppose.'

Simmy couldn't speak. Her head had filled with cotton wool, born of relief and amazement and a renewed desire to laugh for several minutes. She turned to Moxon, who was fending off demands for information from the ever-growing crowd of Hawkshead worthies. 'Call an ambulance,' she told him, after twice trying to get the words out and failing. 'Bonnie says it's all over now.' She could feel hysteria bubbling somewhere in her chest. 'She's done it all without us.'

Chapter Twenty-Six

Mr Lillywhite advanced on the two youngsters, his eyes bulging. 'Who are you?' he demanded of Bonnie. 'How did you get in here? What do you think you're doing?'

She cuddled closer to Ben and scowled up at the man. 'You killed Dan Yates, and half-killed Ben,' she accused. 'You and these women.'

'Nonsense,' said Mrs Lillywhite. 'What a ridiculous accusation.' She glanced at the other woman, looking worried.

'So why are you here? How did *you* get in?' Bonnie felt light-headed from the sense of having nothing to lose. If these people murdered her and Ben, at least they'd be together for ever. And there was no chance at all that the killers would escape punishment. There was definitely satisfaction in that thought. But before that happened, she was determined to put up a fight. 'You came to finish him off, is that it?'

'We're thinking of taking this place on. This is Sheila, the agent. We've been looking around for somewhere all week, and this seems our best option.' Mrs Lillywhite spoke calmly, her words clipped and firm, but her eyes flickered from face to face, and her skin looked bloodless. 'We had no idea at all that there was anybody up here until we heard you moving just now.'

'Liar!'

They all looked at the boy, curled on the ground. His revival was a greater shock to Bonnie than to anyone else. She had believed him to be lost in unconsciousness. The word came out loud and clear, but his eyes remained shut.

'What did he say?' Mr Lillywhite growled.

'He said you're a liar and I believe him. I think you murdered Dan Yates by Esthwaite and kid-napped Ben because he saw you there, red-handed.'

'Sheer fantasy,' snapped the man. 'Childish storytelling.'

'So why's Ben here, then? How did he get here?' Bonnie looked from husband to wife, her face an unwavering challenge. 'You can't even invent a credible denial,' she added with scorn. Beside her, Ben gave a low chuckle of approval. In spite of everything, she was enjoying herself. It got even better when the other woman joined in.

'This is all highly peculiar,' she said. 'How *do* you explain this boy being here?'

'Your guess is as good as ours,' said Mrs Lilly-white. 'I'm telling you, we had no idea he was here. You saw for yourself that the padlock was undisturbed. These children must have got in through a window or something. And the boy's been fooling about, tying himself up, and got more than he'd bargained for. Who knows what kids like this get up to?'

'Liar, liar, liar,' said Ben with growing strength.

'And the man who was murdered?' Sheila pressed on. 'I have been wondering, actually. I knew him slightly – we'd been discussing a plan and I met him once or twice. I've got to organise a

313

seminar about local businesses. I was hoping to use their conference room in the autumn. He told me there were other people who wanted it that same weekend, and we'd have to try and work something out.' She frowned. 'But he was killed before I could get anywhere. It's been extremely frustrating, I can tell you.' She looked at Mrs Lilly-white. 'I did give you the key to this property last weekend. You could have got in, just as this little girl says.'

'And they've kept Ben here since Tuesday,' said Bonnie, wearily.

'No!' Sheila's voice rose. 'Why would they do that?'

'Ask them. They've been doing something illegal and Dan found out – that's my guess. So they murdered him in the woods by the mere, but Ben caught them, so they had to keep him from saying anything, until–' She stopped. Until what? Were they hoping to get away undetected, and then somehow send an anonymous message to the police, so he could be found before it was too late?

It was surreal, making the worst of all imagin-able accusations against two people, who simply stood there with wooden faces.

'Prostitutes,' said Ben, just thickly enough for the word to be in doubt.

'What?' Bonnie bent over him.

His eyes flickered open. 'Girls from poor coun-tries. It's a network. They talked about it. More water,' he finished, his voice expiring.

She jumped to comply. Nothing else mattered. Ben would repeat everything he knew once the police had arrested the couple and taken them away. She didn't have to get everything straight now.

But Sheila had different priorities. 'What did he just say?' she demanded, her eyes bulging. She went up to Rosemary Lillywhite, jabbing at her with a thin finger. 'Have you been trying to drag *me* into this? Was *this* going to be a bawdy house?' She looked around at the echoing room. 'In the middle of a lovely place like Hawkshead?'

'Don't be idiotic,' said Mr Lillywhite. 'Have some sense, woman.'

Ben managed a much better intake of water, swallowing steadily, and letting it do its restorative work. 'Better,' he said. Then he flexed his hands. 'Hurts.'

Bonnie began to wonder how much time had passed, and what was going on outside. The windows only showed roofs and the fells beyond. There were faint voices, but nothing that made her confident that police were there in force, ready to capture the murderers. Despite her determination to take things in the right order, questions were flooding her mind. One stood out. 'How did you manage to write that date?' she asked Ben, with a tender smile.

'Soon as we got here. They didn't tie me up right away. I knew you'd see it.' He returned the smile with interest.

'What?' said Mr Lillywhite.

Bonnie smirked at him. 'You kidnapped the cleverest boy in England, you fool. He wrote that, look.' She pointed at the window, with the mirror-image numerals written in the grime. 'That's how I knew he was here. That's what's cooked

315

your goose.'

Incomprehension was written on three blank faces.

'1780. Wordsworth was here then. We've been studying him together.'

'*Wordsworth?*' Sheila spoke first. It was almost possible to believe she had never heard the name before.

'Poet,' said Ben. Bonnie laughed, not just because it was very funny, but because her beloved's improvement was progressing so prodigiously.

Rosemary Lillywhite approached the window, incredulously. She looked through the glass and down, and saw something that evidently maddened her. 'No-o-o-o!' she screamed, and snatched up a leather briefcase that her husband had brought with him. She hurled it with full force against the panes, smashing three or four of them.

Sheila retreated to the other side of the room, visibly shaking. Mr Lillywhite appeared to be mainly concerned with his bag, which was balancing half in and half out of the window. He stepped forward and retrieved it, before taking a fragile hold of his wife's sleeve and pulling at her. 'Stop it,' he said. 'Think of Tom. Get a hold of yourself, woman.'

Tom? Bonnie gave Ben a sideways glance. 'He's their son,' came the answer. 'He's involved in all this as well.' He made an expression of disgust. 'I thought he was my friend.'

This was altogether new to Bonnie. But before she could ask for further detail, there was a phonecall from Simmy, which she handled with outrageous confidence, and a little while after that there were footsteps on the stairs, and everything was very nearly over.

A man they didn't know led the way into the room, followed by another stranger and then DI Moxon himself appeared. It was highly disorganised and nothing remotely like any police raid they'd all seen on television. Simmy rushed to Ben and grabbed him. 'He didn't believe me,' she wept. 'He said you were safe and sound with Wilf.'

'Tom,' said Ben, with a nod. 'He can do Wilf's voice.'

Moxon stood in stark perplexity at being the solitary police officer at a scene of such complicated and contradictory crime. 'Don't let them go!' shouted Bonnie – not at Moxon, but the two other men. 'They're murderers.'

Their blood up, the men willingly responded. 'All of them?' asked the larger one.

'Not her,' pointing at Sheila. 'The others.'

But the Lillywhites showed no resistance. 'You can't prove anything,' said the husband. 'Not a thing.'

Bonnie's heart thumped. 'Is that right?' she whispered to Ben.

'Of course not,' he told her. 'There'll be evidence galore all over the place. Did you find my phone?'

She nodded. 'They've looked at all the photos.'

He smiled. 'Oh good. That'll be your evidence then. His shoes...' He spoke to DI Moxon, and at last revived enough to sit up straight. 'But for a start you can hold them on a charge of abduction and deprivation of freedom. I hereby press charges against them.'

Simmy had said nothing, after her first outburst. Now she said to Bonnie, 'But how in the world did you find him? That's what I don't understand.'

'Our game,' was the deeply unsatisfactory answer.

Chapter Twenty-Seven

Simmy took an unnervingly unprotesting Bonnie to a GP clinic to have her hand and wrist attended to, while Ben was taken by ambulance to hospital. His dehydration was a cause for concern, as well as possible nerve damage to his wrists from the tight binding. Bonnie had begged to go with him, but it was decreed otherwise. Ben himself promised to call her that evening. 'How?' she shouted. 'You haven't got a phone.'

He rolled his eyes and smiled. 'Trust me,' he said, just as they closed the ambulance doors on him.

Initially bursting with questions, Simmy soon found that a lot of the answers had already been supplied by the afternoon's events.

'It was Tom, then, pretending to be Ben in the shop and giving Barnaby that message?'

'Right,' said Bonnie.

'But isn't it a massive coincidence, that he knows Ben and Wilf? How does he?'

The girl sat up straighter in the passenger seat and sighed. 'I've been wondering that as well. I've never heard of him before. It makes you think his parents might have been out to get Ben all along – but that can't be right. They couldn't have known he'd be at Esthwaite on Tuesday. And why would they have any reason to want him, anyway?'

'Hang on.' Simmy had a thought. 'There was a boy called Tom hiking with Ben and Wilf, and those other brothers. He would have got to know them then. But it still must be a coincidence.'

'He never said anything to me about it,' Bonnie complained. 'All those phone calls every evening and he didn't mention him even once.'

'You talked about your game thingy, I imagine.'

'Nope. That never got a mention, either. I s'pose I did most of the talking. Corinne's been saying I need to do a course or something, and get some qualifications, and that's been bugging me. It was mainly that stuff we talked about.'

'Hmm. So Tom and his mum and dad are here on holiday, and he doesn't want to stay at the hotel with them, so he meets up with lads his own age and talks them into letting him go hiking with them. Where did he go after that? They came back on Tuesday. Where's he been sleeping since then?'

'At the hotel,' Bonnie guessed. 'Melanie told me their room's ludicrously tidy. I bet there's a single bed in there, and they've smuggled him in and needed to hide the evidence.'

'Sounds very odd. Why not just tell the hotel he's staying, if there's a spare bed? And why not just tidy the bed, not the whole room?'

'Dunno, but I bet it's something like that. And

he's been hanging about in that big room upstairs. It might have been him I saw on the
balcony. It's easy enough to hide in a hotel.'

'Gentian would agree with you.'

'Who? Oh, that kid? Seemed like quite a little
character.'

'It makes the Lillywhites even worse, if they involved their son in what they were doing. If Ben's
right that they're trafficking foreign girls for sex,
that's grotesque.'

'Yeah,' said Bonnie uncertainly.

'Presumably, Dan Yates got wind of it all, and
that's why they killed him.'

'Yeah,' Bonnie said again.

'What's the matter?'

'We've not been thinking much about Dan,
have we? Melanie's right about that. We should
make sure she's okay. She'll be feeling left out.'

'Again,' said Simmy ruefully. 'Melanie always
feels left out. She phoned me while I was standing there in Hawkshead, trying to decide what to
do. She's found some emails between Dan and
that Sheila woman.' She frowned. 'What's going
to happen to her, then?'

'Depends, I guess.'

'She's some sort of estate agent. Not the ordinary kind, though. She wanted to have a seminar in
the hotel. Something like that.'

Bonnie was losing interest, cradling her wrist in
a hand still streaked with blood and grime. 'I'm
so dirty,' she moaned. 'Look at me.'

'That's why you need to see a doctor. Get all that
muck washed out of your cuts. And that wrist is
terribly swollen. They might want to x-ray it.'

'I saved him, didn't I? They'd have killed him if I hadn't been there.'

Privately, Simmy thought this unlikely. The presence of Sheila-the-estate-agent suggested no such intention. But why had they gone to Hawkshead with her, anyway? 'You were a hero,' she told the girl.

It was seven o'clock before Simmy had a chance to sit down and drink tea and really think about the events of the past three days. Her mother had firmly ensconced her in the private sitting room, which had uneasy associations with previous brushes with violent death and personal injury. Melanie had phoned again and been invited to come round for a debriefing. Bonnie had gone home to Corinne, lavishly bandaged and perfectly clean. Detective Inspector Moxon had gone quiet.

Russell went to the door when Melanie rang, his newfound security rituals taking far too long. When the girl joined Simmy, she was flushed with impatience. 'What's with your dad?' she demanded.

'He's scared of intruders. It's all my fault.'

'He needs therapy.'

'He's getting it. My mother's got him an appointment. Have some tea and cake.'

'Thanks. That's good about the appointment.' They looked at each other for a quiet moment. 'So – it's all sorted, then? Is that right?'

'More or less. Ben's going to be okay. Bonnie was heroic. Moxon was an idiot. Do you know anything about a boy called Tom? The Lillywhites'

321

son, apparently.'

Melanie shook her head. 'Never knew they had a son.'

'It still feels like too big a coincidence. He invited himself to go along with Ben and Wilf and the others, on their hiking trip at the weekend. Then, when Ben was abducted, he pretended to be him – to that boy Barnaby, in the Co-op. He knew Corinne's car number – I don't know how. It was a trick to make us all think Ben was all right, just doing one of his investigations.'

Melanie repeated what she'd just heard, with supplementary questions. Then she thought about it for a minute or two. 'I don't think it's such a huge coincidence. It's not such a stretch, really, for the Lillywhite boy to hook up with the hiking group.'

'But it is for Ben to be the very person to witness his parents murdering Dan. Don't you think?'

'Maybe.' Melanie leant back into the sofa cushions. 'Well, not really. Ben gets everywhere, doesn't he? Always spying on people and not leaving things alone. It *would* be him.'

Simmy nodded. 'That's true. But it must mean that Tom actually *saw* Ben tied up, in that empty shop, and recognised him. He might even have dreamt up the plan to pretend to be him, to put everybody's mind at rest.'

'That was clever. I was totally convinced.'

'Bonnie wasn't. I saw her talking to Barnaby in a field, earlier today. She must have worked out that it hadn't been Ben at all.' She paused. 'I wonder if it really was him that Ninian saw in that car.'

'Doesn't matter now, does it?'

322

'No, but – well, I still want to know.'

'Never mind. But I'd bet a tenner that it wasn't. Go on with what happened. How on earth did Bonnie manage to find Ben?'

'That's another amazing thing. She saw a date that Ben had scrawled on a dirty window, and she got in through the cellar and found him.'

'Hang on!' Melanie ordered. 'Bonnie was in a *cellar?* Full of coal dust and cobwebs and dirt?'

'Not sure about the coal dust. But plenty of the ordinary sort. She was filthy dirty, with blood from cuts on her hand and cobwebs in her hair.'

'She must have been frantic. You think your dad's got a phobia – what about Bonnie?'

'Pardon?'

'Haven't you worked it out yet? She's totally terrified of dirt. And blood. She keeps it under control these days, but it's still there. I saw her freaking out, a year or so ago, when Corinne made her help with some car repair. She got engine oil on her, just a black streak on her arm, and she went into a real state.'

'I didn't know. I just thought she'd been anorexic.'

'It connects, somehow. But the point is, being dirty is like walking through fire would be to you or me.'

'Well, she did it for Ben.' Simmy wiped away a sudden tear. 'I said she was a hero.'

Again they sat quietly, each thinking hard. Then Melanie said, 'Dan was a bit of a hero as well, believe it or not.'

'Was he?'

'I don't know exactly, but he must have taken a

stand with the Lillywhites, telling them he was going to the police, or something. He'd been googling them, and asking questions, until he'd got a fair idea of what they were up to. He'd actually got a sort of dossier on them. I found it today. They were up here sussing out likely places for running a ... well, *brothel*, he called it.'

'Where did you find it – this dossier? Didn't the police take his computer on Tuesday? That must be routine, surely?'

'They took his laptop, but missed his iPad. He'd left it in the office, so they didn't realise it was his. I went through the history and everything else I could find. It explains quite a lot.'

'How were things at the hotel today?'

'Not too bad. Gentian and her mum leave tomorrow. Mr Ferguson's there till Sunday. They seem to be friends now. I saw the three of them playing cards in the lounge.'

Simmy smiled at the image. 'The news will soon get round – about the Lillywhites.'

'Well, nobody liked them.'

'Can the hotel survive all this publicity, do you think?'

'Bodgett thinks so. He gave us all a bit of a pep talk just before I left. Oh – and he wants you to bring more flowers tomorrow. Those Americans might have gone, but there are plenty of people who still have to be impressed, apparently.'

Simmy put a hand to her mouth. 'But I haven't ordered anything. Where am I going to find enough for two more displays? I should go now and order something.'

'Too late, Sim. You'll have to improvise. It won't

be the first time.'

'Like stealing dahlias from people's gardens, you mean?'

'Are dahlias in flower yet? I thought they were August. It's all crocosmia and delphiniums at the moment.'

'Don't be such a know-all. I suppose I can scrape enough things together from the shop, if I have to.'

'You'll do a wonderful job. You know you will.'

Ben was released from hospital into the arms of his bewildered mother, just after eight that evening. 'Can I use your phone?' he asked her in the car.

Wordlessly, she handed it over.

'Bon? I'm on the way home. See you tomorrow?'

'Okay. I won't be in the shop. My hands don't work.'

'What did you think of the message in the burial ground?'

'Yeah. It was okay.'

'What's up?'

'You nearly *died*, you idiot. And there you are thinking about the game, as if nothing happened.'

He paused, glancing at his mother. 'The game saved us,' he reminded Bonnie. 'It's going to be so mega, when we tell the story. Mum says there's already a couple of reporters hanging about, wanting to talk to me. She says we have to wait until Moxo's given us the go-ahead – but honestly, Bon, this is totally great. I was a real *hostage*. It's given me so many new ideas. My head's bursting with them.'

Bonnie's silence slowly made itself felt.
'What? What's the matter?'
'Nothing,' she said at last.

The publishers hope that this book has given you enjoyable reading. Large Print Books are especially designed to be as easy to see and hold as possible. If you wish a complete list of our books please ask at your local library or write directly to:

Magna Large Print Books
Magna House, Long Preston,
Skipton, North Yorkshire.
BD23 4ND

This Large Print Book for the partially sighted, who cannot read normal print, is published under the auspices of

THE ULVERSCROFT FOUNDATION